Into the
Far Mountains

Other Five Star Titles by Fred Grove:

Man on a Red Horse

Into the Far Mountains

A Western Story

FRED GROVE

Five Star
Unity, Maine

Five Star Western
Published in conjunction with Golden West Literary Agency.

May 1999

First Edition, Second Printing

Five Star Standard Print Western Series.

The text of this edition is unabridged.

Set in 11 pt. Plantin.

Printed in the United States on permanent paper.

Library of Congress Cataloging in Publication Data

Grove, Fred.
    Into the far mountains : a western story / by Fred Grove.
    — 1st ed.
        p.   cm.
    ISBN 0-7862-1330-2 (hc : alk. paper)
    I. Title.
PS3557.R7I58   1999
813´.54—dc21   98-52076

Into the Far Mountains

Chapter One

Jesse Wilder lolled on the blanket-covered straw mattress with his boots off, listening to the raucous drunks from the saloon below, blasting away at bottles on the adobe wall behind the hotel, by now almost an afternoon ritual. A waste of precious ammunition, he thought, when you figured it had to come from as far as California or St. Louis over perilous trails. He batted at a persistent fly, letting his mind wander.

He got up, drank slowly from a bottle of tequila, making a face, wiped his mouth with the back of his left hand, and lay down again, feeling a growing disgust for his continued slothful ways since riding into Tucson from Fort Bowie. He'd arrived with the intention of going on to California, after resting his stock and himself for a spell, an interlude that kept extending, until he'd dawdled away a good five weeks — or was it six? He was drinking too much, and he knew it, back to drifting again, and he saw no immediate end to it as long as his money lasted.

He was beginning to get those awful nightmares again, those old battle dreams. His demons, he called them, which haunted without warning. Sometimes just one would come, sometimes a succession of them, flashing through his mind. Sometimes they'd leave him alone for months, then return in a fury. And he'd be back in the dew-wet woods of Shiloh, the death shrieks of boys like himself tearing at his ears, with the wild Rebel yell: *"Yee-haaa! Yee-haaa-haaa-haa!"* Or deep in the hellish horror at Kennesaw Mountain under the broiling sun, the blue waves of Yankees marching into certain death toward the entrenched Confederates. It was the faces that bothered Jesse, the brave, boyish faces. . . . And there was bloody Franklin. The savage hand-to-hand fighting around the Carter House. And always the following pain and blackness when the bullet slashed his skull and knocked him out of the war. Or he was a prisoner again at Camp Morton. He could actually smell the sickening stink and sweat of the drafty barracks where ill-fed men lay dying. And, last, he was riding the red horse at a dead run as he rushed up to the Juárista camp, after the Hussars of Maximilian's army had struck, and finding Ana amid the carnage. Young Ana, who had no need to die. He wrenched whenever he thought of her.

He often wondered why these torments persisted. Was it his guilt for having survived when all — yes, all — of his boyhood friends had died, either at Shiloh or blood-drenched Franklin? He could only wonder. Yet he knew that the demons would likely plague him the rest of his life. All he wanted was peace of mind. Not richness. Not glory. Just peace of mind.

He'd also been thinking lately of home, back in Tennessee, although there was nothing to go back to there. No family or friends, save one, for a Southerner who'd had to wear the hated blue on the Western frontier in order to survive a Yankee prison camp, and thus was ostracized. That one, Mr. B. L. Sawyer, the family lawyer. He alone understood.

Jesse dozed.

It must have been an hour later, when he stirred to the rushing racket of the twice-weekly, west-bound stage pulling in under cavalry escort. He heard it stop with a jangle of chains and hoof clatter and a hoarse whoaing voice. More voices. The stage's arrival was always the biggest event in

8

town until the next one, unless there'd been a shooting in the saloon. Mentally, he retraced the stage's backward route: Fort Bowie, Doubtful Cañon, the long stretch below the Burro Mountains back to the Mimbres River in New Mexico Territory, then Fort Cummings, and onward to Mesilla and El Paso. These people had to have had some luck getting through, even with an escort.

Curious, bored, he went to the window to watch. Across the street two troopers from Camp Lowell watched, and several sombreroed Mexicans. The stage immediately disgorged two rumpled drummers in bowlers; they made a beeline for the hotel's saloon. Next came a heavy-set man of middle years, a professional-looking man in a dark suit and a light-colored planter's hat, an attire that looked extremely uncomfortable in the afternoon heat. A woman followed. The man offered his hand, but she declined with a little smile and stepped down on her own, an independence that caused the man to shake his head with wry tolerance. She was dressed in a gray traveling suit and a small hat decorated with flowers. An Eastern woman, no doubt. As hostlers unharnessed and brought up fresh mules, the man pointedly directed the unloading of their considerable baggage from the leather-hooded boot in the rear of the stage, while the woman looked on.

Sight of the mules reminded Jesse it was time to feed his own stock. He sat up, pulled on boots, and went out the door.

She was waiting for him again, the pretty young Mexican girl, Elena Murillo. She had huge, dark eyes and hair as black as a raven's wing, which framed a small-featured face, that made her eyes seem all the more prominent. Today she wore a loose-fitting pink blouse, open to the point of her slim shoulders and the curve of her young breasts. He caught the heavy scent of her perfume. At times, she wore the blouse at

9

work in her father's restaurant, but never opened like this. Her proper father would not allow it. She was hardly more than a child. Couldn't be a day over fourteen, maybe thirteen, although she looked older. Just a few years younger than his Ana was when she died. Like a rosebud about to flower, Elena was. Mexican girls matured fast.

He nodded to her and started on, but she touched his arm, smiling all the while. "I've been waiting for you, *Señor* Wilder," she said in accented English.

He smiled at her, aware of much more than a mere friendly greeting. "Julio is the one you should be waiting for," he said. "When he isn't busy in the kitchen, assisting the cook."

She flounced a smooth olive-brown shoulder. "Julio . . . he's just a boy."

He grinned at her total feminine disdain. "But he's older than you. When you're waiting on diners, I can see him watching you from the kitchen. His eyes follow you everywhere. He's a fine young man. Your father has much confidence in him. He told me so."

The dark eyes flashed. More scorn. She put a hand on his arm, stroking it gently. "Can't we talk in your room, *Señor* Wilder? You always so nice. You know how to treat a girl. Julio . . . all he does is gawk at me and try to make funny talk. He's silly. He don' know what to say to a girl. My father says you came from Fort Bowie, where you scouted for the *soldados* . . . that you went into *Méjico*. Fought the heathen Apaches and *bandidos,* and the *soldados* rescued the beautiful daughter of the governor of Sonora from the cruel *bandidos.* Tell me about it, please."

She looked up at him, asking, needing. A rosebud about to burst. He touched his white hair, which hung nearly to his shoulders. Not yet quite thirty years old, he knew that he looked much older. "You should be with someone near your

10

own age, Elena," he said gently. "Not some gray-haired ancient like me. There's a *baile* tonight. I'll bet Julio asks you."

She sniffed.

He knew that, if he let her in his room, she would interpret that as unspoken assent; and, if he made the mistake of kissing and embracing her, his own need would begin to take over, and that would lead to an inevitable conclusion, one he'd regret soon afterward. And once that started, it would go on and on, out of control, and to trouble piled on trouble that would far outweigh the short-lived pleasures. He said — "Some evening I'll talk to you on the patio." — and walked on.

She flounced away, eyes darting fire. But she would get over it, he told himself, and the next time he saw her she would smile at him as usual. Meantime, he must drop a quick word in Julio's ear.

The blaze-faced red horse — that Ana had suitably named *El Soldado* in a time that seemed long, long ago, although less than a year had passed, and a time that would not be again — and Chico, the mischievous Mexican mule, waited for Jesse at the gate of the adobe corral behind the hotel. After drawing water from the well and filling the shallow trough, he dumped shelled corn into nosebags. The mule, in the way of his practical kind, came up eagerly for his feed. The red horse did not. He never did. He held back, waiting. As Jesse slipped the strap over the fox ears, he said, amused: "Now don't you think it's about time you quit reminding me you once ran wild, same as when you dance away from me sometimes in the morning?"

Jesse then threw down plenty of loose hay for them in a corner of the corral. He enjoyed watching them eat, noting that the red ribbon in the horse's black mane was fading

11

badly. Ana's handiwork, it would stay there until it wasted away.

He broke off the thought and closed his eyes for a moment, thinking. Nothing was to be gained by looking back, but how could he not now and then, and with the red horse there to remind him? Together, they had experienced much and, somehow, survived, like old soldiers spared for reasons beyond their understanding. To his mind death had ended a beloved young life down there in Chihuahua, but not a relationship, now not unlike a bequest passed on.

Drifting toward the hotel, he paused to watch the turquoise sky. A roving band of clouds had strayed in from the south over the Rincons. Maybe some rain tonight, maybe not.

He found Julio Barrios alone in the kitchen, busy making early preparations for the evening meal. He was a good-looking young man, slim, straight, dark-eyed, smooth-faced, with a clean smile, not much older than Elena. There was a shyness about him, a deferential manner toward his elders, which no doubt could be traced as gratitude stemming from his tragic past. Apaches had wiped out his family in the Rincons, so the story went. Julio had survived because he was out gathering *piñon* nuts.

Señor Carlos Murillo, Elena's father, a member of the pursuing posse of townsmen, had found a distraught Julio weeping over the mutilated bodies of his parents, younger brother and sister, and brought him home. That was four years ago. He had grown into a quiet, conscientious young man, too reticent for the budding Elena.

He looked at Jesse and smiled a silent greeting.

Jesse said: "There's a *baile* tonight, Julio. Why don't you ask Elena?"

Julio stopped his work. A kind of alarm worked across his

12

face. "Oh, *Señor* Wilder, she wouldn't go with me. She calls me a peon."

"How do you know she won't go if you ask her?"

"I just know." He sounded miserable.

Jesse looked around before he spoke. "Here's something to remember about women, Julio. They don't always mean what they say. Ask her."

Julio hung his head. "Tell you the truth, *señor*, I lack the courage."

"Ask her anyway."

"I don' know how to dance."

"You can't learn, if you don't go."

"What if she says no?"

"She may not."

"But if she does say no?"

"Ask another girl. If nobody asks Elena, she'll be sorry she said no to you."

Julio's face lit up. "I will ask her, *Señor* Wilder. I will! *Muchas gracias*." He kept nodding. "I can see that you savvy women, *Señor* Wilder."

Jesse smiled. "No man ever savvies much about women, Julio. If he says he does, he's either a fool or a liar. But once in a while you have to be a little bold."

His growing boredom turned him toward the plaza, thinking of Luis Vega, Tucson's leading maker of fine saddles and boots, also a good judge of tequila, and always a sociable companion whose connections went back to the old pueblo's early days.

In the beginning today, they talked about the virtues of the double-rigged Texas saddle, such as Jesse rode, as opposed to the center-fire California rig, with long *tapaderos*.

"What you need, *amigo* Jesse," said the affable artisan, always the salesman, displaying his piano-keys smile, "is a

13

fine Mexican saddle," and he gestured to a silver-mounted example with intricate hand-tooled leather.

"It's far too beautiful for my hard use," Jesse said, smiling. This was not the first time *amigo* Luis had urged the saddle upon him. "But I would buy you a drink."

In a *cantina* over tequila, Vega regarded him thoughtfully and said: "*Amigo* Jesse, you are restless *hombre*, I think."

"True. I've loafed long enough."

"A man needs rest after what you've been through. If I may say so, you should have courted the Sonoran governor's daughter, and maybe so by now you would be thinking of getting married and having a family. I have eight children, and another on the way. I love children. They settle a man down."

"You scare me, Luis."

"If you're not ready for a family, you might try something else. Say, looking for gold or silver in the mountains."

"I've never done any prospecting. Never had the time. Offhand, it doesn't appeal to me."

Vega assumed a profound expression. "No . . . that would be wrong for you. That digging in the ground. I cannot see you doing that. You need a family, first. You are just the right age now to settle down. Then you would find a business or trade to support wife and children."

Jesse broke into laughter and signaled for more tequila. "You've overlooked one thing, Luis. I already have a trade . . . it's war. That's all I know, and I've seen too much of that."

"Wait." Vega put an arresting hand on Jesse's shoulder. "Didn't you tell me one time you were a schoolteacher back in the States?"

"Back in Tennessee. A long time ago. Before the war, before Americans went crazy and started killing each other."

"I will think about this some more, *amigo*," Vega promised him solemnly when they parted. "I will think of something."

14

Señor Murillo, short, round-bodied, bustling, ever-obliging, met Jesse at the doorway of the hotel.

"*Señor* Wilder," he said in an impressed voice, "important people are here to see you." He made a sweeping gesture. "They have come a long way . . . thees man and woman . . . from back East."

Puzzled, Jesse could only stare at him. Then he remembered the day's arrivals by stage. The two drummers and the well-dressed man and woman. He knew them not. His bafflement grew. "That's a long way to come for the wrong man. Where are they? What do they want?"

Murillo gave him a *quién-sabe* shrug and led off down the hallway to the lone first-floor suite, where the door was open. There Murillo paused, looked inside, and, smiling, spoke: "Here is *Señor* Wilder." He then stepped back, lingering, perhaps, in hopes of hearing the reason for this intriguing mystery.

Jesse entered slowly and stopped short. The man was standing. He had a huge, domed forehead, a large chin and heavy nose, questioning eyes, and a fleshy, bearded face. His overall impression struck Jesse as being stiffly humorless and pompous, perhaps made so by his profession. His voice was formal and carefully modulated, as if he was accustomed to addressing a roomful of people, as he said — "I am J. L. Russell." — and extended a proper hand. Jesse took it, wondering. "It is my honor, Mister Wilder," Russell continued evenly, "to make you acquainted with Missus Susan Andrews Lattimore."

Jesse removed his hat.

She rose at once, still in the traveling suit of unmistakable quality and styling, which followed the lines of her slender body, and, without the flowered hat, he saw luxurious light-brown hair swept back over her ears and knotted on her neck

15

in a chignon. An expressive, engaging woman, expectancy wreathing her even features, her parted lips, with her blue-green eyes keenly on his face, appraising, he thought, what she might find therein. She held out a quick, firm hand, smiling easily and warmly: "Mister Wilder, I cannot express to you how delighted and thankful we are to find you. Mister Russell is my attorney. You are, indeed, a most difficult person to trace. I feel that God alone has led us to you, 'way out here in the vast reaches of the Southwest. There is no other possible explanation for it." All at once, she looked drawn and tired. Her pleasant, well-bred voice faltered. "I. . . ." She seemed to search for words.

In a state of complete perplexity, Jesse held up both hands in a warding-off motion before she could say more. "There must be some mistake. A mistake of identity."

She uttered a pleasant little laugh of certainty, eyes still fixed on his face. "You are Jesse Alden Wilder, aren't you? Of course, you are. Once a captain in the Army of Tennessee, you served from Shiloh until almost the very end. Wounded and made prisoner at the battle of Franklin, you were taken to a Yankee prison camp." He started to interrupt her, but she went on as if reciting by rote. "To survive the camp, you were forced to serve in the Union Army out West. Later, mustered out, you helped train the peasants of President Benito Juárez in Mexico. You were instrumental in bringing about the defeat of Emperor Maximilian's forces. Shortly after, you returned to the States. At Fort Cummings, New Mexico Territory, you played an active rôle in bringing about the rescue of the post commander's little son, being held for ransom in the mountains, and in destroying the gang of cut-throats holding the boy."

He could only listen, dumbfounded at her knowledge, as she continued without pause. "At Fort Bowie, we've been able to learn on the q.t. . . . thanks to Mister Russell's connection in Washington . . . that you served as scout on a secret mission deep into Sonora that resulted in the rescue of the governor of Sonora's daughter, held for ransom by *bandidos*. All this, after much fighting, including Apache attacks."

She stopped speaking as suddenly as she had begun, still openly studying his face, still smiling, deciding she saw strength and judgment there, qualities she would sorely need in a man. An interesting face, she thought. A young-old face, with the creases and the close-cropped grayish beard. The mouth a bit pensive. A straight, strong nose. Thoughtful gray eyes set wide. Sun wrinkles at the corners. The feature that most invited conjecture into his past was the prematurely gray hair. Why that, at his age, although knowing that he had experienced much? How old was he? Thirty, forty? No, not forty. He had the build of a much younger man.

Meeting her eyes, Jesse saw that she was fairly tall. Her erect posture was remindful of an equestrienne, her clear skin already browned by the Southwestern sun and wind. She projected cheerful determination, physical strength, and quick intelligence. A mature, good-looking woman in her late twenties, he guessed. Maybe thirty. Certainly no older.

He said: "I'm amazed that you know all this about me . . . but why?"

"You've been in a New York paper, thanks to Colonel Taylor, the Fort Cummings commander, who is also a newspaper correspondent and has aspirations to be an author. 'Fighting Dick' Taylor, I believe they call him, based on his Civil War exploits. He's working on a book about President Juárez's victory in Mexico, giving much credit to ex-Confederates who supplied training and leadership. Furthermore, he's written of his gratitude to you and others for going in there and saving his child's life. He describes quite a fight that took place in the mountains above Fort Cummings."

She had answered one question, but not the more important one. He said: "However, I don't understand the reason for all of this, Missus Lattimore. Why you've traveled so far to locate me?"

Her hopeful expectancy had yet to leave her face. With a gracious gesture, she said: "Please sit down, Captain Wilder. Excuse my lack of manners. It's still a difficult story for me to tell, though I should be used to it by now."

He took a chair and watched her expression change to a somber, yet resolute, acceptance.

"Six weeks ago," she began, "my son Jimmy was traveling by stage from Saint Louis with his Uncle Tom Andrews, their destination San Diego. Uncle Tom had shipping interests there. It was to be a great adventure for a seven-year-old boy, brought up in our sheltered life in Philadelphia, where my husband, Rutherford, is an attorney."

"A leading corporation lawyer," Russell interjected somewhat pompously, Jesse thought, which prompted him to wonder why the husband hadn't accompanied his wife instead of Russell, because, whatever this was about, he sensed it dealt with tragedy.

"If I'd known then what I know now about conditions on the trail," she said, "I wouldn't have allowed Jimmy to go. But I was assured there'd be cavalry escorts all the way, down through Texas and Comanche country, and then into New Mexico and Arizona, which was true, and which Mister Russell and I can vouch for, having had escorts all the way, and now recently strengthened. But at a place called Cow Spring, in New Mexico, below the Burro Mountains . . . once a stage stop on the Butterfield Trail . . . many Apaches attacked the party. They killed Uncle Tom and all but one of the escort troopers. Jimmy was taken captive, and the Apaches van-

18

ished. The wounded survivor lived through the attack by playing dead. He told the story to a large party of well-armed travelers coming through next day."

Jesse could see her pain, and he felt for her, and by now he knew the certain purpose of her coming here, and with that, feeling the onset of an old weariness, he leaned forward, forearms resting on his knees, hands clasped, waiting.

She said: "I came as soon as I could, thankful that Mister Russell could accompany me . . . since Rutherford couldn't."

Couldn't. What was more important than hurrying West to search for your little son, Jesse thought, his dislike for the man growing.

"I was in New York, when we received word," she said. "As you know, travel is slow."

"You've made good time," he said, "considering the great distance." He dreaded the answer he would have to give her. There was none other, yet he hated to hurt her.

Time seemed to settle between them as her gaze moved from him to her clasped hands. Then she looked up at him in a most touching and appealing way and said: "Captain Wilder, I've come to ask you to help find Jimmy, realizing it is an enormous task and involves great danger. Money is of no concern. Whatever you ask, I'm prepared to pay. I've been assured that no one else is better qualified. You are an exceptional man of great experience."

"I'm a survivor, Missus Lattimore. Hardly more."

"And, as you say, a survivor," she picked up quickly, "you know this vast country."

"I've been over parts of it, including southwestern New Mexico and down into the Sierra Madre."

"But you do know where one might search for Jimmy?"

"I can't answer that, ma'am. I suppose the Apaches were Chiricahuas, raiding out of the mountains by the same

19

name southeast of here. As Chiricahuas, they also could have gone down into Sonora, in the Sierra Madre. They often raid northern Sonora. Likewise, the Apaches at Cow Spring could have been Warm Springs Apaches, raiding out of their haunts in the Black Range in New Mexico. It's hard to say."

A shadow seemed to fall across her face. "I was hoping. . . ."

Her suffering got to him. "I do know," he said gently, "that Apaches treat captive children with kindness. They do this mainly not out of liking or generosity, but to raise them as Apaches, so they'll grow up to be warriors."

Her eyes flashed. "I can't think of any fate more terrible than growing up to become a greasy Indian."

"Apaches don't look at it that way. And there has been a reported sighting or two of white warriors running with Apaches. What this means is survival. A chance to live. Right now, I'll bet your boy is playing with Indian children. He's eating what they eat. He sleeps in a wickiup. By now he's made friends. It's not an easy life, but Apaches thrive on it. Your boy will take to it."

She sat quite straight. "I want you to know, Captain Wilder, that I have no intention of ever giving up searching for my son. Never!"

"I understand. You have my heart-felt sympathy . . . in fact, far more than sympathy. But it would be unfair of me . . . even unkind . . . to give you false hopes of finding your boy. He could be in one of a dozen camps or *rancherías* from New Mexico to Arizona to Sonora. It's like the old saying of finding a needle in a haystack . . . that impossible."

She was determined. "But I have to have hope."

In the following silence, Russell cleared his throat and said: "Isn't there some way that contact could be made

20

with the Chiricahuas? We've heard much about Chief Cochise. Missus Lattimore would be happy to pay a ransom."

"The Chiricahuas are at war with the Army now. Their only contact is when they fight. There was a time when there was peace. But in Eighteen Sixty-One, I'm told, some Pinal Apaches stole a twelve-year-old boy named Felix Ward, who was half Mexican and half Pinal. The Army questioned Cochise. He said he knew nothing about it. The green lieutenant in charge . . . named Bascom . . . didn't believe Cochise. Bascom informed Cochise he was under arrest. Held in a tent, Cochise promptly knifed his way free and escaped under fire. Thereafter followed a series of blunders on both sides. The Army took some prisoners and hanged them . . . to make matters worse, several were relatives of Cochise. In turn, the Apaches took prisoners at the Apache Pass stage station, finished them off. It's been war ever since."

"What happened to the boy?"

"He survived, but the Chiricahuas hadn't taken him, after all. He's now with a Mexican family here."

Russell shook his head. But Mrs. Lattimore, her face firming a little, said: "Captain Wilder, may I ask you what you would do if you were in my position as a parent?"

He answered without hesitation. "Exactly what you've done . . . come out here, looking for help."

"So . . . ?" She seemed encouraged.

"I would help you, if I could. I understand how you feel. But I don't want to give you any false hopes. Therefore, Missus Lattimore, I must ask you to understand when I say there is nothing I can do. It's an impossible quest. I'm very sorry. Now, if you'll excuse me . . . ?"

He stood and left the room, somehow feeling thoroughly

mean about his forthright refusal, and damning his being powerless to help, taking with him the distressing picture of her dark head bowed, her despairing face sinking into her hands, while Russell glared at him.

Chapter Two

His feeling persisted next morning, when he went down to breakfast, hoping Mrs. Lattimore and Russell weren't in the dining room. Fortunately, they were not. He didn't want to see them. There was nothing he could do about the boy. Yet, in his mind's eye, he still retained the image of her stricken face and bowed head. He wished he could have put his refusal in kinder words, but could not find them. No was no.

Julio spotted him from the kitchen and came to his table, a smile wreathing his eager face.

"*Señor* Wilder," he said, trying to keep his voice low. "It worked just as you said it would. I asked her, and she accepted. The *baile* was wonderful. I even learned to dance a little."

Jesse smiled at him with approval. "I knew you'd make it. Before long you'll be a dancing fool. All the girls will be giving you sidelong glances."

The boy looked down. "A long time that will be, *señor*. Once I stepped on her foot . . . but lightly."

"What did she do?"

"She gave me a hard look. Then she laughed."

"What did you do?"

"I apologized for my awkwardness, then I laughed, and we laughed together."

"That put you over."

The sudden appearance of Elena, coming to work, ended the conversation, and Julio went back to the kitchen, walking a little straighter. It was amusing how she pretended not to know Jesse as she served his breakfast, keeping her pretty face expressionless. He smiled at her, and, when he said good morning, she ignored him. Leaving after breakfast, he glanced back and saw her eyes on him like thrown knives. *She imagines herself a spurned woman,* he thought. *Julio, my friend, you've got your work cut out for you. Good luck.*

After time with his stock, he whiled away the morning in town. Vega was too busy with customers for a drink. It was early afternoon before he returned to the hotel and ordered tequila brought to him on the patio.

Mrs. Lattimore appeared so suddenly he decided she must have been watching him from the dining room. He stood and gestured to a chair. She had changed to a dark blue dress — like the traveling suit, it followed the lines of her slender body.

"I don't want to interrupt you, Captain Wilder," she said in that quite pleasant way she had of speaking.

"You're not interrupting me at all. Please join me."

"Thank you."

"The only soft drink I can offer you is coffee."

"Nothing, thank you."

There was a break in their conversation, leaving each regarding the other. *She's still assessing me,* he thought, remembering their meeting. Feeling uncomfortable, he said: "I don't mind telling you that I've felt like a mean man ever since yesterday, even though I see no way that I can help you."

"I understand, Captain Wilder."

"Like I said, the first question is what band of Apaches has Jimmy. The next is where they're camped. They move around a lot."

She took that in without comment.

"And I have no way of knowing either."

She made a sudden gesture. "If . . . somehow . . . this Apache band could be located . . . I'd pay a big ransom. Any amount to get Jimmy back. If an amount could be agreed on, I could even arrange . . . through my husband . . . for it to be paid in gold coins." She looked straight at him, seeking his approval.

He waited a moment before he spoke, choosing his words with care. "Gold means nothing to an Apache. Gold is taboo. I've been told it's the symbol of the sun, hence sacred to Ussen, or God. They don't understand its value. They've seen white men go crazy at its discovery. It's amusing to them. They can understand the value of many horses or mules or rifles . . . that's something they can see and use."

"Then I would give them many horses or mules or rifles."

"No, I shouldn't have said rifles. The Army would frown on providing weapons to the enemy. I'm afraid we're back to the same two questions . . . which band and where, and how do you ride into a hostile camp to parley without being shot?"

A lull ensued until she said — "There is something I'd like to show you, Captain." — and, taking a velvet-wrapped object from her purse, she removed a tintype. "This is my Jimmy."

He saw a sturdy-looking boy proudly dressed in a second lieutenant's Union cavalry uniform, gloved right hand on hip, left hand on saber. An eager, boyish face staring out at the world with a lurking impishness.

"My father insisted on having a uniform made for his only grandson," she said. "Complete with visored kepi, gloves, and wooden saber made to size. He's had a short haircut. You can't tell it, but he's blond."

"Your father?"

"The late Colonel James R. Andrews. The Fourth New York."

"He's a fine-looking boy." And he wasn't just saying that to please her. But if she expected showing him the tintype to change his mind, she was dead wrong.

"My father passed on early this year. He never fully recovered from wounds received at Gettysburg. If he were alive, I know he would have come with me."

Jimmy named after his grandfather, not his father. The thought nicked at Jesse's mind. "Sorry to hear that, Missus Lattimore." He looked at the tintype again and handed it back to her with an approving nod. "I'd say he's all boy, which is much in his favor right now."

She brightened at his words. "Rutherford says he's too rowdy, which the colonel always said was the way a boy should be growing up."

"I have to agree with the colonel."

Here we are with the ice broken between us, the realization suddenly dawned on him, *me with untouched tequila, and she with nothing while plainly needing a drink.* "I'm going to get you a drink," he said, rising, "and it won't be coffee. Don't go away."

In a short time he set a glass in front of her. "It's brandy mixed with fruit juice. What *Señor* Murillo calls a brandy cobbler. Smoother than the straight tequila I'm having."

She sipped tentatively. "It is good. Thank you. I have had a little rye mixed with cider, my father's favorite."

"I prefer tequila out here because generally it's better than the cheap whiskey that's freighted in from the East. Either tequila or California brandy."

They sipped in silence for a while, as if they'd run out of small talk. Enjoying this, he was reminded it had been years, before the war, in fact, when he'd last had the pleasure of a genteel woman's company. He had loved Sally Jameson, whose ancestry on her mother's side went back to the first families of Virginia, but was too shy to tell her, and then the hotheads tore the nation apart. The bands playing the spirited "Dixie" and "The Bonnie Blue Flag," and the ever-smiling girls waving and the young men stirring restlessly, fearful the conflict would be over before they could enlist. Whether Miss Sally had returned his tender feelings, he never knew for certain, although he thought she had. He'd carried that in his hopes until the day he'd returned home from Fort Leavenworth, after the 6th Regiment, composed mostly of former Johnny Rebs, was mustered out after duty on the plains as so-called galvanized Yankees.

He could still hear Sally's mother's voice ringing like metal on an anvil when he'd called at the Jameson home. "Miss Sally, I'm pleased to say, is happily married and living in New Orleans. Furthermore, I'm honored to say, married to a true patriot of the Confederacy who served his country without turning traitor. Good day, young sir!" She had slammed the door in his face.

Mr. Sawyer, long the Wilder family lawyer, was the only person in town who hadn't turned and walked away from Jesse. Mr. Sawyer, whose benign eyes offset a gaunt face, had regretfully read the provisions of Jesse's father's will: one half to brother Claiborne, of Corinth, Mississippi, and the other half to their sister, now Mary Elizabeth Somerville, of Lexington, Kentucky. Brother Claiborne, who hadn't fired a shot and spent most of the war in Atlanta, thanks to a fat government job, and before Atlanta fell fleeing to New Orleans. "To my youngest son, Jesse Alden Wilder, now serving in the Union Army in the West, I give, devise, and bequeath one dollar."

Either wear the blue or die in a Yankee prison camp. There will be no understanding or forgiveness in my lifetime. On that dismal, but realistic, conclusion he'd headed for Texas, where folks didn't ask what a man's name was back in the States or why he'd left, and soon after that he left for Mexico.

"You're a quiet man, Captain Wilder," Mrs. Lattimore observed.

"At times, I've learned to enjoy quiet. Excuse my silence just now. I àm not ignoring your concern for your son."

"I realize I owe you an apology," she said. "Certainly one is in order. It was wholly unfair of me to take for granted you would dash off at once with a force of straight-shooting frontiersmen and friendly Indian scouts, looking for Jimmy, knowing how to go about it and exactly where to search in this vast, even terrifying, land. Yes, it is terrifying, but beautiful, too." She took a long drink from the cobbler.

"No apology is necessary or expected," he replied, avoiding her direct eyes. "None at all."

"Oh, but one is. You see, I saw you as my only hope."

"It makes a man feel worthy to know that people have faith in him. By the same token, it makes him feel unworthy to know that he can't measure up to those expectations . . . that, in this case, he is merely a mortal man with limited powers."

She stared at her glass, tears on the verge of rising to her eyes, yet withheld. "I must be honest, Captain. When I read about you, and your many experiences, I felt then you were my one hope for Jimmy. I still do. It was pure instinct or intuition. My father used to say that instinct is our deepest, innermost self. What we really feel. What we sense. It's very complex, innate. It gives us direction. Like faith. It's our true inner voice speaking to us." She sipped again and glanced away. "When I told Rutherford, he said I was being ridiculous, overly emotional . . . giving in to an impossible dream . . . that, in the first place, I'd never find you. When I told him I was going out here anyway, he insisted Mister Russell accompany me, which I'm glad he did. But I have found the man I was looking for. It was no impossible dream. I have accomplished that much."

She finished her drink rather abruptly. "Thank you for the cobbler, Captain. I shall remember the mixture. Mister Russell is returning to Philadelphia tomorrow. I have a letter to write to my husband explaining the situation . . . which Mister Russell will deliver."

"You're staying a while?" he asked, rising as she did, somehow glad that she wasn't leaving with Russell.

"Yes, in hope something will turn up. I wouldn't feel right giving up so soon." She seemed to be steeling herself.

He could only nod his understanding of her feelings, at the same time seeing the virtual futility of her hopes.

His eyes followed her as she left. She had a graceful walk. A resolute, lovely woman, now a truly honest woman, and he felt her desperation. It seemed hard not to call after her and say he'd try something. But what could he do? And he was left without an answer. He shrugged off the frustration and went back to his tequila.

He did not see her again that evening, or the next day. By that time he had begun to wonder about her absence. Was she ill? In her crushing disappointment, had she taken to her bed? Inquiring of Murillo, he was told: "*Señora* Lattimore is taking her meals in her suite while she works."

"Works?"

"I should say while she studies and writes. She keeps me busy bringing what books and maps I can find on Arizona. She wants to know all about the mountain ranges and the rivers and where the wild Apaches roam."

"What did you tell her about the Apaches?"

Murillo shrugged. "What could anyone say? That they are like the wind. Now in the mountains. Now on the desert.

29

Now in Mexico, seen only when they attack. What did you tell her?"

"I've told her there is no way I can help her. I know none, though I am very sympathetic about her boy Jimmy."

"Did she show you the tintype?"

"Yes, yesterday. Fine-looking lad."

Murillo played him a sly look. "And you were not touched in the heart?"

"Yes, but not enough to go off on some damn' fool mission without the least chance of finding the boy, let alone rescuing him."

"Also she asks me about buying horses and mules and saddles and guns," Murillo said ominously. "In her mind, I know, she is thinking about hiring men to lead her into the mountains. She is very determined, thees Anglo woman. And also ver' nice."

"The worst possible thing she could do, but it won't be easy to find men that foolish, unless they want to die quickly. This would be a mission for the Army except for one thing . . . the Army's at war with the Chiricahuas. She knows that. I told her, and the Army must have told her, when she and Russell stopped at Fort Bowie coming out."

"Looks like the Army could do something."

"I'd say the Army, though sympathetic, wants nothing to do with rescuing a little boy after what happened some years back in the Bascom affair, which set off this whole damned Indian war."

"Ah, thees Anglo woman," Murillo said, impressed. "She will never give up searching for her little boy. It is sad."

"I notice you say Anglo, not *gringo*."

"*Gringo* is reserved for the rude Americans who come here and insult our culture, paw over our women, and treat us like dirt. You and *Señora* Lattimore respect us. In turn, we

30

respect you, *Señor* Wilder."

"Thank you, Don Carlos. Main thing is, we are friends."

The following morning, after he had finished watering and feeding his stock, he stood by, observing them longer than usual, noting that, like himself, they were filling out again. It was good to see them looking smooth once more, after the hard going down into Sonora. Tying them by their halters, he curried and brushed the mule, thinking it wasn't always fair to care for the red horse first, although a man would favor his mount ahead of his pack mule. He had just finished grooming his horse, careful to curry around the ribbon woven into the black mane, when an unmistakably pleasant voice spoke to him from the gate of the corral.

"I see that you take splendid care of your stock, Captain. My father, the colonel, would approve."

"It's either that or end up walking sometime or not eating if I didn't look after Chico, too," Jesse said.

"May I come in for a closer look?"

"Please do," he said, sliding free the poles that comprised the gate.

She moved toward the red horse and stood back, ranging her gaze over him. "Straight legs. Short back. Sloping shoulder. Long underline. Well-muscled hindquarters. Good balance. Short cannons and pasterns. I like his bold head. He has that look some outstanding horses seem to have." She paused, searching for words. "What is it?"

"Some horsemen call it the look of eagles. Fits him. He's not big, but tough. He once ran wild in Texas. A mustang. I bought him off a dealer in El Paso who swore he'd been broke to saddle. On the contrary, it took the two of us a while to get acquainted."

He saw her eyes catch the ribbon, but she made no comment, and he offered none.

She said: "Being the daughter of a cavalryman, I had a horse when I was growing up. A steady old saddler with a running walk. A leggy dark chestnut called Peter. I was heartbroken when he suddenly died of colic."

"They're a member of the family."

"My father soon got me another horse, named Dexter. I liked him, but no horse could take the place of Peter, my first mount. There was a special bond between us. I could crawl under him and all over him, and he never made a wrong move. Never stepped on me. He'd just stand there patiently, now and then turning his head to see what I was about. I twined ribbons in his mane and tail, and fixed a huge bow in his forelock . . . till he looked like a circus horse. I groomed and fed him every day, cavalry routine, having been told that I didn't deserve a horse unless I took care of him."

"I've heard cavalrymen joke that the Army seems more concerned about horses than troopers. After all, horses cost money. Remounts a hundred dollars or more per head, whereas a private draws only thirteen dollars a month."

Smiling at that, she said: "Furthermore, a good cavalry horse carries heavy loads for a long distance. Besides the trooper, the mount has to tote one hundred pounds of saddle, weapons, ammunition, rations, the trooper's personal gear, picket pins, horseshoes, bridle and halter and saddlebags. And maybe go thirty-five miles a day . . . sixty miles on a forced march. He must be from fourteen to sixteen hands high and weigh from seven-fifty to a thousand pounds."

He had to smile now. "I see that you've been well-informed, Missus Lattimore."

She regarded the horse again, her eyes seeming to linger on the black mane and ribbon. "What is your mount's name, Captain?"

"His true name is *El Soldado* . . . The Soldier. He was a battlefield horse in Mexico. But I mostly think of him just as the red horse. Chico is a Mexican mule, wiry and tough. Sure-footed as a mountain goat. Naturally, has a mule's deviltry. Never been a mule born without that. One night on the mission down into Sonora he broke picket and ate a big hole in the top of the sergeant's dog tent. Happened, the sergeant wasn't well liked, which is not unusual for sergeants, and the troopers roared with laughter and said they hoped it didn't rain that night. I had to go rescue Chico. Question is, why did he pick the sergeant's tent? Because he knew that would cause the biggest uproar. But how did he know? The answer is simple . . . he's a mule."

She stroked Chico's face and murmured nonsense to him.

"Don't walk behind him," Jesse cautioned. "He might kick. You know the old saying . . . a mule will toil in harness over the years for the one chance to kick a farmer through a barn door. So far, we're still on speaking terms, but I give him plenty of room around the hindside. Truth is," Jesse whispered, "I like him. Not that I'd tell him. He might get mad."

She laughed and approached the red horse. As she slowly lifted a hand to pet the blazed face, he snorted and danced away a little, his eyes locked on her. She stopped, saying: "I don't want to rush him."

"Go ahead," Jesse said, "he'll let you pet him now. He first has to make his point, that he used to run wild on the Texas plains. Dances away from me most times when I saddle him in the morning. After that, everything's just fine. He's absolutely trustworthy on the trail. And has never bolted under gunfire."

Gradually, murmuring all the while, taking the halter rope, she stepped nearer, and the red horse stood perfectly still, although with nostrils flaring. "I like you very much," she said, stroking his face. "You're a fine one." When she combed his forelock with her fingers, he still didn't move. "Guess I check out," she said, looking at Jesse. "He smelled me. I passed muster."

"Would you like to ride him?"

"You've read my mind."

"I think I can locate a side-saddle."

"If not, I can do with a stock saddle."

"Say tomorrow morning? Earlier than this . . . when it's cooler?"

She didn't hesitate. "That would be splendid."

"I'll borrow a horse and saddle from *Señor* Murillo, and we'll take a little ride out on the desert."

Her expression told him she was delighted. "I won't keep you waiting," she said.

The rest of the day dragged for him as he kept thinking of her and her impossible purpose. Tequila on the patio merely deepened his awareness.

Next morning she did not keep him waiting. She was there within moments after he had the horses saddled and ready. She in brown riding boots, a blue denim skirt, a man's blue flannel shirt, such as troopers wore, and a sensible, wide-brimmed, low-crowned gray hat instead of another flowered hat, all of which told him that she had come West with the expectation of doing some riding in the rescue of her son. He held the red horse under tight rein, while he gave her a hand up, so there was no dancing antic, then mounted Murillo's chestnut, and they were away, riding south out of town.

They rode along the main road, watching the distant peaks, the horses striding out eagerly, *El Soldado* in the running walk.

Delighted, she exclaimed: "I do believe I could drink a cup

of coffee on him and never spill a drop!"

It pleased him that she liked his horse, and he observed that she sat the saddle well, the mark of a cavalryman's daughter. He wondered if she could equally handle a firearm.

They had gone about a mile before it occurred to him that only she had spoken. He found himself in a pleasant, yet observant, frame of mind, a Spencer carbine in a long scabbard under his right leg, a Colt Navy .36 at his belt. The way conditions were, no road was guaranteed safe passage, east or west, even within a few miles of town. Dust devils danced in the glittering distance and swirled up to the turquoise sky. He pulled rein, when he saw her eyes fasten on an extra-large cactus whose branches nearly touched the ground and arched upward.

"That reminds me of an elephant's trunk," she said, pointing. "I believe it's called a saguaro?" As Murillo said, she'd been reading up on the country.

"You're right."

"How old would you say it is?"

"Old. Very old."

She laughed at his vague reply. "Would you say it's a hundred years old?"

"Older than that."

"Maybe a thousand?"

"Younger than that. But plenty old."

"I can't pin you down, Captain."

He pretended to duck away. "Generalities can cover a wide range of ignorance. That is a very big saguaro. I've been told the fruit is edible, part of an Indian's diet. The inner saguaro ribs are used for making Apache wickiups, with grass, branches, leaves."

"Wickiups?"

"Brush huts. Well adapted to desert and mountain

country. And you don't have to take it with you when you move camp. Just make another one when you get there."

"Very sensible."

"An Apache can flourish where a greenhorn white man would perish."

They continued on, Jesse enjoying her company and her enthusiasm for the desert surroundings. However, it also formed in his mind that, if her purpose in coming was to sway him to organize a search party for Jimmy, when there wasn't a single lead where the boy might be, she was dead wrong, as she had been about showing him the tintype. Nothing had changed. But what if something to go on developed that was definite? Say, the name of the band and where the band's *rancheria* was? He put that aside as wild speculation and buried the thought.

They came to the skeletons of four burned-out wagons. His mount began shying away. The red horse eyed the wreckage and passed on.

"Happened a couple of months ago," he said. "A party coming up from Hermosillo. Ambushed. Never had a chance."

"I remember we passed it, coming in."

Not far beyond, Jesse decided they had gone far enough. He halted and passed her a canteen.

"Believe we'd better head back," he said.

As they rode along, a question persisted, one he was positive to which he knew the answer, but he would ask it anyway to clear his mind. "When you and Mister Russell stopped at Fort Bowie, and you explained your reason for coming out here, did the Army say it would help in any way? I don't believe we went into that, when we first talked. I know Colonel Chilton, the C.O. A fine officer. He dared the rescue mission into Sonora, orders from Washington be damned

36

about U.S. troops on Mexican soil."

She thought for a moment before she answered. "It was as you've told us. The Army's at war with the Chiricahuas. Colonel Chilton was most understanding. He said, in view of the situation, all he could do would be to order all field commanders to look out for a white child upon attacking a *ranchería*."

"You see," Jesse said, "there's just nothing to go on."

No more was said the rest of the ride. When they dismounted at the corral, she said: "Thank you very much, Captain. I enjoyed the ride. It was a relief."

"I enjoyed it, too. Thank you for going."

"I'm very fond of *El Soldado*. Would you consider selling him?"

"Only to you, if I did."

"Which means never. You've trained him well."

"Truth is, he's trained me as well. By now we understand each other. A must in this country . . . knowing what your horse can do."

She gave him a quick handshake, her face growing somber as she walked to the hotel, head down, her eyes, unseeing, on the ground. *She's finally understanding the harsh reality of it.* The thought moved through his mind, staying with him, as he unsaddled, feeling her futility as his own.

Chapter Three

Time crawled. Afternoon heat lay banked in the *cantina*. Luis Vega cocked a gauging eye at Jesse and said: "You are not restless today, but I can see that something heavy is on your mind, *amigo,* because you are frowning. Would it be the pretty Anglo woman at the hotel whose little boy the Apaches have?"

"How did you know that?"

"Everybody in town knows." He shrugged. "Sad stories travel faster than good news."

"I can't think of a more impossible thing right now than trying to find the boy."

"Except mothers never give up. She's traveled this far, and she expects you to search for her little one."

"Don't rub it in, Luis. As much as I sympathize about the boy, I've told her there's nothing to go on. There has to be some starting points. The particular band. Where the band's camped, God knows, and, even if we did know, maybe here today, gone tomorrow, with war going on. Tell you the truth, I don't want to get involved. I'm tired of war."

"Don't blame you." Luis took a long, reflective sip. "If there was something to go on, what might one do?"

"Get some men together, if you could find anybody fool enough to take such risks."

"Men will take risks if well paid."

"Some truth in that. Yet there's a limit to the risks."

After they had sipped a while longer, Vega said: "I have lived here a long time, and, if there is one truth I know about

Apaches, it is this . . . it takes an Apache to catch an Apache."

"Common sense," Jesse agreed. "But where would you find this Apache?"

"He wouldn't have to be a Chiricahua Apache. An Apache from another tribe would do. Say a Tonto or a White Mountain Apache. Or just someone who's lived among the Apaches."

"A Mexican captive?"

"Yes."

"Say, you found such a person. What then?"

Vega shrugged. "That would be a start. He might know where to look."

"Might. Might not, if he hadn't run with Apaches lately."

Vega studied his glass. "There is a Mexican here who lived with Cochise's people. Taken captive as a boy in Sonora and grew up as an Apache."

Jesse threw him a look, but said nothing.

"His name," Vega said slowly, "is Miguel García. Sleeps on the plaza with the other drunks."

"Just a drunk," Jesse said in a dismissing tone, and had another tequila.

It was near sundown, when he returned to the hotel. During supper, he was the lone diner. He asked Murillo about Mrs. Lattimore. "She has asked that her supper be brought to her suite," Murillo told him. "She is still busy with maps and books."

Afterward, as a cooling evening wind curled off the crimson desert, tequila in hand, Jesse sat on the back side of the patio, watching the colors change the sky, aware that his discontent with his way of life was mounting day by day. But where to from here? And, always, he came up against that wall he couldn't scale.

Sudden movement behind the corral in the fading light

drew his eyes. A woman's slender figure. When she turned again, he saw that it was Mrs. Lattimore, apparently out for a walk. She stood facing the east, resolutely, it seemed to him, head high, watching the far mountains — *the brutal mountains,* he thought, *if you went at them blindly, unprepared.* She didn't move, a figure frozen in reflection. She stood there for the longest time until, suddenly, the purple darkness enveloped her, and he saw her no more.

Immersed in thought, he rose and went inside, increasingly unhappy with himself. Getting ready for bed, he still retained the image of her in the gathering darkness. *A lone woman against the mountains,* he mused. *A damned brave woman. Why would the husband of such a fine woman let her attempt this alone?* He dropped off to sleep with that pulsing in his mind.

When he woke up, he realized he'd slept only a few hours, a throwback to his marching days in the Army of Tennessee — forever marching, it seemed then. Column of twos. "Close up! Close up!" A halt in the muddy darkness. Break ranks. Men virtually sleeping where they fell out, almost too weary to draw in their legs to keep from being run over by passing mule-drawn artillery pieces. Up after a few hours. Maybe breakfast, maybe not. Depended. Wait. In position at daybreak. Ravels of smoke rising from the Yankee camp in the misty woods. Springing a surprise attack, they would have a Yankee breakfast this morning and plenty of sought-after Yankee coffee.

Habits experienced in a man's formative years were hard to break. Sometimes they set the rhythm of his life. To this day he was a light sleeper, only in short spans. Fully awake now, he smoked his pipe a long while, looking out at the formless night beyond the window, then lay down again. An amusing thought crossed his mind. So he'd helped train the

40

Juáristas to fight the French, and gone into Sonora as a scout for Yankee troopers disguised as miners to rescue the governor of Sonora's beautiful daughter held by *bandidos*. An ex-Rebel helping Yankees, of all things, and paid $5,000 for it. Some people would consider him nothing more than a mercenary, and a mercenary was just about what Jesse Alden Wilder had become. Except that he'd believed in the Juáristas' cause: fighting for their country against invaders, same as the South had fought on its soil against the North. Except the only reason he'd gone into Sonora was because he had learned some deserters from Maximilian's army had joined the *bandidos*. It was probable these deserters had been in the raid on the Juárista camp where Ana had been killed. He had seen it as a chance to strike one last blow for his beloved Ana, and he had.

Yet, he had no illusions about any of this. He'd seen too much to have any. By now his wars seemed to blend into each other, into one connecting series of experiences without end.

Vega stared at him in near astonishment, when Jesse walked into the saddle shop soon after Vega opened for business. "Have you been up all night drinking with those self-styled heroes who prefer to fight Apaches from the hotel bar and never shoot anything but bottles?"

"Well, I have been up a good part of the night, but sober. Not a bad feeling for a change. I want you to take me to this Miguel García. I'd like to talk to him."

Vega's face approached disgust. "I knew I shouldn't have told you about him. Now you'll get involved in some wild venture, end up scalped, and it will be all my fault."

"I said *talk*. That doesn't mean involved in any way."

"If you had a family, you wouldn't be acting like this."

Jesse showed him a half grin. "Give me time, Luis. Give

41

me time. It takes two, you know."

"There are pretty girls here who'd like a good husband. Even an Anglo. You just haven't looked. Have you been to a *baile* since you came here?"

"Can't say that I have."

"See," Vega scolded, in a triumphant voice, "you haven't even looked for a wife." He sighed, resigned. "So you want to talk to Miguel García?"

"Yes. Thank you."

"Well, you may be sorry. He's not much." Reluctantly, he laid down his awl and took off his work apron.

They walked along a narrow street out to the plaza. There Vega paused, looking around. Eight or ten figures sprawled in the shade against the adobe buildings like so many discarded bundles amid scattered bottles. Some were still sleeping. Others sat with their backs against the walls.

Vega gave a little nod of recognition and crossed over to a man who was sitting up, facing across the square. He was dressed in dirty peasant white, which Jesse remembered from the Juárista days, but he wore moccasins, and his black hair with a red headband hung loosely down to his shoulders like an Apache's. *So, he hasn't shed all his Indian upbringing,* Jesse thought.

"Miguel," Vega said softly, gently, and the man appeared to turn his face away before he could bring himself to look up at Vega and smile dimly.

Just a drunk, Jesse reflected. *Just a drunk.*

"This gentleman wants to talk to you," Vega explained in Spanish.

The black eyes opened wider. "Me? What is there to talk about?"

"He'll tell you."

"What do I know?"

"Let him ask you what you might know."

A kind of whimsical deviltry ran across the dark brown face. "It is hard for a hungry man to say what he knows."

"True, *señor*," Jesse said. "You need some breakfast. Come with us. You are very welcome."

Instead of scrambling up at once, Miguel seemed to weigh the invitation. Jesse caught a glimpse of pride in that hesitation, of a man who had seen better days. He had a strong, rugged, interesting face that revealed the lines and wear of burning sun and wind. A Roman nose gave him a hawk-like aspect. A face that evoked hard times, that made him look older than he probably was, somewhere between thirty-five and fifty, Jesse decided. Surprisingly, for his short stature, Jesse noted that he was thick through the upper body, with a barrel chest. All he needed was a breechcloth and buckskin shirt, and he could pass for an Apache. But the feature that registered most on Jesse was the deep-down expression buried in the black eyes that struck Jesse as unaccountably forlorn and sad, like a cloud over his face.

"Come with us, Miguel," Jesse said, and held out his hand. "You are welcome." He thought: *This suffering man should be treated with consideration. A drunk he might be, but he isn't a beggar.*

Ignoring the hand, Miguel cuffed an empty bottle out of the way, half rolled to his feet, and nodded to them, "Thank you, *señor*." He was lean and straight, even shorter than Jesse had thought. About five feet, two. Again, his age? Neither young nor old.

Vega led off to a nearby Mexican café, and, while he and Jesse drank coffee, Miguel wolfed down beans and tortillas with beer. There was scarcely any talk. When he finished the plate, Jesse signaled for another. He also finished it and another beer. Jesse would have ordered again, but Miguel

43

shook his head no. *"Gracias, señor."*

"You are very welcome," Jesse assured him.

"This is not the place to talk," Vega said. "Let's go over to my shop."

When he left them in the rear of the shop, Miguel seemed to regard Jesse with open suspicion. What would an Anglo want of him?

Jesse came to the point at once, in Spanish. *"Señor* Vega tells me that you were taken captive as a boy in *Méjico* and grew up with the Chiricahuas."

Miguel nodded, stone-faced, plainly not interested in his past.

"May I ask why you left the Chiricahuas?"

"My mother died and then my wife died, and we had no children. Also, I am not a *Tsoka-ne-nde*."

"Tsoka-ne-nde?"

"Cochise's band. The Great Chief."

"When did you lose your mother and wife?"

"My mother died eight years ago. When my wife died five years ago, I left the band."

"I'm sorry. I have felt the same losses you have. Do you miss the Chiricahuas?"

Miguel shrugged. "I told you I'm not Chiricahua."

"So you don't miss them?"

"Why you ask such questions?" Miguel was testy.

Jesse realized he'd get nowhere unless he came to the point immediately. "Do you know about the Anglo woman staying at the hotel? Do you know why she is here?"

The time-lined face the color of earth creased into self-mockery. "How would I know?"

"Gossip," Jesse said.

"There's no gossip, as you call it, on the plaza. Talk is only of food and drink . . . always of drink."

"I see. Then I'll tell you. This Anglo woman lives in the Eastern part of this country . . . far off. She has come out here to find her young son, who was captured by Apaches. Have you heard about the captive boy?"

An indifferent shrug. *Why would he hear?*

"It happened east of here. In *Nuevo Mejico*. Not far south of the Burro Mountains. At a place called Cow Spring. There used to be a stage station there."

Miguel's eyes lit up at that. "Yes. The spring. The water is good. There is always water there."

"This happened not long ago. The boy was with an uncle. They had an escort of soldiers. All were killed except one soldier, who told what happened."

"Why would I hear about this? I told you I am not Chiricahua, and I have no ear for your gossip."

"Yet you were raised as a Chiricahua."

"That did not make me one of them."

"Then what are you?"

"I was born *mejicano*. In the Sonoran town of Bavispe."

"I have been there." Jesse expected him to show interest at that, but, strangely, he did not. "That makes you *mejicano*."

"But I am not *mejicano*."

"Why do you say that?" Jesse asked, puzzled. "You have to be one or the other."

Miguel didn't reply at once. His face seemed to reflect far-away thoughts, and the sadness. "I will come to that." When he spoke again, his voice was heavy with conflict. "When the Chiricahuas raided Bavispe, they killed my father and took my mother and me, two other women, and six children. I remember the hard days that followed. Always in pain. Shivering and quaking with fear before we reached the Dragoon Mountains and Cochise's stronghold. Afraid every step they would kill us. The children who had no mothers were

45

given away. I stayed with my mother. In time, she became the wife of a warrior. Yes, *señor*, I grew up like an Apache. I learned to eat mule and horse meat. I learned to deny myself. I could take a mouthful of water and run up a mountain without swallowing it. An Apache, you know, can cover fifty to seventy-five miles a day at a swinging dogtrot. He can run a horse down. I could do that, when I grew older."

"I believe you," Jesse said admiringly. "You have an extra deep chest, the chest of a runner."

"Then I could. Not any more. I am nothing."

That touched Jesse. "Don't say that. You are a man. You have experienced much, suffered much. Now tell me more about yourself, Miguel. Why you say you are neither Chiricahua nor *mejicano?*"

Almost painfully Miguel went on. "While I was growing up, my captors told me I would soon forget where I came from, that I was a Chiricahua now. One of them was an older *mejicano* boy named Santos. He was very mean. Bad temper. Almost every day he'd tell me I was an Apache. He'd laugh and sneer, when I said I was still *mejicano*. He said he hated *mejicanos*. I thought he said that to impress the Apaches. He was my enemy from the start. Being older and stronger, he would throw me down and twist my arms, like the coward he was. Sometimes a warrior had to stop him, when he tried to choke me. One time I picked up a rock and knocked him out. He never jumped me after that, but I could tell he still hated me even more. He had evil eyes like knives. More than once he swore he'd kill me someday."

Perhaps glad to have an understanding listener, even relieved to have his story told, Miguel appeared to gather his thoughts before he continued. "The Chiricahuas liked to raid during a full moon, when the light is almost like day. They killed *mejicanos* like flies, and the *mejicanos* killed Apaches, when they could. Raiding Mexico is a way of life for Chiricahuas. Sometimes when pursued hard, they would split up and agree to meet at a place. That gave the *mejícanos* too many tracks to follow. Confused them. Sometimes we traveled four, five nights and days without stopping to eat or sleep. They soon found out which ones were men. Some boys could stand it like men. Some couldn't. I was among the young ones who could. It was that or be left behind and killed." He ceased talking, his face softening. "But I never forgot Bavispe, my home, where the singing river flows by and my father was killed. I ached for my home and my people. I never forgot all the time I went on raids into Sonora. I managed never to kill a *mejícano*. Instead, I became a great horse and mule thief. No Chiricahua was better. Even the Great Chief, Cochise, praised me. Even the other Chiricahua bands heard of my power. Santos seemed to hate me even more after that, he was so jealous. I could slip into a corral with horses made nervous by the smell of Apaches . . . quiet them and let them out, and we'd start driving them quietly north. I have what the Chiricahuas call 'power-with-horses.' So they called me the Horse Stealer. I sang horse songs. I sang before we went on a raid. Most times we would go on foot, leaving horses as food for the women and children. The songs were part of my medicine, my power. The songs helped us locate horse herds, and then we lured them to places where we could drive them off. Sometimes we'd rope the horses we wanted, if the horses were slow coming out of the corrals. I can make horses easy to handle. Maybe it's because I don't rush up to them, but gentle them. Let them smell me. My hands and arms, my chest, my hair, my face. I was never bitten. That way I tamed them. I don't know exactly why I have this power, but I do."

"It's a gift you have," Jesse said, meaning it, and hoped

he sounded convincing.

"There is another reason why I have this power. I observed the taboos."

"Tell me."

"When I was sixteen, I was old enough to go on raids as a novice warrior. A child of the water, they called it. I had to follow certain rules or go back to the *ranchería*. They gave me a scratching stick and a drinking tube. I was not allowed to scratch my head with my fingers. I used the stick. I had to suck water into my throat through the cane tube. I was instructed that, if water touched my lips, I would have a mustache. They gave me a novice's war hat with four feathers in it . . . hummingbird, oriole, quail, and eagle . . . but the hat had no power. I had to pack mescal for the warriors to chew and rawhide for moccasin soles and cut firewood and do the cooking. On a raid at night I had to rest on a rock for four days, so I wouldn't go to sleep. Also I had to sleep with my head to the east until I got home. The first four days of a raid I had to go to the front. I could not look back or around. Always straight ahead. The second time on a raid I was told not to sleep through the night, but to get up often and run around in the dark. In the morning I would run up a hill and urinate, then scratch dirt over that place like a coyote does, and howl like a coyote does. That way, the warriors told me, I would be smart like a coyote and stay out of trouble. And every morning they told me to run around camp so I would always be a strong runner. I did that. I was strong."

His speech was flowing now. Again he paused.

"Go on," Jesse urged.

"As a novice, I did as I was told. I never spoke unless spoken to. I never laughed, even when something was funny. I never complained when hungry or thirsty or tired. I was not allowed to eat warm food on my first two raids. If I cooked it,

48

I had to let it get cold before I ate it, or I couldn't learn to control horses. For the same reason, I wasn't allowed to eat entrails. My horse power must go back to my training as a novice."

"But not all warriors have this horse power?"

"True. Not many do."

"So you never killed any *mejicanos* because you thought of them as your people Yet you insist you are not *mejicano*. Why is this?"

Miguel frowned and proceeded slowly, solemnly. "I will tell you now. But don't think I was a coward . . . I became a warrior. I killed three *pindah-lickoyee* enemies . . . White Eyes. One was a soldier in a blue uniform. He tried to kill me. The *méjicanos* fought the White Eye soldiers in the big war long ago, when many White Eyes invaded *Méjico*. He was an enemy of my people."

"Who were the other White Eyes?"

"One was a miner. I shot him, when we attacked a camp. They were digging for the forbidden yellow metal that makes White Eyes crazy. The other White Eye was in a wagon train we burned on the San Pedro. A huge man with a black beard. I killed him with a knife. He kept cursing me as we wrestled. He was strong, but I was quicker. We killed them all that morning on the San Pedro."

He was talking like an Apache warrior now, boasting a little, Jesse thought. "When did you change your mind about being *mejicano*? How did this happen?"

"When I went back to Bavispe after my wife died. I even dressed up like a *mejicano,* with sombrero and boots, fancy shirt and leather pants, and rode into the plaza on a good bay horse. I saw an old woman there. I asked her if she remembered the raid and my family. All she remembered was the raid and my mother's first name, which was Rosa, and one of the other women. Then she looked at me with scorn, turned her back, and walked away from me. I went over to an old man and asked if he remembered the raid. He said he did and my name was Miguel García. That made me feel good. At last I was back among my own people! Then he said . . . 'But the Apaches made you like them. You have lived among them too long. You will lead them back here. You are not *mejícano* . . . you are Apache.' And he spit on the ground, and walked away. After that, nobody would talk to me. When I went up to them, they turned their backs and walked away. Nobody invited me into their homes. Not one. Some *mejícano* soldiers came. They told me I had better leave. I hung my head and rode away. Now you understand when I say I am nothing."

His infinite sadness stirred Jesse. "You are still a man. What happened wasn't your fault."

"Makes no difference."

"What do you do for a living?"

"As little as I can. It is not much of a living. I exist. Since I am good with stock, sometimes I work as a teamster on short hauls to the mines in the mountains. Sometimes I cut wood. Once a *pindah* officer in blue uniform asked me if I would serve as a guide for the soldiers at Fort Bowie. I am not a traitor to the *Tsoka-ne-nde,* even though I am not one of them. I also remembered the long-ago war in my *Méjico* against the White Eye invaders, and I said, no."

"Which shows you are still a *mejícano* at heart."

Miguel looked down. "Makes no difference. In Bavispe, my country, I am still an Apache, an outcast. Sometimes I help good men like *Señor* Murillo break a young horse or mule. I still have horse power. I can thank the Chiricahuas for that."

Jesse sensed that Miguel was getting tired and more depressed as he said: "I have talked too much about the old days. It makes me feel bad. My heart is on the ground. Maybe I should go into the mountains, stretch out under a pine tree, and give up. Let Ussen the Breathmaker take my spirit. Ride the Ghost Pony to the Happy Place. Let the wild animals have my worthless body. Let. . . ."

Jesse stopped him abruptly. "Don't talk like that. You're tired. Here." He held out several *pesos*. "There is much more to talk to you about, Miguel. Take this. Go buy yourself some clothes. Get a room somewhere. Rest. Eat good. Take a bath. You'll feel better. Meet me here this same time in the morning."

Miguel blinked at the silver adobe dollars without taking them, as if a particle of pride restrained him.

"Take them," Jesse insisted. "I want you to enjoy yourself." He pressed the coins into Miguel's lax hand and started him toward the door.

When Miguel had gone and Jesse told Vega what he'd done, the saddle-maker frowned and shook his head. "You did the wrong thing. He'll just get drunk."

"I told him to meet me here tomorrow morning."

"He won't. You'll have to go find him."

"Maybe so. At least, I'll know whether he's reliable or not."

Vega stood back in sharp surprise. "What do you mean . . . reliable?"

"Whether he can be trusted or not."

"Trusted? How do you mean?"

"Maybe . . . to lead a search party into the mountains."

Vega put hands to his ears. "No more. You can't be saying this, *amigo*. It's crazy."

"Right now, it's just a thought."

"A crazy thought," Vega scowled, and returned to his work.

Jesse raised a dry smile. "Of course, it's crazy. See you in the morning, Luis." As he went out, Vega's voice followed him. "Above all, don't be a fool. You can't take this on. It's too much for any man."

He was in long-legged stride for the hotel bar when Mrs. Lattimore, the Anglo lady, as he was beginning to think of her, hurried in from the direction of the corrals.

"Oh, Captain Wilder," she said, somewhat breathlessly, "I've been looking for you, hoping I'd find you."

"My good fortune."

She smiled. "Always the Southern gentleman."

"Back in Tennessee, remember, I'm considered anything but a gentleman because I once wore the Union blue. What is it?"

"I thought I'd do some riding while I await further word from my husband. Might even buy a good horse. *Señor* Murillo has kindly asked a local horse trader to bring up several horses for me to look at. But I'd like your opinion before I do anything. The man is here now with three horses."

"Glad to."

They went out to the corral where a white man waited with three horses, their halters held by a Mexican boy. The trader, his whiskered jaws working on an enormous wad of tobacco, his eyes sharp, touched the brim of his hat and said — "Ma'am, here is the horse I think you'll like." — and led out a leggy, dark chestnut of light build. "Only six years old. Foaled in Arizona. A fine animal. Well-bred. A one-owner horse. Local businessman. Sold when he got too old to ride."

As she strolled around the horse, Jesse saw her give it the keen sizing up one would expect of a cavalryman's daughter, then she said to him: "What do you think?"

"Let's see," he parried, thinking suspiciously: *Who was too old, the rider or the horse?* At first glance, the gelding looked fit enough. Nice head, nice shoulder. But. . . . "Will you lead him around a little, sir?" he asked. Something bothered him.

The trader obligingly led the chestnut in a circle and back, while that elusive something still bothered Jesse. And he said: "Let's take a look at his mouth."

"Help yourself," the trader obliged, sounding confident.

He thinks I don't know how to read a horse's teeth. Jesse opened the horse's mouth and peered intently, studying the teeth in detail. *"Señor,"* he said, turning to the trader with a slow smile, "I know this has been a good horse in his time. But his lower nippers are round or nearly so, as thick as they are broad, and the corner teeth are getting round. This faithful old traveler is about twelve years old, and he's getting a little down in weight. That's what bothered me first."

The trader, looking shocked and annoyed, recovered and gazed up at the sky. Turning to Mrs. Lattimore, he swept off his sombrero and bowed from the waist. "I just bought this horse a few days ago. Was told he's six. I did look at him. Just reckon my eyesight ain't what it used to be. Looks like I got skinned. Ma'am, I assure you I wouldn't. . . ."

Why, of course you wouldn't, Jesse said to himself, amused, *if you got caught at it,* amigo.

She displayed a forgiving smile. "What else do you have, sir? What about that dark bay?"

He led the bay forth, back to his old bluster. Again, strolling, she eyeballed the prospect. "I like his shoulder and head and his legs are straight. Good back. He's a shorter-coupled mount than the other horse, but I'm told that shorter-coupled horses do better in the mountains and rough country than the larger, longer-coupled type. He's not pigeon-toed, cow-hocked, or knock-kneed. Underline is long. Has a deep chest. How old is he, sir?"

The trader shrugged and backed off, apparently to avoid

being caught again. "Ma'am, to tell you the truth, I don't exactly know. Just had 'im a week. I know I liked the way he moved. My eyesight bein' what it is, maybe the gentleman had better take a look-see at him."

She turned appealingly to Jesse, who opened the bay's mouth and peered at length. "This horse has a full mouth," he said presently. "I've heard traders say that when a horse has all his permanent teeth. Let's see now . . . the cups are worn from the two middle teeth and shaded into the next tooth on both sides of the middle teeth. I'd say this horse is about six years old. No older."

"I figgered he was about that," the trader said, nodding all around, going along.

Jesse could see that she liked the bay, and so did he. She looked at the trader. "How much do you want for this horse, sir?"

He gazed down, scuffed a boot in the dust, looked up, and said: "Seein' as it's you, ma'am, I figger I could let this one go for two hundred."

She blinked at the price. "I think, sir, you'll have to come down from that." There was some horse trader in the colonel's daughter.

"Oh, I don't know, ma'am. He's a mighty good horse."

"Why not ride the horse first?" Jesse broke in. "See how he travels. You might like him, might not."

The trader dug him a hard look, but had to nod agreement.

"You can use *Señor* Morillo's side-saddle," Jesse said. He bridled and saddled the bay, gave her a hand up, and she reined away.

She turned the horse left and right. "He's in the correct leads," she said over her shoulder. "Somebody has schooled this fellow."

"He's a fine animal," the trader said. "Sure caught my eye. Cost me a pretty penny."

Jesse smiled to himself. *You bought him for a song.*

She rode off at a trot. The bay appeared to travel smoothly. After about fifty yards, she went at a canter, then a gallop. A stretch of that and she slapped with the reins and took him into a dead run, leaning low over the flying black mane.

"That lady can ride," the trader said, impressed.

Likewise impressed, Jesse watched her ease off after a short run, bringing the horse down into a lazy gallop, and then a trot, ending the tryout by walking him, blowing, up to the watchers.

"He handles and rides nicely," she said, dismounting before Jesse could hand her down.

Independent, he thought, and unsaddled.

"Ma'am," the trader said, smiling magnanimously, "reckon I can let you have this fine traveler for a hundred seventy-five."

She took that in, considering.

Jesse, who was standing behind the trader, shook his head, no.

She said: "I can't go that high, sir."

"How about a bargain one-fifty?"

Again, Jesse cautioned her.

She merely shrugged.

"Ma'am," the trader implored, "I can't give this fine horse away."

"I wouldn't expect you to. I will pay a fair price."

The trader pretended to consider, gazing off, jaws working fast. "Tell you what I'll do. I'll let him go for one-forty. Can't beat that. How does that sound to you?"

When Jesse prompted again, she made as if to walk away.

Before she had taken three steps, the trader said: "One-thirty-five."

She kept walking. By now she had the trader jumping up and down. "One-thirty!"

She didn't stop.

The trader was desperate. Pumping both arms, he virtually shouted at her: "The bay is yours for a hundred-fifteen!"

She stopped, glanced back casually, and was going on when he threw up his hands and said: "You can have 'im for a hundred even . . . but I won't go a cent lower." His flat tone told Jesse that he had finally reached rock bottom.

When she turned, she regarded the trader with an expression that Jesse thought would make just about any man wish to please her, and he nodded to her, and she said: "Thank you, sir. I'll take the bay. Write me out a bill of sale, and I'll get your money."

Afterward, while she and Jesse stood by, further admiring her purchase, she asked curiously: "Where did you learn to read a horse's teeth?"

"My father taught me. He was mainly a mule trader. Also raised 'em. Sold to cotton farmers in Alabama and Mississippi, but he kept and sold a few saddle horses. Where did you learn to rock back and forth like that when buying a horse?"

She gave him a matching smile. "My father was also a regimental remount officer at times. Occasionally he'd take me along when the Army was buying. I soon learned that horse dealers are real burglars, except they operate in bold daylight and would skin their sainted mother if they could."

He laughed. She could make a man laugh. He appreciated that. It was a substance of life from which, he realized, he'd been on short rations for too long.

"Well," she concluded, "I'd better see *Señor* Murillo about boarding my horse. After that, I'll need to buy some horse furniture."

He laughed again. "Spoken like a true cavalryman."

Chapter Four

While making his way to Vega's shop next morning, Jesse asked himself point-blank: *Why am I doing this? Why do I persist? Miguel is obviously just another drunk. Why bother the poor man? Why not let him be? He's content with his life. Luis is right. It's crazy . . . if not crazy, it's not even remotely logical in view of the few known facts about the Lattimore boy's capture.* Nevertheless, he continued on, expecting, yet not expecting, to find Miguel there.

He wasn't.

"You really didn't think he'd be here, did you?" Vega asked, pinning Jesse with an I-told-you-so look.

"Yes and no. To be honest, more no than yes, but still a chance."

"About the chance a one-legged man would have of winning a butt-kicking contest. So what now?"

"Think I'll go look for him."

Vega groaned.

In the plaza, Jesse looked around, scanning the reclining figures. No Miguel.

He asked a Mexican, sitting cross-legged against a wall: "*Señor,* have you seen Miguel García?"

No. He had not. His tone said he wasn't interested in Miguel or anyone else.

Jesse asked another man, who answered: "*¿Quién sabe?*"

At that point the man next to him spoke up. "Who are you?"

"A friend," Jesse said. "He was supposed to meet me

this morning at Vega's."

The man tilted his head back. "Miguel to meet you? To meet anybody?" He grunted disdain. "Well, *señor*, I will tell you this only because you say you are a friend. Miguel went to María's house last night. I saw him go in."

"Where's María's house?"

The man pointed. "Down that street where the big mesquite stands in the front yard."

Jesse thanked him and walked across the plaza, musing. Miguel had a little money, so he got himself a woman. You could expect that. At least, he was young enough to want a woman.

He passed a rock-walled well and a wooden water trough and found the mesquite tree a short distance on. There was no litter in the yard, and the door of the neat, one-story adobe was painted a light blue. Did that mean anything? He rapped politely on the door.

A long silence. He knocked again.

A stout, middle-aged woman opened the door. Her face looked soft and matronly.

Jesse removed his hat, smiled at her, and said in Spanish: "Is Miguel here?"

Her black eyes regarded him suspiciously, warily. "Why you want him?"

"I'm a friend. He was supposed to meet me this morning at *Señor* Vega's saddle shop, but didn't show up. I hope he's not sick."

"Miguel sick?" She moved her shoulders, a gesture which said that would be unusual, hesitated, and called: "Miguel, there's a man here to see you."

Silence. A long silence.

She called again. "There's a man here to see you. An Anglo. He says he's a friend."

A listless, disclaiming voice answered. "I have no Anglo man friend."

"Tell him," Jesse said, "I'm the Anglo he talked to yesterday who took him to breakfast." Better, he decided, not to mention the money, although the woman must have shared it.

"Go on back," she said.

Miguel lay propped up in bed, barefoot, his left hand cradling a bottle of beer. A sour smell pervaded the room. But he wore a new gray shirt and trousers, which told Jesse he had enough self-respect to want new clothes. His rugged face looked the same: forlorn and cast down.

" 'Morning, *señor*," Jesse said, taking a chair. "I hoped I'd see you at Vega's shop."

Miguel averted his eyes.

"Why didn't you come?" Jesse asked.

"I was drunk. I'm still drunk."

"It was your money to do with as you liked. I see you bought some clothes. That's good. Did you take a bath, too?"

For an instant a hint of laughter stood in the coal-black eyes. "María made me take a bath before I got in bed with her. She is very clean, that woman. So you know I came here to a woman."

"Why not? You're a man. It was your money."

For the first time Miguel looked directly at Jesse. "You're not mad because I didn't come to Vega's?"

"Not mad. But disappointed that you didn't keep your word."

"I didn't say I would meet you at Vega's."

"But you didn't say you wouldn't. I thought it was understood. You used to be a Chiricahua warrior known as the Horse Stealer. I thought fighting men kept their word."

"Time is not the same to an Apache as it is to a White Eye.

60

An Apache says he will be at a place. He may mean tomorrow or the next day. I have seen this thing the White Eyes and *mejícanos* here use to tell time, this shiny round thing called a watch. An Apache goes by the sun and the moon and the growl in his stomach. He will stop right there and kill a mule and eat it . . . if he's not in a hurry, he will cook it. If he's being chased by White Eye soldiers or *mejícanos,* he will eat it raw and go on. Maybe take some meat with him."

"Well," Jesse said, smiling, "the sun came up this morning, and you weren't at Vega's. I've been told that Apaches also go by days, which is the same as counting suns."

"That is true. When a war party is ready to go into *Méjico,* the chief will give a buckskin cord to an old man and tell him about how many days they will be gone. Maybe thirty, maybe more. The chief tells the old man to tie a knot in the cord each day. When the knots on the cord are within ten days of the return, then the camp can expect the war party any time."

"Do you believe in Ussen, the Chiricahuas' Supreme Being?" Jesse asked as a way to keep the talk going.

Miguel nodded. He wasn't about to shout it out, Jesse sensed, like some recent convert in backwoods Tennessee.

"Then tell me," Jesse said, "why do Apaches raid into *Méjico?*"

"They raid for need and because the *mejícanos* are enemies who pay bounties for Apache scalps."

"Doesn't Ussen tell you not to kill people and take their possessions?"

Miguel actually smiled. "Ussen does not command Apaches to love their enemies. Apaches are honest. The White Eyes say love your enemies, but kill them anyway. It is also a sacred obligation for Apaches to avenge wrongs. Any time the *mejícanos* kill an Apache, there must be a revenge war party. Not just one life, but many lives must pay for that one

Apache the *mejicanos* killed. A relative of the dead Apache will ask a leader to organize a war party and call for volunteers. If the war party brings back a *mejicano* prisoner, a relative of the dead Apache will torture and kill the prisoner."

"So that's how it works," Jesse said, sensing that the conversation was about to ebb.

Suddenly Miguel asked: "Why you come here? Why you do this? Why you make this talk?"

"There are still some things I want to know."

Miguel sat a little straighter. He took a long swallow from the bottle and belched. "These things go back to the Anglo woman and her son, don't they?"

"They do."

"But why?"

"Because you know the mountains. Because you know where the different Chiricahua bands camp."

"Not any more. Only Cochise, the Great Chief, knows. I know where his main stronghold is in the Chiricahua Mountains, and his favorite camp in the Dragoon Mountains, where he is now. He is not afraid. He camps where he pleases, that chief."

"I suppose you know Cochise personally?"

"Yes. I admire him. He praised my horse power. The raiders I was with always brought back many *mejicano* horses and mules. I have told you this."

"I remember. Do you think Cochise would know what band has the Anglo woman's little boy and where they're camped?"

"Maybe. But Cochise himself would not take a white boy. He takes only *mejicanos* and a few desert Indians."

"Why only *mejicanos?*" Jesse asked, to carry the talk forward, although the answer was obvious.

"Because they make good Apaches."

"But you didn't stay a good Apache. You are an exception."

"I stayed Apache as long as my mother and wife lived. Oh, there were times when I felt like a warrior, when my horse power worked and the older warriors said my power was strong and they had plenty of meat . . . that made me feel big for a time. Now, as I have told you, I am nothing. I belong to no people. I'm an outcast."

"I don't see it that way," Jesse insisted. "In your heart you are *mejicano,* which is good. *Méjico* is your country." He let the silence between them build while Miguel worked on the bottle. "Now tell me this," Jesse said, choosing his words carefully. "Since Cochise probably knows which band has the little boy, do you think Cochise would tell you where the band is camped?"

Miguel's answer was to set the bottle down hard. "I would never ask the Great Chief that, in this bad time, with war going on with the White Eyes."

"Why not, Miguel? It would be an act of mercy. You could tell him the Anglo boy's mother is prepared to pay a ransom, say, of many horses and mules, for the return of her son. They can always use more stock, can't they? You could ask the Great Chief if he would send a runner with word to that band. Or he could order the band to give up the boy for the ransom. What do you think he would say to that?"

Miguel stared at the brown bottle. "There is another reason."

"Why? You said he remembered your power."

"True. You see, even the Great Chief cannot rule another band. He cannot tell them what to do."

"But Cochise must have much influence."

"True. But each band is its own power. Each Apache man can do as he wishes. No chief can tell him what to do except on the war trail. Then what the war chief says, the others must do. The other men can't talk back to the chief." Miguel looked weary. He called to María for more beer, and, when she brought it, he seemed to sink back into his gloomy mood as before. As an afterthought, near apology, he asked Jesse if he would like a beer. Jesse declined with thanks.

Enough had been said between them for now, Jesse sensed, Miguel conversing mainly in fluent Spanish, now and then resorting to a little English. Maybe too much had been said, judging by Miguel's melancholy face. Jesse saw him as an intelligent man, and that acuteness increased his suffering. Jesse stood and held out his hand. "Remember, you are a man."

Miguel's eyes seemed to say it didn't matter.

Jesse was at the doorway when Miguel's sudden voice arrested him. "How old is the Anglo boy?"

Jesse looked at him. "Seven."

Pain passed over Miguel's face. "The same age I was when the Apaches killed my father and took my mother and me and the others away. It was the worst time of my life, *señor,* my mother's, too. She never let go of my hand all the way back to the stronghold. Some Apaches rode horses. The captives walked. Our shoes wore out. Our feet bled. When we lagged, they whipped us. For the first time we ate raw mule meat. We didn't like it. To this day I don't like mule or horse meat. Never eat it. At night she held onto me. Put her arms around me. Two of the younger children died on the way. The Apaches threw their bodies into the brush for wild animals to feed on. Didn't even cover their little bodies with rocks . . . while their poor mothers wailed. We went on." He was speaking without pause now, the words rolling. "None of us expected to live. Later, some of the women wished they hadn't. Those the Apaches didn't take as wives became

64

slaves. A hard life. Looked on as low *mejicanas*. That is the way it was, *señor*. How could I ever forget that?"

"You can't," Jesse said, feeling for him. "It is part of your life. Try to think of other things. You are a man, Miguel."

Miguel lay back and closed his eyes, miserable to his core. He said: "Over and over my little mother say to me when I grew older . . . 'Remember your name is Miguel García. The Apaches will call you the Horse Stealer, but your true name is Miguel García . . . you are *mejicano*. And remember your father. He was a good man, Eduardo García. For years he was the *alcalde* in our village. He was good to people . . . remember that. Don't forget him . . . that good man . . . my husband . . . your father . . . Eduardo García. It gives me strength to say his name. Don't forget him. That way he lives through us.' Her mouth would turn bitter. 'These heathens killed him . . . that good man . . . your father.' Although she accepted her fate as a captive, she always called the Chiricahuas heathens to me. My blessed little mother." He was weeping. "Gone now as the wind that passes over her grave in the mountains. Gone."

Understanding, feeling much of what Miguel felt, Jesse quietly left the room. He'd never seen a man more sad. On his way out of the house, María, her eyes wide and downcast, said: "Miguel hurts inside, *señor*." She placed a hand over her heart. "It is hard to explain."

"I understand," Jesse said, and left.

As he walked toward the plaza, a sudden insight struck him. It was so powerful, so revealing, he stopped dead still. He and Miguel shared a common, painful burden that would never be entirely healed within themselves — both were pariahs, cast out by their people because of senseless war.

Chapter Five

A scream flung Miguel awake. He jerked up, his body taut. Yet the house was still, and María slept by his side, her breathing as unbroken as a child's. Where had it come from? He heard nothing now. Beyond the narrow window the black night clamped down, not a slither of light anywhere on the street. No voices. No sounds of a struggle out there. Where had it come from? It was piercing, that cry of death. Unforgettable. He checked himself, suddenly remembering. He'd heard it many times before in his torn dreams. He knew that scream.

And then, bit by bit, fragments of familiar, violent images began taking shape, and now, in a rush, he saw the scene clearly. He fought to push it from his mind, to deny it, not let it form completely, but it came on anyway, ruthlessly, and stayed there. It was part of his past, part of his life, as the friendly Anglo man had said. And so he let it roll through his head again, still as vivid as the first time he saw the Apache, dragging the screaming woman out of the house by her hair and, whooping, slashing her throat, and the gushing blood making a muddy stream on the dusty street.

He closed his eyes and lay back, unable to shut out the first horror of his childhood. The second one, moments after, when he saw his father fighting another Apache. His father going down, stabbed through the heart. Blood everywhere. Somehow his pleading mother was spared with a few others, and they were whipped out of Bavispe at a run to the terrifying yells of the Apaches.

As much as he sought to rub out the horror, it continued to unfold again in detail. The Apaches with white and black stripes painted across their faces, over their noses, and under their eyes. Some used red paint. Some painted their whole face red. Some the whole body. Some wore little white dots around their mouths. Everything they did was terrifying. They tied up their hair up in a bunch on top of their heads. They all wore long breechcloths down to the middle of their thighs.

They never seemed to tire. When water was short, they put stones in their mouths to start saliva. The women dared not complain. A few begged. His mother did not. She was too proud. When a woman or child slowed the march, the Apaches lashed them with whips. If a child could go no farther, a woman carried the little one. His mother was strong and brave. She saved his life. She also helped others. She was a small woman, but her heart was big, his mother.

Another horror rose to his mind. When closely pursued by Mexican soldiers, a woman gave birth to a boy. As soon as it was born, the Apaches tore it from the arms of the sobbing mother and threw it in a cañon for fear it would cry at night and reveal their camp to the pursuers.

Although the Apaches often beat the women and were cruel to them in every way, they didn't rape them. He discussed this now in his mind. As a boy, he didn't know the meaning of the word then; later, he would learn the Apaches didn't rape because they said that it brought bad luck. For that, thinking of his mother, he was thankful. But there was nothing more to be thankful for on that suffering trek — that never seemed to end — to Cochise's stronghold. When his feet bled, his mother tore cloth from her long skirt for bandages. When he was hungry, she stole food from the warriors' sparse supplies at night. When the Apaches killed a mule and stopped only long enough to eat it raw, his mother coaxed him into chewing some of the stringy meat; he detested it, but it had given him strength. When he was thirsty, she showed him how to get water from cactus. They chewed the inner parts, and barrel cactus was like watermelon. When he started to cry, she shushed him and held him close. When he ripped open his arm on a catclaw bush, his mother peeled an ear of prickly pear cactus for a poultice, laid it over the wound, and wrapped it with cloth, and his arm got well. His mother. Her name was Rosa. She was brave and good, his mother. *Remember, your name is Miguel García.*

There was a big celebration, when the victorious war party reached the stronghold. The feast was big. Miguel smiled wryly to himself. The Apaches even cooked some of the mule meat. There was plenty of other foods that Miguel soon liked: dried berries, fruits, nuts, deer meat, bread made from ground acorns and mesquite beans. The victors distributed the spoils of their raid.

Victory dances lasted four days and nights. When all the warriors had been recognized for their deeds, there was a round dance and a circle dance. On the fourth night the men and women danced in separate lines, alternately approaching each other and moving apart. Two warriors had died in the raid on Bavispe. Their names were not mentioned. Another wry smile. The Apaches were afraid to mention the dead because they feared ghosts. It was strange. Miguel had seen enough violence not to believe in ghosts. You did not turn into a ghost, when you died. Where you went, he wasn't sure, but you didn't become a ghost.

It was after the fourth night that an Apache warrior took Rosa for his wife. That was good, in a way: her life was saved from toil as a slave. So was Miguel's, but then they were no longer Mexicans. This made Miguel weep as he recalled his murdered father.

This night he kept thinking of his dead mother, buried among rocks down there in the Chiricahua Mountains, buried so she faced the rising sun each morning. Ashes and hoddentin, the sacred potion of the tule, sprinkled in a circle around her grave. Buried like an Apache and she wasn't Apache. She was a Christian. Many times he saw her make the sign of the cross, his little mother. Every boy needed a mother. His had saved his life.

Miguel paused. The little Anglo boy captive had no mother to look out for him. He'd probably die, if he wasn't already dead. What would a little Anglo boy know about eating cactus? And who would adopt a *pindah* — a White Eye boy? He'd never heard of that.

It was getting daylight, and the long, painful journey back into the torture of the past had tired him all through. He slept now.

Jesse found the saddle shop closed, and Vega, as expected, in the *cantina* drinking beer. Jesse had the same.

"I looked for you this morning," Vega said, eyeing him curiously. "Have you given up on Miguel?"

"I found him yesterday. He was at María's."

Vega grinned knowingly.

"We talked for a long time," Jesse said, "adding much to what he told me in the shop. I feel sorry for the poor man."

"How do you mean? He has chosen to be what he is . . . a drunk . . . when he could find steady work, if he wants it. He's honest. He's very good with stock. Give him time and he can gentle the wildest horse or mule."

"I know. He has what the Chiricahuas call horse power. You might call it a gift. I knew a slave back in Tennessee who had it."

"A gift or unusual patience?"

"Guess they go together."

"You haven't answered my question, *amigo*. Have you given up on him?"

"I understand him now. I didn't before. He's a troubled man. He told me he's not an Apache, and he's not a *Mejicano*."

"How can he say that? He's accepted here as a *Mejicano*."

"Did you know that Apaches killed his father, when he and his mother were captured? Happened in Bavispe."

"I didn't, but I'm not surprised."

"He left the Chiricahuas, when his wife died. He has no children. His mother died before his wife did."

"I don't see how he can say he's not a *Mejicano*."

"Good reason for that. When he left the Apaches, he rode down to Bavispe in Sonora, where he was born, hoping for acceptance and understanding . . . a reunion. They remembered the raid, all right. They remembered him as a boy, and they remembered his family. But they said he was an Apache. They didn't trust him. They said he'd lead the Apaches back to the village. After that, everybody turned their backs on him and walked away. One man spat. So he's an outcast. He feels he has no people. In a way, he's like a man without a country."

"Can't he go back to the Chiricahuas? Not that I'd want him to be a heathen Apache again."

"He could. But he's not an Apache. He doesn't want to be one. After all, they killed his father and made his mother and him captives."

Vega placed a reflective hand to his chin and was silent. Another long moment and he said: "What are you going to do about him?"

"I'm going to do him a favor and let him alone. It's been

70

painful for him to talk to me of his past. He says his heart is on the ground. That he's nothing. It's sad. He's a broken man. He has nothing to go back to. I feel sorry for him."

Always the thoughtful one, Vega said: "Maybe it's good for him to talk to somebody who listens. To get this out of him."

"It just brought it all back again. He's been through a great deal of hell, losing his family."

Jesse found himself avoiding Susan Lattimore. When he saw her dining alone, or sitting on the patio, or strolling in the evening, her eyes always turned toward the distant mountains, he purposely went in another direction, and felt shamefaced as he did. Although she had seemed to manage her emotions well in public, notably without family or old friends for support, it was difficult for him to continue facing her when he could offer her not the slightest encouragement — after she had journeyed so far to find him, mistakenly assuming that he, and only he, was the one man who could rescue her son. The mere thought of her impulsive, yet instinctive, action, as she had revealed, caused him unrest and even some guilt. He had gone so far as to think of throwing up everything here and going on to California — a cowardly dodge, he soon decided. He couldn't ride away from all this and always wonder what had eventually happened. Neither could he continue to avoid her much longer. Meanwhile, his interest in Miguel as one who might be able to help had faded completely. There was nothing anyone could do.

He was drunk again, and it hadn't helped, only made it worse, fanning the flames of his memory. His mind kept flashing back to the past, night and day, denying him even a little rest. He was reliving bloody events from the cruel days, complete in detail with the same fears. Restless, driven, he returned to the plaza and spoke to the derelicts he knew, hoping for relief. They only laughed at him. "What are you doing here, Miguel? You should be with your woman. Go away. Don't bother us."

He had no answer. He wondered if he were losing his mind. He walked the dusty streets a while and ended up again at María's. He still had some money left from what the generous Anglo man had given him. He drank some more and fell in bed, knowing the bloody past would stalk him again soon after dark. He kept thinking of the little White Eye boy. To survive, he would have to learn to live like an Apache. If he played with the Apache kids, he would learn, and he might make it. If he didn't, he was doomed. It had been difficult for Miguel at first, but then he had his mother. This White Eye boy didn't. His mother was at the hotel.

He groaned in understanding and tried to sleep, and before long the tortured night began. He was, it dawned on him, trying to reconstruct his reality, lost in an alcoholic haze for so long. It was a step-by-step journey from murky darkness into light. An awakening. The Anglo man had pierced that darkness with his story about the little White Eye boy. It had struck a spark inside him, and the spark would not go out, causing him to summon the memory of his own survival alongside his brave little Mexican mother.

Something had to change; he sensed that. He saw it coming, when, with a gesture of finality, María sat down beside him, took his hand, and looked him in the eye and said in her softly patient voice: "Miguel, you can't go on like this. You're just fading away. Look at you! Your face . . . your body . . . you are all bones. Do you want to die?"

He couldn't meet her eyes. "All I know is I am nothing. I

have no people to go back to. I have nothing to live for."

She drove her voice at him. "As a little boy you and your sainted mother walked clear from Bavispe down in Sonora to the stronghold in the mountains. The Apaches were cruel to you, yet you survived. You became an Apache warrior, known for your horse power. You even killed some White Eyes. And you say you are nothing?"

He didn't answer.

"Listen to me," she said. "You are kind to me. Far kinder than the *padre*, who tells me to change my ways or burn in hell. You treat me like a woman. I am grateful for that. Life is hard for a woman like me. No family. Few friends. You do that because you are a man, a decent man. You must remember that. If a man isn't really a man, he is nothing. But not until then. You are a man. . . . You can't go on like this, or you'll die . . . you will, I know. Quit feeling sorry for yourself. Do something with your life. Do what is in your heart, Miguel. Be the good, strong, decent man you are."

Leaving him, she walked quickly from the room. He sat there long after she left, still troubled, thinking, but, when he got up, it was as if he saw himself for the first time.

Jesse saw to the red horse and mule, ate an early breakfast, took some weeks-old newspapers to his room, and settled down to see what was happening back East and in San Francisco.

The morning was half gone, when he heard a knock at his door.

"*Señor* Wilder," Murillo said. "*Señor* Vega is with me. He wishes to see you."

Jesse opened the door. "Come in, both of you."

Murillo nodded good morning, saying: "I have things to do."

73

"Sit down, Luis. What is it?"

Vega remained standing, an odd look on his face, "It's Miguel García. He was waiting for you at the shop, when I opened. He said he wants to talk to you."

Jesse felt his pulse jump. "Did he say why?"

"He offered nothing beyond that. He asked if I would find you, and I said I would. He's waiting at the shop."

"Was he drunk?"

"Didn't look drunk. Just haggard as hell, and very calm."

"Let's go."

Chapter Six

Miguel was waiting by the doorway of the shop. A thin, drawn shape, although the deep chest still gave the impression of dormant strength. He held his head high as he watched them approach. No turning away and averting his eyes as he had that first day when they had found him on the plaza among the sprawling vagrants. He wore the same clothing Jesse had noticed at María's some days ago, but today everything looked freshly washed.

Jesse extended a hand. Miguel took it firmly. Both nodded. Neither spoke.

Vega said: "Come inside. Go on back where you can talk."

They walked back and took seats on a bench, facing each other. Each seemed to grope for a beginning.

"What is it, Miguel?"

He didn't hesitate. He said in Spanish: "I will go see Cochise in his stronghold. I will ask him about the Anglo woman's little son. This I will do, *señor*."

Jesse's head came up, and he leaned back, totally unprepared for such a surprising turn. He had expected Miguel, seeing a soft touch, to hit him up for more money. Maybe even a horse or mule. By no means had he thought Miguel, a drunk, capable of such a startling decision, of such a personally demanding decision. It would be extremely dangerous, moreover, if the Chiricahuas now considered him a Mexican after virtually deserting them.

"Well, that's good," Jesse said, feeling a catch of excitement and wonder he still wasn't quite sure yet could be true.

"You are the only man who can help. The boy's mother will be grateful, and she will pay you well."

Jesse continued to study the man. In contrast to Jesse's previous talks with him, Miguel seemed calm and deliberate, settled in purpose. While still wan and tired-looking, his body soft from prolonged drinking and inactivity, his old "I am nothing" state of mind had vanished. Why the reversal? Apparently, he'd come to some sort of personal end of the trail. A remarkable turnaround, Jesse thought. It took time for a man to change for better or worse. In these few days Miguel had got a grip on himself, found himself again.

"Yes, I will do this thing, *señor,*" Miguel said in a voice that seemed almost sing-song to Jesse. Like something rehearsed to build up courage.

Jesse stared at him hard, some of his awe fading at the change of tone. "Hold on, Miguel. Are you sure you really want to take this on? It's dangerous as hell. You left the Chiricahuas . . . never went back. They must think you're a traitor, living now among their enemies in *Méjico.* They may shoot you on sight. You'd better think about this some more before we go to the Anglo woman."

Miguel shook his head. "I am not drunk, *señor.* For once, my head is clear. It has been clear for some days. Cochise will remember my horse power as the Horse Stealer. I know the dangers in going back. Some Apaches were jealous. But I will do this thing."

"But why . . . why?"

Miguel's set expression didn't change. He spoke calmly. "It is not for the Anglo woman's money. I don't want her money. I can make a living here, if I want to. I can exist."

"Lately, it seems you haven't wanted even that."

"That is true."

"Now you have changed your mind. Why?" To Jesse, it

76

was strange. He'd tried to talk Miguel into going to Cochise; now he feared for him. He could very well get killed. "I don't think you realize what you're getting into."

"I do. I am not a fool, *señor*."

"Still, why do you want to do this? Why this sudden change of heart? Tell me, Miguel."

Miguel let the silence hang between them, locked in his own thoughts. Whenever reality hit him, and he wavered from his purpose, the image of his mother filled his mind and the terrible clarity of the cruel misery they suffered on the way to the stronghold smote him.

"I've been thinking," he said after a while. "It is the boy. The little White Eye boy, meek as a little rabbit, afraid, always hungry and thirsty. Once I suffered what he has suffered. Only I had my mother. He has no mother to look after him. He will die before long. He may be dead now."

Jesse looked at him without speaking, marveling.

"I will need a horse and pack mule, and other things, and a fine gift horse for the Great Chief."

"You'll have whatever you need."

"A rifle or carbine and plenty of shells, if it happens they try to kill me."

"We'll get into everything later. We'll go to the Anglo woman now and tell her you will try to help find her boy." Still, he delayed, allowing Miguel the chance to refuse.

Miguel's answer was to turn to go.

As they walked toward the hotel, Jesse tried to sort things out, thinking ahead. *False hopes. False hopes. She'll get sky high over this, and God knows how it will turn out. It's very likely Miguel will be shot the moment he enters Cochise's camp.*

At the hotel Jesse inquired about Mrs. Lattimore.

"I think she's in her quarters," Murillo said, at the same time casting curious eyes on Miguel. "Always busy. Reading maps and writing letters."

"Carlos, kindly tell her that I'd like to see her and that I have a man with me."

Murillo's black eyes bored deeper into Miguel. He returned in a minute. "She will see you. Her door is open." His wondering gaze followed them.

When they reached her doorway, Jesse rapped lightly, and her pleasant voice bade them to come in.

She rose to her feet as they entered.

"Missus Lattimore," Jesse said, "this is Miguel García. There is much to tell you."

Her eyes wide, she extended Miguel a gracious hand. He took it briefly, awkwardly.

"Please sit down," she said.

Without further preliminary, Jesse said: "When Miguel was a boy down in Bavispe, Sonora, Chiricahuas raided the village, killed his father, and captured him and his mother and others. They walked all the way to Cochise's stronghold, a terrible experience. So he grew up as an Apache, yet he never forgot that he was a Mexican. His mother died eight years ago, and, when his Apache wife passed on five years ago, he left the Apaches and has not gone back. He has no children." Jesse pursed his lips, aware of the total stillness in the room. "The point is this. Miguel says he will go see Cochise, the Great Chief, and ask him if he knows what band has Jimmy and where their *ranchería* is."

Her eyes suddenly opened wider, and she uttered a little cry and stood up, hands clasped. Tears traced down her cheeks. "This is so unexpected," she said, choking with emotion. Her voice broke. "So wonderful. So wonderful, indeed. How can I ever thank you, Miguel?" Of a sudden, she strode across and hugged him impulsively. Miguel, taken aback, accepted the embrace woodenly.

False hopes. The words rang through Jesse's head. He said in a matter-of-fact voice: "There is no assurance that Cochise knows where Jimmy is. Or, if he knows, that he will tell Miguel. However, Miguel is willing to go. He will need a good horse to ride, horse furniture, a pack mule for supplies, a rifle, and a fine horse as a gift for Cochise."

"He shall have whatever he wants," she promised. "Everything! And I will pay you well, Miguel. Just tell me how much."

At that, Miguel looked lost and bewildered.

"He speaks a little English," Jesse explained. "But his Spanish is excellent. Much better than mine. Although we've talked about this, we haven't discussed pay."

"Then please ask him."

Jesse looked at Miguel. "How much pay do you want?"

Miguel shrugged. He seemed almost indifferent.

"It's up to you, Miguel. You're the one taking the risk."

Then, unhurriedly: "Fifty *pesos* now. To leave some money with María. I will need some things. If the Great Chief tells me where the little boy is, tell the Anglo lady she can pay me one hundred *pesos*. If the Great Chief tells me nothing, she will owe me nothing. But I would keep the horse and pack mule and rifle, if she so wishes."

When Jesse relayed that, she said: "That isn't very much. Whatever he wishes. When does he want to leave?"

"Soon as we can get an outfit together. Should be able to pick out the stock today. That way he can leave in the morning."

"Very well. Just let me know how much you need. You know, Captain, now that something is actually being done to find Jimmy in answer to my prayers, I can't help being curious. Why is Miguel doing this? It's so unexpected. So incredible. So dangerous and out of the blue. By the grace of

God and one Miguel García." She gave Miguel a dazzling smile of gratitude.

"It's sure not for money. It's Jimmy. Miguel feels for him. He was Jimmy's age, when he was captured. He and his mother and the others were fearful every step the Apaches would kill them. If it hadn't been for his mother, he would've died from hunger or thirst. What this comes down to is he wants to help."

"How noble of him!"

"He's been through his own private hell. You might say, he's like a man without a country. After his wife died, he went back to Bavispe. He thought he'd be welcomed, and he'd have a home. Instead, they said he'd been gone too long and become an Apache, and they turned their backs on him and walked away. They said he would lead the Apaches back to their village. He's not an Apache, doesn't want to be, and his own people have rejected him. But he's decided to do this. Maybe it's a healing for him."

"That's very sad. Tell me how did Miguel learn about Jimmy, and how did you come to know him?"

"*Señor* Vega, the saddle-maker. He told me about Miguel. We found him on the plaza with drunks. I fed him. Gave him a little money. I talked with him twice. A long time. I asked him about going to see Cochise. He said he couldn't do that. I gave up, seeing how troubled he was. That was several days ago. He must have thought long and hard about this." Jesse shook his head wonderingly. "Then today, to my surprise, he told Vega he wanted to see me. I saw him, and now we're here."

"But the danger to him?" she questioned, giving Miguel a worried look. "Going back after being gone those years?"

"Miguel has what the Chiricahuas call horse power. Has a way with horses and mules. Can make them do what he

80

wants. He was the greatest horse thief in the tribe, and they had some good ones. Even Cochise praised him."

She insisted on going with them. They tried two traders before they found the right horses. With Miguel doing most of the sizing up, walking around the horses, and Jesse looking into their mouths to determine their true age, and Mrs. Lattimore adding her expertise, they bought a short-backed dun with straight legs and a good head and for the gift horse an eye-catching, high-stepping, black gelding with a blazed face. The dun was seven years old, the black five. The dun cost seventy dollars, Jesse backing off long enough to bring the hands-wringing trader down from a hundred, and the fine-looking black went for a hundred and ten.

While this was going on, a conclusion had been firming in Jesse's mind. He'd drawn Miguel into this, and, rightfully, he owed him a helping hand. *Once again,* he thought, *I'm about to plunge into a venture without precedent.*

"Now for a good pack mule for Miguel," Susan Lattimore said.

Before the trader could show them an animal, Jesse said: "We don't need a mule. I have a good one, a tough little Mexican mule. I'm going with Miguel." This he repeated in Spanish.

She and Miguel swung around at him.

"*Señor,*" Miguel protested, "ride into the stronghold with me, they'll kill us both."

"I'm not quite that foolish. I mean I'll go part way. Set up a camp. Wait for you. That way you can travel light. After you see Cochise, you may have to light out of there fast."

"Remember, the White Eye war is going on."

"There are always risks."

She was instantly opposed. "You don't have to go, Captain. Why do it?"

"I feel I owe him that since I got him into it."

"Oh, my. A duty-bound Southerner." Her voice contained the hint of an old sadness of something gone by.

He took it as mockery and, feeling a flash of anger, said: "A debt is a debt. He's risking everything, going in there, even if he was raised as an Apache and went on their raids."

"All right, if that's how you see it."

So it was settled there, still somewhat reluctantly on her part. Afterward, they led the horses to the corral behind the hotel, then returned to town where she personally saw to the horse furniture Miguel would need, including saddlebags, canteens, and supplies to go on the mule, and a good second-hand .40-70 Sharps carbine, which she examined closely. "It doesn't show a lot of hard knocks," she said. "You look at it, Captain." He did, and agreed.

"A deserter probably sold it and his horse and the furniture," Jesse commented, "then headed for California. There's always a good market out here for weapons and good government horses."

"And may I ask what weapons you'll carry, Captain?"

"For one, a Yankee-invented killer. A Fifty-Six-Fifty Spencer carbine. Holds seven rounds in the magazine. Insert a shell in the chamber, and you've got an eight-shooter."

"And," she finished, "you ear the hammer back for each shot. It can reach out accurately up to four hundred yards. It has a tubular, spring-loaded magazine that inserts into the butt of the stock. Very handy."

He held a knowing grin on her. "I believe you've had instructions."

"My father used to talk about it. How deadly the Spencer rifle was against infantry."

"We Rebs first ran into the Spencer rifles at Hoover's Gap, Tennessee." He wasn't grinning now. "And again at Franklin. It was like a continuous sheet of fire."

"I didn't mean to make light of how it was used," she amended quickly. "Like General Sherman said . . . war is hell. I hate it. My father hated it and passed on early because of it."

"I didn't think you were making light of it," he assured her. "More than once I was lucky to have a Spencer with me down in Mexico. For a side arm, I have a Colt Navy Thirty-Six, converted to metallic cartridges."

It was mid-afternoon when all preparations were made. Miguel said he would be at the corral by daylight. As he started to leave, she spoke up. "We've talked about everything but the distance, Captain. How far is it to the stronghold?"

"I'd say about three days' ride, or less. It's in the Dragoon Mountains." He looked at Miguel.

He nodded.

She was suddenly bursting with more anxiety. "How can we be sure Cochise will be there?"

"Good question," Jesse agreed. "I hadn't even thought of that. Just assumed, Miguel seemed so certain." He asked Miguel in Spanish, and then Jesse said to her: "He says Cochise will be there. It's his favorite place this time of year, and easy to defend."

She still wasn't convinced. "What if cavalry from Fort Bowie attacks the stronghold?"

"I doubt that Fort Bowie even knows where it is."

They left Miguel on that note and walked in preoccupied silence back to the hotel.

"Captain," she said, "will you be my guest at dinner tonight?"

He accepted with thanks, sensing that she was realizing

further the meaning of this ride into Apache country.

In his room, checking weapons, he learned that he was short of shells for the Spencer, which called for another trip in the town. On the way back, he dropped in to see Vega. The saddle-maker's face stiffened at the news.

"I was afraid something like this might happen," he said. "It is very dangerous. Only two men."

"Miguel knows every foot of the way. I have confidence in him."

Vega threw up stained hands. "But why is he doing this? Not many days ago he was a common drunk on the plaza."

"Why does a man take a different road in life sometimes? A new resolve? He's quit drinking. He wants to do something. He says he feels for the little White Eye boy because he was once a captive himself at the same age. It is quite a turn-around. That's about all I can tell you, Luis."

As they parted, Vega flung an arm around Jesse and gave him a powerful *abrazo* that made Jesse grunt. "Go with God," Vega said solemnly. "I will pray for you every day, *amigo*."

"Thank you, Luis. We'll probably need it."

Susan Lattimore, dressed in a high-necked, beige dress of a style far beyond Jesse's limited knowledge, greeted him with a warm handshake. Her blue-green eyes shone with grati-tude. No somberness tonight. They had wine, and more wine. They chatted about many things, avoiding tomorrow, anything but tomorrow. He was aware that her eyes never seemed to leave his face, which made him somewhat uncom-fortable. Her expectant expression was a study in hope, a mother's unquenchable hope, he thought. He wished he could feel more of her optimism, but he could not. He'd seen too much of the brutal border country and beyond, stretching back to El Paso and Chihuahua. Still, Miguel offered one slim chance, and you took the one chance you had in this game, no matter the odds. As much as he marveled at Miguel, he still couldn't quite fathom the little man. Was he a little daft? In place of not having the acceptance of his own people, was he trying to recapture his childhood before the Bavispe raid? Or, reliving the ordeal of the captives' cruel trek to the stronghold, was he retaining the living image of his beloved mother? Maybe even Miguel didn't know exactly what drove him, what vague force.

At last their talk dwindled. It was time to go. Jesse thanked her for the dinner, and, as they drifted away from the restaurant, he escorted her to her quarters. There was an awkward moment as he said: "Good night."

"Good night," she said. "I thank you and Miguel with all my heart. God bless you and guide you."

Chapter Seven

Jesse hadn't expected her to see them off in the morning, but there she was, materializing out of the filmy grayness as he and Miguel finished saddling.

"I cannot find enough words to thank you again for going," she said in her earnest voice. "God bless you. And needless to say, please stay alert at all times."

She kissed Jesse lightly on the cheek and would have done the same for Miguel. When he drew back, wooden-like, she sought his withheld hand and shook it warmly.

They rode off to the east with a wave, just as the sun was breaking through the pearl-gray sky.

Miguel set the course. This morning he was dressed like an Apache: a red headband around his black hair, which hung to his shoulders. A sensible, long-sleeved, loose-fitting white shirt. Breechcloth, buckskin leggings, and moccasins. The Sharps carbine hung in a leather case under his right leg, close to his right hand. A long knife was at his belt.

At least one of us looks like an Apache, Jesse approved.

Miguel's dun took to the gravelly going, alongside the red horse in the running walk, the trotting Chico bringing up the rear on a long halter rope. Miguel led the black gift horse on a shorter halter.

Hardly a word was exchanged as the early haze wore away. Miguel watched the trail and the mountains. Nothing stirred.

This morning Jesse took along his worn leather-cased Blakeslee Quickloader cartridge box, tied to the saddle horn, instead of on a leather sling over his right shoulder when in use and affixed to his belt. It was a comfortable piece of equipment which he had carried in Mexico. Presently, seeing Miguel eyeing it with interest, he explained its name and operation and drew the sheathed Spencer and demonstrated.

"The Quickloader holds ten tubes of seven cartridges each. When the carbine is empty, you withdraw the magazine from the butt stock, slide in cartridges from a tube, put the tube back, reinsert the magazine, and lock the cover plate. You can load this piece with a cartridge in the chamber and make it an eight-shooter. The magazine has a spring that keeps the cartridges pushed forward. After firing, the trigger guard is lowered to eject the empty case and bring up a new one. You ear back the hammer for each shot, like this. This gives a rate of fire of sixteen shots a minute." Jesse smiled. "But keep that up very long and the barrel can get too hot to hold. You use a bandanna."

Miguel nodded. "Beats old muzzle-loaders."

"This gun has one dangerous habit," Jesse said, with a crooked grin. "Bang the butt down too hard when fully loaded, it's been known to go off, with fatal results to the holder. So I'm careful not to bang it. Sometimes I carry it with only one cartridge in the chamber. Today it's fully loaded."

They made good time and camped early in the cool timber on the murmuring San Pedro. Good water, plenty of wood. Miguel proposed a big fire before sundown, so after sundown there would be no flames to be seen from a distance, and they'd have coals for cooking. Jesse asked if Miguel thought they had been sighted, and Miguel said he'd noticed no movements, no mirror signals, no smoke. Besides, he shrugged, only two riders were no threat.

"But they might want these good horses," Jesse reasoned.

Miguel nodded. "Tomorrow," he said, "will be different

as we ride deeper into Cochise's country. Old feelings will come back to me. Tonight I feel nothing." His eyes posed a question. "Do you believe me when I say that? This *feeling* thing?"

"Yes. It's like when you know your enemy is out there somewhere, but you don't know how close or how far."

Miguel seemed pleased to hear that. "You have the same feelings?"

"Maybe not in the way you do. You were brought up like an Apache. No doubt your senses are keener than mine. The feelings or meanings in what you see. A bird takes sudden flight. A bush moves. A ravel of dust in the distance. What you smell and hear. What you taste."

Miguel nodded approval. "Where did you learn these things?"

"As a young man in the Anglos' big war a few years ago, far to the East. People in the northern part of the country fighting people in the South. The North called it the Civil War, the South the War Between the States. A terrible war. I fought for the South. I soon learned the enemy was close by. Then on the plains, fighting Indians who always rode horseback. Then down in *Méjico,* helping train *Presidente* Juárez's *méjicano* peasants fighting the Emperor Maximilian's mercenaries. Did you ever hear of *Presidente* Juárez?"

Miguel didn't answer. However, his thoughtful expression said maybe so, maybe not. He couldn't be sure. Maybe he didn't know what a president was.

"He's a great man," Jesse said. "As *presidente,* he's a great chief. You would be impressed, if you saw him and talked to him."

"You talk to . . . this great chief of *Méjico?*"

"Once. He's not a big man, but he seems bigger than he is. Has a short, stocky body and a strong face with black eyes. A man of purpose. Fit to be *presidente* of your *Méjico*. He's not *mestizo*. He's true *méjicano*."

Miguel was much impressed now. "Me . . . I'm no *mestizo*." He said it proudly, as if sharing that with Juárez made him feel important as a man, which Jesse thought was good for him. "What did you say to him?" Miguel asked. "Why were you there to see him?"

"I asked him not to execute Emperor Maximilian and two *mejicano* generals who had fought Juárez." No need for Jesse to say that he had been a citizen general in Juárez's peasant army, that he had been known in Mexico as *el soldado del pelo blanco,* the Soldier with the White Hair. *No need to go into that,* he thought.

"Who was this emperor?"

"It's a long story. He was sent to *Méjico* by the French, who wanted to set up an empire in *Méjico*."

"Who are the French?"

"It's a country far from here in what is called Europe."

Again the maybe so look. "What did Juárez say when you asked him?"

"He told me to leave. Soon after that he ordered Maximilian and the generals shot."

"You mean like this?" Miguel held a forefinger to his temple.

"Not that way. *Méjicano* soldiers lined them up against an adobe wall and shot them. Many people wanted them spared. Like I said, *Presidente* Juárez is a man of purpose. He kills his enemies."

"Just like Apaches." Miguel nodded.

They were cooking, while they talked — Jesse working in a little English when his Spanish faltered, and Miguel picking it up fast. Boiling coffee. Frying thick slices of bacon in a skillet. Miguel had brought a large sack of tortillas. Except for the absence of detested Army hardtack, which Jesse, like every horse soldier he'd known, viewed as the creation of some fiendish misanthrope who also hated the Army system, they were eating a cavalryman's rations tonight. Jesse was enjoying this being out, and he sensed that Miguel did likewise. In addition, there was dried fruit in the packs for later and tinned food if needed. Jesse had tequila in a saddlebag. As usual, he would like to have a couple of drinks before they ate, but it wouldn't be fair to open a bottle around a man coming off liquor. Miguel still had the shakes at times.

"Where were the other places you learn these war feelings?" Miguel asked, passing more tortillas.

"Not long ago. Down in Sonora. Fighting *bandidos* and Apaches, who I assume were Chiricahuas. I must say the Apaches sharpened my feelings considerably."

"Why did you fight them?"

"They jumped us on the way down. I was a scout for some White Eye soldiers disguised as miners. Their purpose was to rescue the only daughter of the governor of Sonora held for ransom by a big band of *bandidos*."

"Why like miners?" Miguel was just full of questions. He was also intelligent and a good man in the field. Jesse was beginning to like him.

Jesse explained: "I believe you said you'd heard about the big war when the White Eyes invaded *Méjico* and took *Ciudad Méjico?*"

"Yes."

"Well, because of that war *Méjico* is sensitive about any White Eye soldiers below the border. So the soldiers dressed like miners. There wasn't much time. The *bandidos* had threatened to kill the girl and her *duenna,* if the ransom wasn't paid soon."

Miguel's interest grew. There was a pause as they started on the bacon and dipped tortillas in bacon grease, between drinking coffee from tin cups.

"Where the *bandidos* hold the girl and her *duenna?*"

"They had built a walled stronghold out of an abandoned *hacienda* near La Gloria in the foothills of the Sierra Madre."

"La Gloria," Miguel said, nodding, his tone reminiscent.

"Below Bavispe and Bacera. The Bavispe River flows nearby."

"Ah . . . Bavispe . . . Bavispe," Miguel repeated, his eyes sad. "And the singing river."

Jesse felt for him. *He'll never get over being turned away. Time will help some, but it will always be there, like an old wound that never quite heals.*

"The White Eye soldiers saved the girl and her *duenna?*"

"Just by luck, we found a cave that led into the *hacienda,* and got them out. After that, it was a wild, running fight for a while. We took position. They even charged us. We lost some men. But we stayed together and marched on. Not far from the border another band of *bandidos* jumped us. We broke them, with help from White Eye soldiers, dashing down from the border. Feelings? And more feelings. Sometimes I feel like all I've ever known is war. War makes a man old. There are times when I feel like an old man."

Miguel stared at Jesse. "Although your hair is white, you don't look old. You don't act like an old man."

Jesse laughed. "Thank you, Miguel. This is a good camp. Tonight I can feel young, and tonight you have no feelings of danger."

Miguel's gaze remained absorbed with Jesse in unspoken curiosity, as if to ask: *A man this young so gray?*

Jesse didn't explain. Why tell him it had changed almost overnight after Ana was killed in the Hussar attack, leaving

91

him in numbing grief and shock? It had taken him a good while to let go and accept what had happened. It was too personal a thing to tell. Too much going back. Too much history. Let it be.

The coals died to dull eyes, and they sat there just listening to the night sounds. When a nearby coyote barked and raised its voice, quavering and high-wailing, joined by a chorus farther away, Miguel laughed and said — *"¡Cantad, amigos!"* — and, for Jesse's benefit quickly: "Sing, friends! I always used to bark like a coyote, when I approached a camp. Three times I would bark. That way they knew the Horse Stealer was coming. I was known by the three barks."

"I doubt if a White Eye could bark like that if he tried," Jesse said.

"I practiced. Would a White Eye practice?"

They were to take turns, standing watch, Jesse first, Miguel insisting on the last one preceding dawn. Before Miguel lay down, he made a bed of grass on which to place his blanket. He was, Jesse saw, preparing himself, rehearsing Apache ways. Tomorrow would be different from today, with plenty of *feelings*.

It happened soon after Jesse's first watch, just after he had pulled off his boots and was drawing up a blanket against the nippy air. He heard the red horse snort and move and halt, blowing through his nostrils. Jesse sprang up, reaching for the Spencer. A shadow emerged instantly to his right, pale in the moon glitter — Miguel in his light-colored shirt.

Suddenly Miguel's amused laugh broke the quiet. "A coyote was scouting our camp. Your horse saw him before I did. Your horse . . . he stand watch like man, that horse. Good horse."

The rest of the night passed quietly.

★ ★ ★ ★ ★

Next day the country began to rough up. Jesse sensed Miguel was leading them at a more watchful, slower pace, although he did not say he was. In fact, he said very little. Nothing moved out there except antelope now and then, white rump patches bobbing, and red-tailed hawks sailing the perfect turquoise sky, or the skirts of a whirling dust-devil churning up reddish-yellow dust. But, Jesse reasoned, it was what you didn't see that mattered first in Cochise country. You would have to assume that they had been spotted.

About noontime, when they halted, Jesse said: "What are your feelings, Miguel?"

"Stronger, my feelings are. I won't sleep much tonight. I will be thinking about tomorrow."

"That goes for both of us. Why don't I take the last watch? You might sleep better."

"Better this way. I take the last watch again."

"Did you see anything today that told you we've been sighted?"

"Nothing. But stronger the feelings came."

Jesse's smile was wry. "That's enough."

The Little Dragoon Mountains heaved up before them the next morning, flanked on the south by a great mass of huge boulders, scattered and piled as if flung about carelessly by a giant hand. Through field glasses, Jesse could see a narrow trail winding into the boulders. Miguel wisely led them around all that upheaval, keeping to their right, on toward the Dragoon Mountains proper.

Well before dark, they rode up to the roofless, stone-walled ruins of the Dragoon Springs stage station, which sat on a gentle rise. *Pretty country,* Jesse thought. Grass belly-high to a horse rolled away to the northeast. Looking around, he saw the rocky mounds of four graves and glanced at Miguel for an answer and got a shrug. The stageline was another dream the war had killed, Jesse mused. After watering at a spring about a mile away in a draw, they pick-eted close to the station and made a supper fire. The stock would be corralled inside later. Here, it was agreed, Jesse would wait for Miguel to return from the stronghold.

Sitting around the fire, drinking coffee, Miguel said Jesse should wait two days for him and no longer.

"If I don't come by then, I am dead."

"I refuse to think that way," Jesse told him flatly. "I will wait three days for you, or longer. Hell, yes, I will."

"You are good man, *señor*, to say that."

"I got you into this. I've got to get you out."

"I get many strong feelings today. All day I think about the old days, growing up as an Apache. I think about my dear mother. How she saved my life, when I was a little boy on the long walk to the stronghold." He looked off into the darkness, his face a mirror of sadness. "To my mind also comes my old enemy, Santos, and how he hated me."

"Was he alive when you left the Chiricahuas?"

"Still alive, still full of hate. By that time he had become a minor war chief. He was jealous because I was the tribe's greatest stealer of horses. He sneered, when I left. Called me a traitor."

"What did you do?"

"I just laughed. Reminded him that every Chiricahua is a free person except on the war trail, when he must obey the war chief. Those watching nodded. I mounted my horse and rode away. I expected him to follow me. Try to ride ahead and ambush me. But he didn't. He was afraid of me."

"Do you fear Cochise?"

Miguel gazed into the fire before he answered. "This may

sound strange to a White Eye. As powerful as Cochise is, I do not fear him for what he might do to me. I respect him. He knows that. He honored me for my horse power. He knows I never lied. He knows I was a good Apache. He knows I was generous."

"That should help."

"It is Santos that concerns me, and the others."

"The others? What others?"

"Santos has some followers. A few minor warriors. That concerns me, and if Cochise will tell me anything."

Jesse felt a stab of guilt. Miguel was risking everything by going back. He had nothing to gain for himself. Besides his old enemy, there could be others who considered him as nothing more then a traitor, asking their chief for the unheard favor of returning a captive, a hated White Eye at that.

These thoughts plagued him into the night.

Chapter Eight

It was time to go. A crisp morning, bright with promise. Jesse wasn't superstitious, but he hoped it was a good omen.

When Miguel had saddled, they shook hands.

"Good luck," Jesse said. "I'll wait here, and I'll be watching."

Miguel mounted and rode off, leading the eye-catching black gelding. He didn't look back.

Jesse put the red horse and mule on picket for grazing. After a reasonable time, he would bring them in and saddle the horse and pack up. It was wise to expect the worst, which might be Miguel slamming in here on the run. Anything could happen. They might have to fort up for a while.

Later, that done, he rode to the spring and filled canteens. Loping back, he checked the Spencer and settled down to waiting and watching the way to the stronghold from his lookout on the highest stone wall, the Quickloader with him. With good luck, Miguel would be back by late afternoon or the next day. After that? He gave a mental shrug.

In the beginning, it was gladdening for Miguel to see familiar country again, yet equally depressing as the morning passed, because it also raked up the past. He rode steadily, reasoning that he must have been discovered by now, meanwhile noting little signs around him. The leaves on the ocotillos had changed from rich green to bright yellow as the cool nights and shorter days of autumn set in. This also assured him that Cochise would be at his favorite camp this time of year, which the Chiricahuas called Earth Reddish Brown. He was confident of that.

As the sun advanced, he saw nothing that disturbed him in the grassy vastness. If anything, the brokenness unfolding before him was too peaceful. It might mean a false peace. He would not be surprised, if Chiricahua riders suddenly appeared and dashed up to demand his reason for being here. Because he had left the tribe, they might sneer at him, kill him, and take the good horses. Killing the famed Horse Stealer would not be like killing a relative, even if he had lived among them for years, had married a Chiricahua woman, now dead. He was no more than a lowly *mejicano* whom warriors delighted in killing like flies or squashing like bugs. He knew their thinking.

The old consciousness of not belonging, which he had kept at a distance these past few days, assaulted him again. He was nothing. If only the people at Bavispe had opened their hearts to him and welcomed him back, he would have fought for them and showed them how to defend themselves. But because they had suffered so much for as long as the oldest villager remembered, and before that handed-down memories of bloody Apache raids for many, many years, they dared not accept him. His being alive was proof enough that he was an Apache. And their greatest fear was that he would lead the heathen Apaches back to murder and rob them again. A justified fear, he realized, because it had happened once at another village. Only once — but once was enough to feed their fear and keep it alive — a captive returning, pretending friendship, staying long enough to learn the strength of the village, if Mexican soldiers were posted nearby, then leading the Apaches back. They felt they could not afford to trust a returning captive, no matter what he said or how he was dressed. They had suffered too much, his poor people by the singing river. Thinking of them, and understanding them, he felt his eyes grow wet.

Save for the low chanting of the wind or a hawk's cry or the brittle crack of hoofs on rocks, he rode through a world of silence. Pronghorn antelope moved like cloud shadows in the distance. Either he would be killed, or he would ride out of here. It was that clear in his mind. But he would not surrender meekly or beg for mercy as he had seen villagers react on Sonoran raids, when as a child of the water he had turned his face to look the other way, helpless to aid the helpless. He had become a warrior, a man, and he was still a man. If they jumped him today, he would fight. The very thought of his mother sent him strength. His mind kept swinging back to her and how she had lived and what she had said. All along, he realized, she had sought to instill courage and pride in him. *Your true name is Miguel García. Remember that.* She had accepted her fate; he must his. It could end here today or not. He belonged to no people. *And yet,* he thought, *I will do this thing.*

Gradually a new understanding seeped into his thoughts; it continued to glow all through him, a wonderfully warm and peaceful feeling, adding to his purpose. It told him further why he was riding toward Cochise's stronghold. It had been there a long time, in the back of his mind, waiting to be recognized at the right and needed moment. It was because of his blessed little Mexican mother and how she had pulled the two of them through that he was here. He was doing this thing to honor her life, directed by Ussen to honor her blessed memory. Because of her, unknowingly at first, he sensed, he had offered to help the little captive White Eye boy. Her spirit, sweet and strong, had guided him. He would — Ussen, or God, granting: to him they were both the same.

He looked back at the trailing horse, the black hide shining as if greased, the proud head held high, alert to everything. Indeed, a fitting gift for the Great Chief. Miguel's eyes then told him he was nearing the long corridor that led to the entrance of the rocky stronghold. And still no movement, no sign, which surprised him with the White Eye war going on. And then he smelled wood smoke faintly on the wind, the sweet scent of juniper burning. He smiled to himself. Their *ranchería* was closer than he'd expected.

Coming to the opening of the wooded corridor, he halted. He knew he must have been sighted. But he would wait.

Nothing happened. No signs. But he looked like an Apache. Why should they worry? He could be from another band. Nonetheless, a chill ran up his spine. Be much easier to kill him when he rode farther on. By now they had recognized the Horse Stealer, who had deserted them.

He rode at a walk, eyes searching, seeing no life, yet sensing much in the wooded distance. He knew the place well. He entered a dry wash cluttered with broken rocks and small boulders. Around him rose oaks and junipers. He felt the cool touch of a light breeze on his face, and he got the smoke smell again, stronger this time. So the camp wasn't far. Just then the black started tossing his head, yanking on the halter rope. Miguel tightened his lead, and the black settled down. The two horses were creating a clatter now, which was good. *Let them know I am coming close.*

Abruptly he pulled reins. It was time for him to give his old signal of the Horse Stealer, the tribe's greatest thief, and he lifted his head and, tightening his throat, barked three times like a coyote. Sharp, high barks. They were good barks. Very clear. You couldn't tell them from a real coyote, he was sure. The Horse Stealer could still do it.

He rode on, deeper into the shadows. In the timber it was almost like early dusk in places. Not seeing anyone was starting to wear on him. Would they simply shoot him from ambush and take the horses — would that be all? He spurned the thought, because once he had been one of them, and he could steal more horses and mules than any man. They would wonder why he'd returned. To make sure of his presence, he barked three times again.

He did not know how far he had come when the figure of an Indian man appeared not far ahead, blocking his way, rifle ready, shaping up so suddenly he might have sprung from the rocky earth. Although Miguel was looking ahead, still the man's suddenness surprised him. He felt a sharp jolt of fear. But he didn't halt or show uncertainty. You couldn't show fear before an Apache. He'd spit on you, maybe kill you right there.

Therefore, he rode steadily toward the man, whose face was in shadow, halting only a few steps away.

"You heard my signal," Miguel said boldly, "so you know who I am. The Horse Stealer. I've come to see Cochise."

Not until then did the Apache turn full front, whipping around, as if to startle Miguel.

Miguel jerked, a cold chill coursing up his neck. It was none other than his old enemy, Santos. The worst of luck. But he would not let Santos stop him.

"I know you," Santos sneered. "The mighty Horse Stealer, who left his people, who deserted them."

"I left of my own free will. No one . . . tried to stop me. They remembered when I was a warrior. How I killed White Eyes . . . and brought back many horses and mules from *Méjico*. How I did on the war trail . . . never complained. Did as I was told." The somewhat guttural language, not spoken in years, had come to him unevenly at first, in bursts and pauses, and hanging sounds. But now it was flowing, quickened and recalled by his utter contempt for Santos. "Besides the many horses and mules, I brought back weapons, blankets, clothing. I was always generous. They remembered that." His voice rose. "What have you done? You, the big *mejicano* hater, though you are *mejicano* by blood. The cruel one who picked on little boys."

Santos beat his chest. "I'm a warrior. I've killed many *mejicanos* and White Eyes."

He was bragging and knew it. If Santos was a warrior, he was still a minor one.

"You don't look like a warrior," Miguel taunted him. "You've grown fat. Your movements are slow. You can't run up a mountain. Your shoulders are hunched. The sneer on your face is fixed. Your eyes keep looking away. Your front teeth are yellow and broken. Did someone break them, or did you fall down, drunk on *tizwin?*"

Santos puffed up. "I'm a lookout for the camp. I am trusted."

"I guess you can do that," Miguel belittled him. "A boy could do the same. Maybe in time Cochise will let you watch the horses."

Santos was furious. "Why have you come back? You have been gone long time. Why do you want to see Cochise?"

"That's for me to tell Cochise. I have a gift for him, this fine black horse. Now carry that word to the Great Chief."

Santos pretended to turn to go. In that instant Miguel saw his burning wish to kill him. Miguel drew the Sharps carbine. "Don't try it," Miguel warned him, "or I will kill you here."

Sneering, Santos turned away and started off at a heavy-bodied trot. After a short way, he stopped and looked back, sneering, eyes flinging hate, and trotted on again.

Tension gripped Miguel, while he waited. His days of drinking seemed to come upon him all at once. He was sweating hard, hands shaking, unable to control an uneasy weakness. He needed tequila, he needed beer — anything. Guilt hammered him unmercifully, and he damned himself. He fought himself. His thoughts raced. Would Santos dare not report to Cochise? Miguel didn't think so, although the man would stop at nothing to harm him. But if Santos did not return before long, Miguel would go ahead on his own. He prayed to Ussen.

He made certain the carbine was loose, brushing his right hand. His shaking all but ceased as he willed himself together, prepared to ride on unbidden, when he saw two Apaches walking toward him, taking deliberately slow steps, it seemed. One was Santos. The other Miguel recognized after some moments as Antone. A burly man. Half Mexican, half Apache. A Santos follower. Two of a kind. Not much of a warrior, judged through a once-warrior's eyes. Miguel watched them warily for their intentions. If they tried to flank him, he would shoot one and ride over the other, then go on boldly to the *rancheria*. That he must do. He felt himself tighten, seeing Santos's upper lip curl in further contempt. He saw them trade quick glances. They were, Miguel sensed, trying to decide whether to jump him here. He laid his right hand on the carbine.

Suddenly he saw Santos's face change into what for him was an imitation of a smile. The other tough pose, the glances, had been all bluff to scare Miguel. And Santos said: "Cochise said to let the traitor come on. Follow us."

Miguel snapped back. "You lie as usual, Santos. If Cochise had called me a traitor, he wouldn't let me into the camp."

Santos sneered and started off, Antone beside him, moving faster this time.

Walking the horses, Miguel kept a careful distance from the pair. After some distance, he began to see blackened circles where he had once camped. Remembered little happenings sprang to his mind: where he had brought in a deer and shared it; where his brush wickiup had stood, his wife, Josefa, busy with cooking; where his little mother, always busy, had worked on a hide saddlebag. Thinking of his wife and mother made him feel bad, mixed with a haunting warmth, a depression he forced aside to concentrate on what lay before him.

More armed warriors materialized along the trail. They eyed him coldly, suspiciously. The few he remembered showed no glint of recognition, even though they must know him. A war with the *pindahs* was going on, and he had left them some years ago. What did he want here?

Santos walked with a swagger now. It wasn't often, Miguel reminded himself, that his old enemy was the center of attention. Today he was involved in something that concerned the Great Chief.

The camp was farther back into the forest than usual, chosen for defense in time of war. Santos gestured for Miguel to halt, and he and Antone disappeared in the depths of the scattered wickiups.

Miguel smelled cooking fires, aware that women and children were intently watching him, their warm and curious faces like bright copper. Some remembered him. Their eyes told him, and their faint smiles told him more: the Horse Stealer had shared what he had. He'd been brave. He'd not lied. He wasn't mean. But why had he left them? Maybe Miguel discerned glimmers of regret; maybe he didn't, only wished it. Sitting here on his good horse, showing the watchers a friendly face, holding the prancing black, he could feel the pull of these war-like and generous people, each like a shield for others. Their way of life was hard, even when times were better than usual. They would lose the war with the White Eyes eventually. What would happen to them, then?

He feared for them in the approaching world dominated by White Eyes. He had lived among them. He missed them, still, in some ways. Yes, he did. But he wasn't one of them, and so he had left them. He simply didn't belong here. He was out of place.

Santos came, strutting back through the camp. Nobody seemed impressed. One old man smiled. Stopping before Miguel, Santos drew himself up and said haughtily, pointing away: "Cochise will see you over there. Follow me."

He led off to a secluded place under a large oak tree, free of boulders and brush. There was a low rock ledge, like a bench, in the shape of a half moon.

"Wait here," Santos said importantly, giving his broken-tooth sneer. "I hope the traitor knows enough to be dismounted when the Great Chief comes."

Miguel glared back at him without speaking and dismounted, knowing well the proprieties. You never took a position that was above the chief. You did not look down upon him. Never. To do so would indicate assumed superiority. No one was superior to Cochise, great leader of the *Tsoka-ne-nde* band of Chiricahuas, who ruled the Dragoon, Chiricahua, and Dos Cabezas Mountains and the broad deserts in between.

Presently, Miguel saw the tall figure of the chief approaching, his step light, clad in breechcloth, beaded buckskin shirt, a bright headband, and hip-length moccasins with turned-up toe pieces. Black hair fell past his shoulders. A boy trailed him.

Miguel felt a quick sense of boundless awe and respect, even liking, although neither did you invade his person with a hug nor stand close to him unless he chose it that way, or offer your hand unless he extended his first. Usually, he spoke first, unless a scout was bringing news.

Watching, Miguel noted Cochise's wide shoulders and strong frame. The black, vigilant eyes. The long, somewhat narrow face and firm jaw. The high forehead and high cheekbones. The large, wide mouth, usually compressed. The strong, straight nose. In all, an austere, impassive face, rather arrogant, the face of a chief. Cochise had the quick movements of a fighting warrior, on foot or horseback. He had changed little, if any, since Miguel had left the band five years ago.

Cochise paused, his eyes reading, assessing, questioning, and curious, traveling from Miguel to the good horses, dwelling there, appreciating.

Miguel waited for him to speak.

"I remember you," Cochise said in a level voice. "Why have you come back?" When he didn't offer his hand, Miguel knew the chief was suspicious, which, in all fairness, was logical and his right.

"I will tell you, Great Chief. But first . . . I have brought this fine black horse . . . it's a gift for you." He was still stumbling a little in speech, which was a bad beginning. It made him sound uncertain. He took a grip on himself.

"Still the Horse Stealer?" Cochise's tone was amused.

"I didn't steal this one."

"I have learned that people who present a gift first want something."

"True. I want something, but it's not for me. It's for another person, who bought this horse in Tucson for you as a gift. But first, I hope you will accept the horse? It's an honest gift." He was doing better now, his speech flowing, his voice even.

Cochise moved up to the horse. He looked into the black's eyes for long moments, as if reading inner equine qualities there: obedience, courage, durability. He stepped back, his gaze taking in the front legs, judging. Moving on, he ranged his eyes slowly over the black's short back and sloping shoulders, the shoulders of a runner, the muscled hindquarters, and sound back legs.

Miguel followed all this, fearing that, if Cochise suspected trickery, he would refuse the horse, and their talk would end there.

"I will take the horse," Cochise announced, walking back. He waved the boy forward. Miguel released the halter rope, and the boy led the high-stepping horse away, back through the watching camp.

Cochise sat down on the ledge and nodded for Miguel to do likewise, which was nearly as good as a handshake. Miguel tied the dun out of the way and sat down.

"Why," Cochise began, speaking in a flat voice, black eyes leveled, "should I believe anything you say? You left us, yet you grew up among us. Some call you a traitor. Why should I believe you?"

"Because I never lied. Because I went on war parties, did as I was told, and learned I had the horse power. Because I fought as a warrior. Because I killed three *pindahs*. Because I was not a coward. Because I was generous. When I shot a deer, I shared it. I did not forget the old people." Cochise nodded to that. "When the war parties returned with stock and goods, I shared what I had."

"You did," Cochise said. "I remember. Generosity is not forgotten."

"I'm glad you remember, Great Chief."

"But why did you leave us?"

Miguel felt the desire to look at the ground, to avoid the riveting black stare, but knew he must keep his own eyes level. And he said: "My mother died. My wife died. I had no children. I am not a Chiricahua. So I left."

"Where did you go?"

"To Tucson."

"What did you do there?"

"Sometimes I broke young horses. I drove wagons. I even cut wood. It was not an easy life."

"Some of what you do is women's work," Cochise said disdainfully. "You should have stayed here and remained a man."

"Perhaps," Miguel replied, and for an instant felt the pull of the old ways, and the persuasive power of this great leader.

"Instead of Tucson, why didn't you go to *Méjico?*"

"I did. I went to Bavispe, where I was born and where my mother and I were stolen . . . and where my father was killed."

Cochise showed no regret. "What happened?"

"They turned their backs on me, walked away. Said I'd been gone too long. Said I was an Apache. Said they were afraid I'd lead a war party back to the village. They told me to leave."

"Yet you were never asked to lead a war party back to Bavispe, were you?"

"That is true. I was not."

"They lied so you would leave!" Cochise drove his right fist into his left palm. "All *méjicanos* lie! One reason why they have always been our enemies. Why do they offer bounties for our scalps?"

Speaking carefully, Miguel said: "The people in Bavispe told me that once a captive did lead a war party into a village upriver."

"That must have been a *Nde-nda-i* war party. It was not one of mine. Captives never lead my big *Tsoka-ne-nde* war parties."

"I did not mean it was. But it made them not trust me."

Cochise was scornful. "I believe I can understand that,

knowing how *mejicanos* think."

"There is another reason why you should believe me, Great Chief. People in Tucson learned I had lived as a Chiricahua. There was much talk. They stared at me and pointed. An officer from Camp Lowell, the new *pindah* soldier post in Tucson, came to see me. He asked me to serve as a scout for the soldiers. He'd pay me twice a soldier's pay, give me a good horse, a blue uniform, and carbine. I'd ride at the head of the column. I refused. After that, an officer from Fort Bowie came. He asked me to serve as scout and lead the pony soldiers to your camping places. He offered me much money. I still refused. I am not a traitor, Great Chief. I still have feelings for your people, even after your warriors killed my father and made my mother and me captives."

Cochise nodded matter-of-factly, meaning that was the way of life. "What else happened to you?"

"Some time ago I grew depressed. I started drinking. I was a drunkard on the plaza until a short time ago, when I quit drinking."

"What did you drink?"

"What the *mejicanos* and *pindahs* drink . . . tequila and beer."

"No *tizwin?*" Cochise smiled, and Miguel remembered that the chief was a ready drinker himself at celebrations but never out of control.

"Their beer is a form of *tizwin*, but maybe not as strong. You don't have to drink it as soon as it is made, like *tizwin*. Some of it is shipped in barrels from the *pindah* country. Some of it is made in Tucson."

"Why did you quit drinking?"

Miguel didn't answer at once. It was hard to explain, for him to put clearly in a few words. "I finally realized I was killing myself. And about that time this thing came up." He was having to fight off the shakes. He must not show weakness in front of Cochise.

"This thing?" The chief leaned toward Miguel, the black eyes like spear points.

"A *pindah* woman has come to Tucson from far back where the sun rises. She tells a sad story. Apaches took her little boy captive. The little boy was with an uncle escorted by *pindah* soldiers." Cochise was showing scant interest, only irritation. "This happened at Cow Spring, the big spring south of the Burro Mountains, on the old trail the *pindah* stages travel. One soldier lived to tell the story."

"So?" Cochise was only mildly interested.

"The *pindah* woman will pay ransom for the return of her little son. A big ransom."

"Why come to me?" Cochise flared. "You know we *Tsoka-ne-nde* don't capture white children. Only *mejicanos* or maybe a Pima or Papago." The downward curve of his lips said he held the last two tribes in even lower respect than Mexicans.

"I know. I. . . ."

Before Miguel could go on, Cochise interrupted. "How do you know Apaches took the boy?"

"Who else is fighting the *pindahs* around here?"

Cochise frowned. Miguel sensed that the chief was getting uncomfortable, holding back. "Still, why come to me?"

"Who would know better than you, Great Chief of the mighty *Tsoka-ne-nde?*"

"You forget there are other bands besides mine. The *Tci-he-nde* to the east. The *Nde-nda-i* in the Sierra Madre."

Miguel could see that Cochise was growing more restless. He might end their talk any moment and nothing gained. Yet that very unease could mean that he knew more than he wanted to say. Thinking that, Miguel realized that he must talk in a more tactful manner.

"Then it was a *Tci-he-nde* or *Nde-nda-i* war party?"

"This I have heard," Cochise replied, "and only this. A war party of *Nde-nda-i* took a *pindah* boy captive at Cow Spring and wiped out the rest. A good thing, since we are at war. This is not the first time the *Nde-nda-i* have taken *pindah* captives."

Although encouraged, Miguel groaned to himself. The worst band. The most fierce. The *Nde-nda-i*, the so-called Enemy People. Living in the harsher Sierra Madre, they depended more on raiding than the other bands. Mean people, it was said, who prowled like coyotes and lived any place. So mean and thieving at times that kindred Apaches avoided them.

He trusts me, or he wouldn't be telling me this, Miguel reasoned, thinking fast. *He believes that I refused to guide the* pindah *soldiers to his* ranchería. *He knows I've never lied.* Knowing that left Miguel humble and thankful, and not a little proud.

"Is the little boy alive?" he asked.

"I do not know. Little I know about this. There are more important things than a *pindah* captive for me to think about."

"Is it known where the *Nde-nda-i* might be camped?"

Cochise hesitated, still loath. "North of Cow Spring, in the Burro Mountains, where they have a hunting camp for drying meat before Ghost Face time comes."

Miguel knew the location instantly, a favorite place in a remote cañon by a stream fed by the Sweet Spring. Rough country. Good protection. Thick with juniper and oak. Good feed for deer. Plenty firewood. Good grass in the cañon and on the slopes.

Was Cochise going to tell him more? There was yet one

missing piece of information he sought, and he was almost afraid to ask it.

"Great Chief, who might be the leader of that war party?"

Cochise stared at him in open-mouth surprise. "Who else but Juh?"

Miguel didn't bat an eye, while cold fear and dread squeezed his heart and mind. Juh, called The Monster by other bands. Notorious for torturing captives. Had he spared the little *pindah* boy? Most likely it would have depended on his mood. Maybe it was already too late.

"Ah, yes," Miguel agreed genially, "I should have remembered."

Abruptly Cochise came to his feet. "Now that you know, what do you intend to do about it?"

"Go to the camp. Tell the *Nde-nda-i* about the ransom."

"When you say *Nde-nda-i,* you mean Juh. Only Juh speaks for his band. He will laugh at you, then kill you on the spot. Squash you like a red ant. They've never ransomed captives, and neither have we. It would be a sign of weakness, of giving in to the enemy. It's an insult to ask."

"The mother of the boy will offer many horses and much trade goods."

"You're a fool to try it, Horse Stealer. You must have learned this bad thinking from the *mejicanos* in Tucson." He turned away. One step and he looked around, smiling thinly. "That is a good horse from the *pindah* woman. I appreciate a good horse." His pleasantness faded in another moment. "I suppose she would pay you well, if you get her boy back?"

"She would. I would be rich."

"What do you get for just coming here?"

"Nothing, if you had told me nothing. One hundred *pesos,* now that you have told me where the boy is."

"A hundred *pesos* isn't much. My words should be worth

more than that." He was being sarcastic, amused.

"That was all I asked. She would have given me much more."

Again Cochise turned away, and again he flung around as if still not convinced. Yet his face held more bafflement than suspicion. "If not for money, why are you doing this?"

"You forget, Great Chief, that I was once a captive boy. How my mother and I walked all the way from Bavispe to your stronghold. How many times we went hungry and thirsty. How your warriors whipped us whenever we lagged. I would like to save a little boy's life as my mother saved mine. I will do it to honor her memory . . . my mother. That is why."

Cochise held his gaze on him so long and intently, seeming to search his mind, that, for an instant, Miguel feared he was going to strike him. Then, little by little, Miguel saw the taut, questioning features ease, and Cochise turned and took slow steps toward the camp. Their talk was finished. The Great Chief seemed wrapped in deep thought.

Had Miguel just witnessed understanding?

Chapter Nine

Miguel stepped to his horse and mounted unhurriedly, deliberate about it. Let them see that the Horse Stealer was not afraid. With a swinging glance at the diminishing figure of the erect Cochise and the still-attentive watchers, he rode off at a walk.

As the humming sounds and the vicinity of the camp fell away and he entered the darker mantle of the woods, he knew that he was safe, thanks to Cochise, while within the long corridor. However, he could not shake the sensation of pending threat and unalterable change. He was leaving one world for another. The White Eyes would call this a savage world, yet they, too, enjoyed killing. He would not see the *Tsoka-ne-nde* again, conscious that he was honestly concerned and sad for them, despite their violent ways, despite what they had done to him and his family. Their free-roving way of life was doomed. There were too many White Eyes, who would force the band onto a reservation or kill them all in the attempt. And, thinking thus, he knew that he didn't trust the White Eyes any more than an Apache.

He rode at a trot now, aware of time slipping by. Afternoon shadows filled the forest with gloom. He came to his old camping ground, which he had noted coming in, and could not let his eyes linger there. It was too much, already bringing upon him again a flood of painful memories: these, also, he was leaving forever. To offset his feelings, he rode faster, anxious to get all this behind him and reach the stage station before dark. Now and then he spied the ghostly figures of sentinels.

He jerked. Was that the sound of horses back there? The clack of hoofs on rocks? Glancing over his shoulder, he saw only deep shadows and interlacing timber. Nothing moved. Halting to listen, he heard no sounds. His hands shook. He was getting shaky again. His meeting with Cochise had drained him. He hurried on. For what seemed like a long time, it was like this: halting to listen, hearing no pursuit, then riding on at a fast trot.

To his relief, he rode free of the corridor. It was late afternoon. More time had passed than he'd realized. The sun was a copper shield sliding behind the Dragoons. He would reach the station while there was still light. It strengthened him to know that *Señor* Wilder would be watching for him. He did not doubt that.

He kept the dun at a fast trot, sparing him for a long run, if necessary. Before long he reached the ruts of the abandoned stage road and, heartened, followed hard upon it. Often he looked back for signs of pursuit, seeing no dust, no horse shapes. This open country, with the Dragoons now on his left, was his ally. His encouragement swelled. He'd be at the station soon.

Feeling more assured, he began to plan ahead, beyond this day. Letting his mind mull over what Cochise had warned: Juh would kill him. Captives had never been ransomed. It would be certain death to ask. It was an insult, and he would ride the Ghost Pony. He knew he could find the hunting camp; it was like a picture in his mind, having been there many times. That was the first thing. After that? Make the offer and fight for his life? If he escaped, he wouldn't lead White Eye soldiers to the camp — that would be breaking his word. Better to die. He was thinking like an Apache now. Maybe Juh would still think of him as the famous Horse Stealer, known and respected by all the bands? Maybe Juh didn't know he'd left Cochise's band — that would help? Next to a warrior, Apaches respected a great horse thief. Maybe he could convince Juh to take many horses, say, if Miguel brought them to a certain place, far from any soldiers? If not . . . maybe the little boy could be rescued? That was the wildest thought of all. Miguel stopped himself. And maybe the little boy was already dead, cast aside for the wolves and coyotes? He shuddered, hating that possibility.

Lost in thought, feeling the peace of this serene afternoon with a cool breeze wandering out of the Dragoons like a whisper around his ears, and his good horse traveling at a steady trot, he hadn't looked back for a short while. When he did now, he went stiff with fear. He saw not only moving yellow dust; he saw horses. Three horses. Coming fast. It was Santos. He knew. Come to kill him at last, now that he was beyond the shield of Cochise's protection.

He clapped heels, and the dun struck off at a gallop. Looking back after a bit, Miguel saw the three hadn't gained. Neither were they out of carbine range. A waste at this distance. Hanging low to present a smaller target, he urged the willing horse into a run.

He heard the first crack of a rifle behind him, and about the same instant something struck the flinty ground on his left and went whizzing off. Glancing back, he saw a bloom of darkish white smoke. As the dun widened the distance between the pursuers, Miguel heard no more shots. It was easy to know their thinking. In time, they were going to run him down. Three to one. He could imagine the relish on Santo's ugly face. Grimly, Miguel rode on. He'd have to ease his horse off the run before long. But so would they. An endurance race. Could the dun outlast the three? His carbine was a single-shot. In a close fight, there wouldn't be time to reload.

He felt a surge of hope when he sighted the low, dark shape of the stage station on a grassy swell. Then it happened all at once, without a shred of warning. The eager dun was striding hard, barely skimming the rough trail, head low, outrunning the Apache ponies. His horse seemed to take a wrong step. Suddenly, roughly, he broke stride, but not stopping. He limped along gamely, favoring his left front foot. A knowing crashed through Miguel — a pebble! His horse had likely picked up a pebble in his shoe on the trail. Miguel reined down to a slow, labored gallop, which they couldn't hold long, and they went on in that troubled fashion. Miguel looked back. The Apache ponies were gaining, close enough that Miguel heard whooping. Time was upon him. He'd have to make a stand. Better to dismount and fight? He couldn't shoot straight and reload fast enough from a moving horse. But, afoot, they would ride him down.

From the wall Jesse saw this moving dust before he heard the single shot on the wind. Two streaks of dust. A little streak in front, coming hard. Miguel. By God, he'd made it! Behind him more dust, coming as hard. Three riders.

Needing a better angle on the three riders, so Miguel would be out of his line of fire, he moved farther along the wall. Raising the Spencer's sights, he fired one round.

Nothing changed. They were too far. He'd have to wait, hoping Miguel could stay ahead. Jesse inserted a shell in the Spencer's chamber, which gave him eight shots with seven in the buttstock magazine.

Long moments. Watching. Everything came into sharper focus. The dun was outrunning the Apaches. Could he hold that pace? Even as he watched, the hopeful scene changed. The dun broke stride — what the hell! — limping now — but still coming on. A game horse.

The Apache ponies were gaining. His experienced eye told him the range was about five hundred yards — too far yet for carbine accuracy. But maybe the sound of firing would slow them down. He fired two rounds without effect.

The Apaches were closing the gap fast, Miguel sticking like a burr. Another hundred yards he'd be in deep trouble. Now! Jesse started firing, earing back the hammer for each shot.

One pony broke down. He emptied the gun, withdrew the empty magazine from the buttstock, slid in seven cartridges from a tube, put the tube back in the Quickloader, reinserted the magazine, and locked the cover plate — all this in quick, practiced motions.

Crouched low in the saddle, Miguel heard a single crack of sound. Yet he felt nothing and didn't look back. Then, late, he realized the shot had come from before him. *Señor* Wilder! The Apaches carried single-shot rifles or carbines. They wouldn't waste a bullet at long range. He glanced back and found them nearer. He flinched at the crash of two more shots from the stage station. A rush of moments and he heard rapid firing. Glancing back, he saw one pony go down. The other two riders did not let up. He could see Santos in the lead, beating his mount at every leap. Miguel's own poor horse couldn't last much longer. He'd have to pull up and fight. Another quick, backward look. Antone was closing fast, holding his rifle high.

Wilder was firing rapidly now. The game dun was finished. Old instincts of survival took over as Miguel drew his horse down. Jerking the carbine free, he slid from the saddle and tried to keep the horse, still crippling along, now fighting the reins, between him and the two Apaches. Wilder's carbine was a steady banging in Miguel's ears. He saw the rider

117

trailing Santos throw up his hands and fall. Santos rode untouched. Wilder ceased firing as Santos closed.

A wild knowing spun through Miguel's mind as he saw Santos, coming for him, weaving his horse back and forth with knees and rawhide reins. His enemy could ride. Screeching the familiar Apache yell. Screeching his hate. As if long ago, Miguel's mind flashed, when they were boys, it was Ussen's order of things to be that it end like this: between him and the bully Santos, to the death. Kill or be killed.

Miguel got ready, breathing in gulps. This had to be. He saw Santos leap from his horse and come charging, rifle ready, no letup to his screeching hate. Miguel squared around and leveled the carbine, still holding the reins. As he did, the horse lunged, and Miguel's shot flew wild.

Santos pointed his rifle and screeched in triumph, charging faster. Miguel ducked and threw the empty carbine at him as Santos's rifle went off. Miguel heard a clunk as his carbine struck high. Santos's shot was wild. Miguel felt no pain.

But Santos was getting up, wiping blood from his face. He dug for the knife at his belt. Further destiny, Miguel flashed, that this end with knives, Apache-fashion, at close quarters. Miguel knew it would have to be done very fast. He was weaker than Santos, weak from drinking and idleness and riding. Summoning his waning strength, he drew his long knife and, whooping like an Apache, ran, leaping at Santos instead of circling as knife fighters did, looking for an opening.

He knocked Santos down with his shoulder, but missing with the long knife. Santos reared up, slashing. His knife nicked Miguel's left shoulder and blood ran.

Santos yelled at the sight and had to stop and sneer. "Traitor . . . you die!"

"Not by you . . . you scum!"

There was so little time left, Miguel knew he had to get in close. He feinted with the knife. When Santos dodged, Miguel charged straight at him, slashing. Santos, surprised, stepped back.

Miguel was faster. Then, feinting and slashing, Miguel felt his blade catch Santos's throat. He jerked with all his strength, hearing Santos's cry as he went down.

All at once it was finished.

Miguel looked down at his old enemy, blood streaming down his heaving chest. The hate still smoldered there in the black eyes, but it was fading fast as Santos's cruel life was fading. After these many years, it was finally over between them, as Ussen had ordered.

Pressing his wound, Miguel retrieved his carbine, found his horse, and, taking the reins, began making his way to the stage station. In the distance, he could see a waving figure atop the wall. *Señor* Wilder, his good friend.

Chapter Ten

She regarded them with wide-eyed astonishment and bursting relief as they entered the room, dusty and smelling of horse sweat, and sat down at her outflung invitation. Wordless for a moment, she tendered them a glowing smile and said: "Thank God you're back and safe! I've worried day and night." Concern hurried her speech. "Miguel, I see that you have a bandage on your upper left arm. We must get you to a doctor at once."

He smiled wearily. "*Señor* Wilder. Him good *di-yin,* good medicine man." He patted his bandaged wound. He had to search for the English. "Put on prickly pear . . . just like Apaches do. Feel good. Now I call him *amigo* Jesse."

"I'll still take him to a doctor, though I think he's all right," Jesse said. "Prickly pear keeps a wound clean. Fortunately, it's not a deep wound."

"So you got into a fight? Not with Cochise, I pray?"

Miguel shook his head vigorously. "No Cochise. Was old enemy. Him no more now." Uncomfortable talking to this pretty *pindah* woman in his awkward English, he looked at Jesse to explain further, and Jesse said: "An old enemy, dating back to Miguel's boyhood days, and two other killers chased him after he left the stronghold. There was a knife fight. Miguel won."

Miguel waved an interrupting hand. "You watch from stage station. You shoot." He raised both hands, simulating firing, and clapped his hands. "*Bang, bang.* You shoot

120

Santos's friends." He waited for Jesse to go on. Jesse confirmed with only a nod.

"There was no pursuit?" she asked.

"None after Miguel's fight," Jesse explained. "We camped that night inside the Dragoon stage station and started back next day."

"And Cochise?" she inquired softly, looking at Miguel.

He turned to Jesse. "You tell the *señora*."

"There is much to tell," Jesse began, feeling he must not raise her hopes too high, must tell it with clarity devoid of emotion and no more. This was only another beginning, and each time the circumstances got tougher. "What Miguel did was very brave, going in there. Cochise was cool but friendly. He remembered Miguel as the great Horse Stealer. He accepted your fine horse. No doubt that helped. At first, he was reluctant to say much about any Apache captives. In a nutshell, Missus Lattimore, after Cochise questioned Miguel and there was much roundabout talk, Cochise told Miguel that *Nde-nda-i* Apaches . . . not Cochise's band . . . attacked at Cow Spring and captured a white boy. By all reasoning, the boy has to be your Jimmy."

Her face lit up as if caught in a swift ray of light, and she raised her eyes to heaven and then closed them, weeping softly, her shoulders shaking, hands to her face.

He wanted to reach out to her, yet that would only add fuel to her nearly impossible hopes. Instead, he said: "The *Nde-nda-i* are camped now in the Burro Mountains. A hunting camp. They're getting in meat for the winter. That's all Cochise said."

She looked up then, eyes brimming. "You know where the camp is?"

"Miguel does. At a place called Sweet Spring."

"And we can go there?" she said, almost child-like, just a

mere ride into the mountains. "I will pay whatever the Apaches want."

"Miguel and I have talked about this by the hour. What might be done. What can't be done. And, believe me, the hazards."

"Oh, yes," she agreed, dabbing at her eyes with a handkerchief. "What can be done? The first thing, bring in the Army, now that we know where Jimmy is being held?"

"Bringing in the Army would be the last move we should make." Jesse was emphatic. "If the Army acted on what we know, the Apaches would kill every white captive in camp. I mean, if the Army attacked, and it would. There's this war going on."

"Oh, no," she sighed.

"An approach has to be made, sure, but any big show of force would ruin everything. However, we'd still need a small group of picked men. Out of sight, while the approach is made. You see, this is far different from talking to Cochise. This time we're dealing with Chief Juh. His *Nde-nda-i* are called the Enemy People, Miguel says. They live in the Sierra Madre, when they're not raiding north of the border. Juh is considered the most war-like of all the Chiricahua chiefs." He wouldn't add to her stress and tell her Juh was despised by many Apaches for his brutality. "Juh is no statesman like Cochise. If not for the terrible blunder of the Bascom affair I told you about, Cochise's people would be at peace today. Cochise even had a contract to supply wood to the stage station in Apache Pass until that blundering fool, Lieutenant Bascom, came along."

"What can we do within reason?" she pleaded. "I hate to ask you and Miguel to do more. You've done so much. I'll pay whatever this Chief Juh wants with the exception of arms, as you've told me, and you've said gold is taboo."

"There's another thing. Cochise reminded Miguel that Chiricahuas have never ransomed captives. To do so would be a sign of weakness. However, Cochise has never taken white captives. Mainly Mexicans and others from the lesser Arizona tribes to make slaves. Juh is a different breed of chief."

"But what is there to do but offer horses and mules and goods for Jimmy?"

"That's certainly the most sensible way."

"And if that doesn't work?"

"Depends on Juh's mood, Miguel says. He might say no and walk away. If he doesn't want stock and goods, what would he want unless it was guns? Or he might drag out the parley to get the chance to ambush us."

"Oh, my. A dreadful alternative."

"There is one other possibility left us, should he turn down the ransom. It depends on the location of Juh's camp. The terrain."

"I believe you're talking like a cavalryman now, Captain."

"I am. Could be . . . everything will come down to making a dash into the camp and grabbing Jimmy on the run. Go in shooting."

She clasped her hands and looked down with troubled eyes. "I'm so grateful for what you and Miguel have done. Now, here I am needing you to do more." She visibly shook off the thought. "It's too much. Far too much. I won't do it. I can't. It's more than an imposition. It's again a matter of life and death."

She broke off, and the silence clamped down and held until Miguel stirred and faced Jesse and said in Spanish: "Juh is not Cochise. Juh is bad about torturing prisoners. But he has a weakness . . . he is greedy. That is known. We say so many horses for the boy, or say a fine horse like the one for

Cochise. Will bring horses or horse to a certain place. Let him pick the place. If it is bad place for us, where he can murder us all and take horses, too, we parley some more. We do what the White Eyes call beating around the bush." He took a long breath. "Tell the *señora* . . . this brave mother . . . I will go to Juh's camp, and I will make the talk. I will do this thing, *amigo*."

Jesse held his eyes on Miguel. This courageous little man amazed him again. So utterly damned cool about chancing his life. And so Jesse looked at her and said: "Miguel says he will make the talk, as he expresses it. He will go to Juh's camp and make the talk for ransom. He will do this thing . . . this brave thing. Not that he called it that."

Her eyes seemed to melt. She began to weep a little. "I am so grateful, Miguel. How can I thank you enough? You're risking your life once again for my only son."

Miguel said no word. Just regarded her gently, nodding understanding.

"But not alone," Jesse said. "We'll back him up."

Her eyes locked on him. "Just how do you mean?"

"Keep him in sight. If he's attacked, we attack."

"You keep saying *we*."

"We'll have to muster some picked men. Not many. Fifteen. Twenty. Men who can shoot and ride. Pay them well."

"About how far are the Burro Mountains?"

"About a hundred and fifty miles."

"It's so far. About the men? You say fifteen or twenty. Why not more? Say thirty?"

"Off hand, I doubt we could find that many reliable men. I'd rather have ten or fifteen good riders, crack shots, good with horses, good in camp, men who know the desert and the mountains . . . a tight little band . . . than a much larger outfit blundering around, making as much noise as a herd of elephants. No grumblers or whiners. Usually they don't show up the first day or two in a detail of column. Absolutely no drunks, like the bunch that holds target practice on bottles behind the hotel."

She smiled. "I can understand why. How will you go about this?"

"Pass the word in town. It will get around fast. It's news. Big news. Tell *Señor* Murillo what we're going to do. What we need. Now, it's going to be costly."

"Fortunately, cost is no matter."

"I mean horses, pack mules, horse furniture, weapons. Rifles or carbines and side arms. Supplies. And there's the matter of pay. Not before we go, but when we get back. If we pay 'em to sign up, some would vamoose or go on a big drunk."

"Let me know what you think would be fair pay."

"We'd better talk about it."

"When do we start things rolling, so to speak?"

"I'll tell Murillo right away. Ask him to pass word for volunteers to report to the hotel, starting in mid-morning. You and I and Miguel will decide on the men. Interview them one at a time in here. You should be in on that. Murillo can help us select stock."

"I realize speed is imperative. Much time has passed."

"Just so we don't go off half-cocked," he said, getting up. "We can go over the details this evening. Now I'd better get Miguel to a doctor."

They were gone almost before she could thank them again. And, looking after them, she felt a great lift of hope, and wonder.

125

Chapter Eleven

They began stringing into the lobby by nine o'clock. A motley bunch. *But this is good,* Jesse thought. *You want a mixture. Pick the best.* It was already getting noisy. Some garrulous drunks — laughing, joking. To them, the mission was just a lark. *Boys, let's go out and shoot us some greasy Indians. Have a little fun.* Mostly Anglos. A few Mexicans. He saw a black man standing far back. A few quiet men, hard-faced. Others with the bearing of military experience, which could be helpful or not. Maybe a deserter or two. Likewise an outlaw or two, on the dodge from back in the States. In time, they'd feel safe to use their right names. He'd never served in an outfit yet, North or South, that didn't harbor some bad apples, hiding behind uniforms, ready to rob a comrade or desert with mount and arms at the first chance.

By the time Jesse was ready to speak to them, some twenty-five or thirty men had gathered. *Señor* Murillo had, indeed, passed the word.

"You've heard in general what this is all about," Jesse began. "We're going to form a small band of dependable volunteers to go into Apache country. Not Cochise's range, down in the Chiricahuas. But farther east, into the Burro Mountains, New Mexico Territory. Our purpose is to ransom a seven-year-old boy recently taken captive at Cow Spring, south of the Burros on the old Butterfield stage trail. The boy, whose name is Jimmy, is the son of Missus Susan Lattimore, who has come West looking for a way to get her boy back." His words produced mutterings. Some men exchanged doubting looks. "This will be a tough ride," Jesse said. "You may get into the fight of your life. But we'll go well-armed. You'll be furnished arms and mounts and all necessary horse furniture." The terminology drew identifying grins from former horse soldiers. "You'll have pack mules and plenty of supplies."

"How many men you want?" one spoke up.

"Ten . . . fifteen . . . maybe twenty. Depending on what shapes up. Men who can ride and shoot. Handle stock. Stick together. Hell or high water. And follow orders. No complainers."

"Fifteen . . . twenty?" a drunk burst out. "Hell, you'll need a hundred, at least. Count me out, boys." And he staggered outside.

Jesse smiled. Some laughed.

"I'm not promising anybody a rose garden." Now was the time to bring in the pay. "Every man will be paid five hundred dollars, when we get back, in addition to keeping his mount, equipment, and arms. The money will be on deposit with *Señor* Murillo here, when we leave. Guess I don't have to remind you that's a lot of money on the frontier."

"You mean we get paid, if we ransom the boy? What if we don't? Just get in one helluva fight gettin' back to save our hides?" The speaker was a long-jawed, bearded Anglo.

"We're not thinking along those lines. But you would get your money, regardless of how we come out."

"Fair enough. Sure beats Army pay at thirteen bucks a month."

"What about supplies?" another asked.

"About what you would expect. However, much better than Army field rations. Bacon, coffee, tortillas as long as they last. Absolutely no hardtack, even if we could get it." The horse soldiers guffawed. "We'll take flour, dried fruit.

127

Plus light grain for the horses and pack mules. I figure it's a three-day ride to the base of the Burros. We may be down to cactus pulp for horse feed before we get back. Any more questions?"

One of the drunks Jesse remembered seeing busting bottles behind the hotel grinned roguishly and asked: "How about some advance money, friend. Say, fifty bucks?"

Jesse knew this was coming. Chuckling, he said: " 'Fraid not. Somebody might forget to report for duty. Or might even get his directions confused and end up in California."

That evoked some grins.

"Any more questions?"

"How soon you aim to pull out?"

"As soon as we can put everything together. In a very few days."

"How about takin' a little jug of whiskey along for snake bite?" a bleary-eyed man asked.

"I'd never deny a man a drink of whiskey on the trail, if he needed it . . . was sick, say. As for the curing of snake bite, I believe there are more reliable ways. But if a man shows up drunk, he'll be discharged on the spot, to make his way back here alone. Something to think about in Apache country."

"Fair enough, I reckon. Man can always use a phlegm-cutter in the mawnin'."

When there were no more questions, Jesse said: "Now, if you gentlemen will line up down the hallway, you'll be interviewed one at a time. *Señor* Murillo will show you in to Missus Lattimore's quarters. I am Captain Jesse Wilder, late of the Confederate Army of Tennessee and down into Chihuahua and Sonora. I will be in charge of the outfit. Miguel García will be chief scout."

"García . . . that common drunk!" A Mexican was sneering.

128

"Not any more. He's been all over the desert and mountains where we're going. Knows it far better than any man here, including me."

"Can you trust him, *señor?* Understand he used to live with the Chiricahuas. Was one of 'em. A captive. Grew up with 'em."

"He can be completely trusted for reasons which I won't go into here. I know the man."

Still sneering, the Mexican walked out. All but one of the other Mexicans followed.

Murillo ushered in the first volunteer, a heavy-set, round-faced, amiable Anglo, hat in hand. His hands looked as big as sledges. His clothing was worn. Everything about him spoke of hard times, but in no way did that diminish his broad smile and easy nature.

"Please, state your name, where you're from, and any previous military experience," Jesse said. Susan Lattimore sat on his right, Miguel on his left.

"Cal Truett. Farmed back in Ohio. Served with Uncle Billy Sherman when we marched through Georgia. Didn't win no medals. I was a farrier, and a durned good one, if I do say so. I can put shoes on anything that walks on four feet. Excuse the language, ma'am, but a farrier naturally develops the power of speech, handlin' rough stock, an' it just pops out."

"May I ask what you're doing 'way out here? I suppose the same question could be asked of all of us."

"Figured I was plumb wore out with farmin'. So came on the lookout for gold, an' it's been one crop failure after another, you could say. Soon as I get me a stake, I'll be goin' back to what I'm good at, dull as farmin' is sometimes. With five hundred dollars, I could buy me a pretty good little farm an' have some left over."

"Come back in the morning, Mister Truett. There'll be a list posted in the lobby. Thank you for volunteering."

"You're mighty welcome. I sure hope everything works out for you, ma'am."

As he went out, Jesse looked at Susan, and she nodded quickly, adding: "We'll certainly need a good farrier." Jesse and Miguel agreed. Jesse wrote down Truett's name. "I don't think I should ask the rest where they're from. A touchy question to some men. I'll cut it out."

"Mister Truett looks in need of clothing and shoes or boots," she said. "I'll include an allowance for each volunteer, part of the equipment. We'll tell them, when they're accepted."

The next man cut a formidable figure. Tall, rawboned, black hair down to his shoulders, full beard, alert black eyes set deep in a hawk-like face, not as old as he looked. He carried a heavy rifle of a make new to Jesse. He said his name was Ben Hardin, and he had grown up in Missouri. "Learned to handle mules. I'm a mule man. I know how to pack a mule so the load rides easy." His voice was low and steady. Like Truett, he could use new clothing. "I hunted buffler in Texas till I got tired of the slaughter, the stink, an' the flies," he told them. "Still tote along my Sharps Big Fifty here. More like a memento now. But it can still reach out there further'n anything the Army's got. Came in right handy a few times gettin' out here. Few rounds of Old Betsy and troublemakers of various breeds kept their distances."

Jesse had heard of the Sharps and its hitting power and range — some said, up to a mile. He suddenly wanted that for the outfit.

"Why Arizona?" he asked.

"Just driftin'. I'd like to settle down. Maybe raise cattle.

Don't think I'm cut out diggin' for gold or silver."

"Any Army service?"

"Union cavalry in Missouri. First sergeant. My family split over the war. Father favored the South. So did my younger brother. Died at Corinth."

"Sorry about your family and brother," Jesse said feelingly, and told him to check back in the morning.

"What do you think?" Susan asked, and Jesse said: "He looks like a steady man. Any man who made first sergeant earned it the hard way. Knows men. That long-range Sharps might help. And he's good with mules and is a packer."

So Ben Hardin passed.

A slim young Mexican with a flashing smile came next. Miguel interviewed him several minutes in rapid-fire Spanish. After the man left, Miguel said in his improving English: "His name Juan López. Grew up here. Says in love . . . needs money for marriage. Little work here for young man. Not much jobs. Good rider, says. Breaks horses. Says will do what we tell him do. No complain. Poor all his life."

"What do you think?" Jesse asked.

"Will make good hand with horses, this man López."

"He's acceptable with me," she said.

Jesse nodded consent. "This brings up a point we have to decide soon. We can't offer Juh anything but horses and mules. Neither can we drive a remuda of horses into the mountains with any secrecy. Shall it be what Miguel took to Cochise . . . one fine horse? Or say several fine horses?"

"If only one horse," she said, "I'd favor a fine stallion, an impressive-looking horse. Another black such as Cochise took, or a blood-red bay. A rangy, powerful animal, realizing, of course, that a stallion will be difficult to handle around other horses."

"We could hobble him at night," Jesse said. "Maybe tie

131

him, too. I like that better than the bigger problem of driving a bunch of horses. One impressive horse will stand out. A good-looking gelding would do as well, besides being easier to handle."

Miguel nodded, adding: "And two good mules."

The following volunteer, a white man in a greasy buckskin shirt and leather britches, eliminated himself almost as he entered, one of the loud-mouthed drunkards who hung around the hotel tavern. He appeared loaded now as he made an exaggerated bow and swept off his broad hat for Susan Lattimore's benefit. "I'm a fightin' son-of-a-buck," he announced. "Can mount up, ready to ride in fifteen minutes. You betcher boots. I can shoot the head off a rattler at fifty yards with a six-shooter."

They detained him no longer than one perfunctory question.

After him, an evasive, yet somehow impressive, individual who spoke in a literate voice of generalities. Late of Texas, naming no particular place. A Confederate veteran, naming no outfit or where he had served, while speaking with controlled anger of the Lost Cause. A tall, mannerly man, well dressed for Tucson. Cool gray eyes in a long face. Jet-black hair and carefully trimmed beard. He made Jesse think of border gamblers he'd seen in El Paso who carried hideout guns. He said his name was Jeff Donaldson, and he had been considering California when "this worthy mission came up."

Another man was quick to the point. Short, muscular, black-eyed, of driving energy, feeling flamed in his sunken face as he clipped: "I'm William Brakebill. A miner. Lost my entire family six months ago back in the Catalinas to Apaches. Wife . . . two little boys. Butchered, they were, while I was out lookin' for deer! I'm ready to join you, and promise I won't hold back in a fight. I will help any way I can.

132

I'd love to knock off some Apaches. Been hopin' for a chance to get back at the brutes." As he spoke, his eyes seemed to smolder and throw off sparks.

"We're very sorry about your family, Mister Brakebill," Jesse said. "You have any idea what band or tribe was responsible?"

"Not a trace. The Army figured it was a war party passin' through. To me, an Apache's an Apache. They're all the same."

"Usually, the Catalinas are too far north for Chiricahuas to have done it. Our purpose is to avoid stirring 'em up. We want to bargain for the boy's release."

Brakebill's voice was blunt. "Well, do I go or not?"

"We'll let you know in the morning. Be a list posted in the lobby. Thank you for coming in, Mister Brakebill. We understand your feelings."

All three took pause, after he left. "Wants to kill Apaches," Jesse mused. "Seems trustworthy and fearless, but maybe too eager."

"There's time to think about it," she said. "I feel so sorry for him. His entire family! His life will never be the same."

"We can't take a man because we feel sorry for him."

Jesse caught the exaggerated military stance the moment Murillo showed in the next volunteer. Apparently, he was trying to impress them. Standing at attention, he spoke in a thick voice: "My name is Nick Crider. Grew up in Pennsylvania. My father was a storekeeper. Too dull for Nick Crider, tyin' up Missus Smith's groceries, weighin' things while she kept an eagle eye on the scales and my thumb. So I became a railroader, just to see the country. When the war came along, what to do but join the cavalry and march to the sound of the guns. At Brandy Station it was charge and counter-charge. Yes, sirree. Smoke and dust so thick it was hard to tell Yank from Reb. Reckon we showed them fancy Southern gents a thing or two as we sabered and shot our way back and forth."

For some instinctive reason, Jesse asked: "What was your outfit?"

And, for some reason, Crider seemed to hesitate before replying: "The First Pennsylvania. Was mighty lucky that day, the way troopers kept gettin' unhorsed. Made it through the war. Yes, sirree. After the ruckus was over, tried rail-roadin' again. Too tame for Nick Crider. Took off. Headed west. Enlisted at Jefferson Barracks, Missouri. Ended up in the Fourth Cav' at Fort Bliss, back in El Paso. Discharged a few months ago." A nonchalant shrug. "Still headed West."

You would think, Jesse reasoned, that a recently dis-charged trooper would be wearing part of his uniform, say the pants. And how much of this Brandy Station stuff was bullshit? Then he caught himself. Why be so critical of Crider? He fit the pattern of many other men Jesse had seen, himself included, turned into rolling stones by the war and the breakup of families. Restless. Embittered. On the lookout for better times and fortune. Sometimes to escape the drudgery of backwoods farms. From service on the plains Jesse remembered the appropriately called "snowbirds" who enlisted for food and shelter during the winter months, then deserted when spring came, taking a good horse and horse furniture and arms.

Crider did present a soldierly appearance. Parade-ground erect. Hard-bodied. Big hands. Tough. A brawler's pitted face. Pale eyes as hard as polished stone. Middle thirties or older. And glib. Could probably talk your arm off. But somehow beneath all that Jesse sensed a hidden violence. The pitted face was like a map of his past.

Crider left as he had entered, in the military posture. There was no immediate acceptance of him. Nobody spoke.

Quickly, following in line, a volunteer whose earnestness impressed at the very beginning. A gaunt, sandy-haired man of nearly middle age wearing side whiskers whose air of self-reproach overshadowed his gentle hazel eyes. "I'm from Ioway," he said, accenting the last syllable. "My handle is Enoch Tatum. One time it was the Reverend Enoch Tatum. Nobody got invited to more sit-down Sunday dinners than Preacher Tatum. Nobody baptized more sinners. Sometimes I'se afraid I'd run out of water. And then the devil slipped up in the guise of demon rum." He smiled kindly, showing a likable face with a toothy grin. "I left under a dark cloud of my own sin, defrocked, kicked out of the little church in the wildwood I'd helped build with my own callused hands. I've wandered West ever since, seeking redemption, salvation from sin, from demon rum."

"Any military service, Reverend?" Jesse asked.

"I was chaplain of an Ioway regiment. We won the war, but I lost the one I came to of my own makin'."

"Any family?"

"Just an old uncle. No woman would have me."

Silence grew heavy, all three, Jesse sensed, feeling for him.

"Do you think you could be of help to us?" Jesse ventured.

"I do, indeed. When I heard about the little boy as a captive, I felt an instant wish to help. This may be my redemption, a long time comin'."

"What all can you do?"

"Any chore around a camp. I grew up on a farm. Used to hard work. Can fix anything that's broke, from harness to a wagon wheel. In the Army I learned about weapons and also helped with the wounded. I don't mind usin' a weapon, if it's for a good purpose. And," he added, grinning, "I'm always in good humor."

The reverend was refreshing after Crider. "How often do you get drunk?"

"It's not so much that I get drunk often. I can hold my liquor, which is part of the problem. Be better if one drink made me sick. Sometimes I go a long while without a drink. It's that, once I start drinkin', I don't stop till the bottle's empty, and then I'm drunk. Nothin' worse than a drunk preacher." He struck a devout pose, hands clasped, which Jesse couldn't decide was sincere or hypocritical. "The Good Book tells us . . . 'Wine is a mocker, strong drink is raging . . . and whosoever is deceived thereby is not wise.' Proverbs . . . Twenty, one."

Susan broke in. "I believe somewhere in Proverbs, we're also told it's all right to give strong drink to someone who is about to perish, and wine to those heavy of heart."

Tatum beamed. "Very good, dear lady. Proverbs . . . Thirty-One, six. It was that very verse, however, that led to my downfall. I was heavy of heart over losin' out to a cornfield rival for a country girl's heart. I took a drink, then another drink. It was on Saturday. I commenced to feel self-righteous, an' come Sunday morning I preached a sermon that shook the rafters. I called attention to who was in pursuit of other men's wives an' sometimes not havin' to run very fast or far to make the catch" — a sly wink now — "an' who'd traded off a colicky buggy horse to an innocent stranger hurryin' by, an' who shortchanged a widder woman outta her egg-an'-butter money every Saturday at the village grocery, an' Sunday mornin' sang the loudest in the angel choir. Well, folks, I've been on the wander ever since, lookin' for a way to get back into the good graces of the Lord. Believe me, it ain't easy."

He waited, a hopefulness filling his homely face.

"There'll be some liquor on the trail," Jesse said. "I won't try to prevent a man from taking along a private bottle. But,

136

as you heard me in the beginning, anybody who gets drunk will be discharged on the spot. A drunk could put the whole outfit at risk."

"I understand. Haven't had a drink in a month. Now, God bless all you folks." He departed, smiling.

In quick succession entered Jason Long and Henry Webb. They offered little about themselves beyond service in the Union cavalry as teamsters in Virginia and working on river boats. Although nothing was said, Jesse perceived some sort of connection between the two. There was just this sameness about them, their slack indifference, their reticence, whereas most volunteers talked freely. Long, the older of the pair, had a domed head and shifty brown eyes set in a hard face. Webb had hooded gray eyes, thin lips, and was paunchy. Jesse wondered if their names were aliases.

Again, he called himself to taw. What the hell did it matter that neither man wanted to say much? If they had a past, why make it public? What counted was could they fill the mission's need for reliable men?

When the next man was slow in appearing, Jesse went to the door and, hearing rising voices, was surprised to see that the line had thinned considerably. A number of men had dropped out. Before him a black man and a white man apparently had been having words.

"I'm next," the white man said.

The black man started to speak up, but held back.

Jesse looked at Murillo. "Who's next?"

Murillo pointed to the black man.

"Come in," Jesse told him.

The white man exploded — "Be god-damned if I'll foller a nigger!" — and stomped off.

"It's all right," Jesse assured the black man. "Come in."

He said his name was Gabe Jackson. Although he spoke in

a hesitant voice, soft and low, as if sizing up the situation, there was nothing servile about him. Nor was he arrogant. He did not look down or slouch, holding the remains of his tattered old hat. He stood a good six, two and straight, and, although his clothes were thin and toes showed through his shoes, he didn't look like a beggar. Just poor. It was his bearing. Here, thought Jesse, with swift perception, is a freedman! His hair was woolly gray, and his broad face and good jaw presented an acceptance of life, come what may. Confront it.

"Where are you from?" Jesse asked, his interest growing.

"Alabama," was the reply. "Ah'm a freedman."

"That's good," Jesse said.

"Was freed befo' de big wah."

"How'd you get by? What did you do?"

"Fo' a long time, Ah jus' lived in de woods. Knocked down rabbits. Got tired uh that. Started West. Cut wood fo' steamboats. Ain't nothin' a man can't do if he sets his mind to it. Ah can even read! Ah took care a broken-down, sweet ol' bachelor preacher in New Awlins fo' a long time. De Reverend Lazarus Dobbins, bless his soul. He'd come theah fo' his health from New Yawk. Had a little pension. Said it was cheaper theah, an' he felt better theah. He teached me to read, he did. It was like a big door swingin' open an' de golden light streamin' through. Oh, my, it was wonderful! Ah slept in de same house. Ah took good care of 'im. Cooked, cleaned, washed, heped 'im git up an' down. An' we prayed together, an' he teached me. Sometimes we'd take a carriage an' Ah'd drive de reverend aroun' town. Made 'im feel good an' me proud." A low chuckle. "Made other niggers jealous uh me. Den my sweet ol' friend up and died. It was sad. No family. Jus' me. I was with 'im. He didn't leave much. A few clothes, a little furniture, some books, an' cooking utensils. A lawyer man, he come to de house. Claimed he had Mistuh Dobbins's will. Ah reckon he did, but why didn't he come to de funeral? Ah was the only one at de funeral, me an' de undertaker.

"Well, de lawyer man looked all aroun' de house, nose stuck in de air. Said it wasn't much, an' it wasn't, an' he left. When he come back to de house ag'in, he had de law with 'im. Big pistol wobblin' on his belt. De lawyer say he gonna take ever'thing to sell fo' funeral expenses. Ah tol' him Reverend Dobbins had left de books to me befo' he die. An' de lawyer, he laugh an' say . . . 'No. Niggers can't read.' Ah picked up de Bible an' started readin' right off from Genesis. Spouted it off, jus' like it is in de Good Book. His eyes got big as fried eggs. Den he say . . . 'Niggers not supposed to read, nohow.' When he started to take my Bible, Ah say to him . . . look in de Bible. It say . . . 'To my good friend, Gabe Jackson, who cared fo' me. Reverend Lazarus Dobbins.' De lawyer, he looked. Kinder got 'im, it did. Well, he let me have de Bible, took ever'thing else."

As he quit speaking, Susan Lattimore clapped loudly, and Jesse and Miguel smiled. "I'm glad you, at least, got your Bible," she said.

Gabe Jackson smiled back at her gratefully. It occurred to Jesse that was probably the most the black man had said to any one person in a long time, since the death of his friend.

"Well, Gabe, how do you think you can help us on this mission into the mountains?"

Gabe Jackson appeared to think about that. "De reverend, he always tell me . . . 'Be hones', Gabe. Don't lie an' don't steal, an' de Lord will reward you. If you feel like lyin', jus' keep yore big mouth shut. If you feel like stealin', jus' keep on walkin' by, put temptation behind you.' He used that word a lot to me. That's what that sweet ol' man tol' me." He looked

139

down and up, seeming to gather his thoughts once more. "An' heah Ah've already lied once today. You see, Ah ain't no freedman. Ah's a runaway. Run off befo' de big wah. Lie git behind me! An' Ah also say Ah never fired no guns. Ah ain't no soldier man. So what have Ah done? Ah worked a world uh mules in de cotton fields befo' I run away. An' sometimes dey worked Gabe, contrary as mules kin be. But de main thing is Ah understands 'em. An' ag'in, Ah ain't no freedman. Ah'm a runaway."

"You have nothing to fear from me or anyone here," Jesse assured him. "My father freed his slaves before the war back in Tennessee." Jackson looked relieved, and Jesse asked: "What else can you do besides handle mules?"

"De longest Ah evah been without food . . . four days. Water . . . three. Ah kin do without. An' when times git better, Gabe Jackson can make the bes' co'nbread you evah ate . . . an' that's no lie, An' biscuits, too. I kin cook anything. Clean game."

Now he waited, and he wasn't begging. Just waiting. *A damned good man,* Jesse sensed.

Jesse looked at Mrs. Lattimore. She nodded. They looked at Miguel. He assented with his eyes. Then Jesse nodded and said: "Come back in the morning and look for your name on the list."

Gabe Jackson was in. He thanked them with a broad smile and left, walking straight.

A few more volunteers trailed in. By now, Jesse saw, they were about at the end of the line. Evidently some had grown tired waiting and gone to the bar, judging by the noise from that side of the hotel. He was beginning to feel discouraged, figuring they wouldn't get a dozen good men. Of these last ones since Gabe Jackson, none seemed eager to help or was qualified by military experience or time spent on the frontier in other endeavors, such as freighting or working on stagelines or ranches. What else was there to do, unless it was mining? Nevertheless, he took down their names and thanked them. Maybe one or two would do.

Murillo waved in the last man, who seemed interested enough. He said his name was Theodore Shelby. Straight from Boston. He came out flatly and said he'd been an Abolitionist before the war, and hated the South over slavery. He was of slight build and intense with darting, humorless gray eyes and a hedge of unruly yellow hair, cut short, that stood up prickly straight, and bushy eyebrows of the same shade. An impatient, wiry man, judging from his restless manner and crisp voice.

"Any military service?"

"Massachusetts infantry regiment, from Malvern Hill to Gettysburg. Wounded. Invalided out of the war. After that, an orderly in hospitals, where I saw all over again the effects of slavery . . . that peculiar institution . . . of good men maimed and dying to prevent it."

"Why join us?"

"I'm broke . . . flat broke. *En route* to California."

"Can you ride and handle a horse?"

"Not since my days as a boy on a stony farm."

"This will be much tougher."

"I won't complain. I can learn."

"I remind you I'm a Southerner, as I said out front. Will you mind serving under my command, at the direction of Missus Lattimore?"

"Don't reckon so."

"We've all had to make adjustments, Mister Shelby. Come back in the morning. There'll be a list posted in the lobby. We thank you."

Jesse sat a few moments before turning to Mrs. Lattimore

and Miguel, thinking a man with a cheerful disposition would be better. Then he said: "Do you want to go over these right after lunch?" They did. "Some may drop out."

She thanked them both, buoyed up as usual. Looking at her, Jesse hoped there was more here today than had met his veteran's eye and insights: some of the dregs of the frontier. Well, they would have to do.

Chapter Twelve

It was late afternoon, when Miguel left his friends at the hotel, and, thinking he needed rest, wearily started for María's. There was a Mexican there, a customer, sporting a fancy leather vest and shiny black boots and big sombrero. He was just leaving as Miguel walked up, and he cast Miguel a knowing glance and a disparaging look around. This man was running her down! It angered Miguel. He would never do that. What else could she do to survive? She had no husband. No children to look after her. Last night, his first back after the long ride to see Cochise, he had downed only one beer, when he returned here, too worn out for more. He had slept like a dead man. But tonight he was going to get drunk; he needed that after these trying days of body and mind, and many more awaited him.

She greeted him casually.

"Is it all right for me to be here tonight?" he asked, as was his custom.

Her shrug said it didn't matter. He could stay or go.

"That man who just left. Who is he?"

"A teamster. New in Tucson. From Los Angeles. Thinks he's a beeg man from the beeg city. Tried to talk me down, like I should be pleased to have a man of his importance here."

Miguel could feel his anger mounting.

She said: "He tried to talk me down. I told him, no. He stayed. But he was rough, and he wanted me to do some things I never have and won't." Miguel's anger must have

143

shone in his face, because she laughed and said: "Why should you care?"

"He had no right to treat you like that."

She spread her soft hands, resigned and tired. "What choice do I have?"

"I would like to stay here tonight. Will you feed me and get me some beer?"

"Don't I always?"

"You do, but I should ask first. You're not a slave, and I'm not your master."

"I'm not much."

"Don't talk like that. You're a good woman."

"Hah! Better not say that to the *padre*."

"The Church takes care of the *padre*. He's grown fat and lazy. Knows little about real life. How people suffer. How hard life is. I have no respect for him. He's not the true spirit of the Church."

Suddenly she became alarmed. She made the sign of the cross. "No, Miguel! No! You must not say that about the *padre*. God will punish you. Don't say that again!"

He felt like laughing. "True. Ussen will punish me for many things before I die, but not that. I will say no more, but I have spoken the truth. Now, please go get me some beer. Here is money."

She frowned and regarded him curiously. "You said *Ussen*."

"That is the Apache name for God. Means the same. Though we're at each other's throats, we worship the same God."

She arched her eyes at him. "You say you're not Apache, yet you still have some of their beliefs."

"I guess," he reflected, "you could say I'm part Chiricahua and part *mejicano* the way I think . . . but not

144

either one. A lost soul." He didn't want to discuss this further; it bothered him. "Now, go get me some beer."

She started to leave, then held up. "That bandage on your arm. I keep thinking about it. You haven't complained, and you've been far too tired to tell me what happened. Did the great Cochise harm you?"

"Not Cochise. An old enemy and two others trailed me, after I left the stronghold." He summed up briefly the chase and the knife fight and Jesse Wilder's rôle.

"Why, Miguel," she said in increasing awe, "you're a hero, and you wouldn't have said a word, if I hadn't asked about the bandage."

He dismissed it. "Go get me some beer. I'm tired and thirsty." He pretended injured pride. "Does a hero have to beg?"

She was smiling as she left the house, which made him feel better about what was building up in him. But to hell with the fat *padre*. He was no true messenger of Ussen.

When she returned, she insisted that he eat something. To please her, he ate lightly of beans, tortillas, squash, and fruit. After that, he began drinking, feeling still terribly worn down; only his inherent toughness and durability and early training as an apprentice warrior, coupled with his purpose, had enabled him to endure the long ride and to face the Great Chief. And, finally, as Ussen had planned, to kill his old enemy, Santos. The realization stung him, ashamed now that he had let himself regress so far physically. Yes, he could thank the stern, older Chiricahuas for his survival, also part of Ussen's purpose to prepare him.

"So you rode into Cochise's country," she said, "and you really saw Cochise?" A note of wonder in her tone. "Did he remember you?"

In a general way, she knew part of his history, his growing

up as an Apache, and his being turned away at Bavispe.

"He remembered me. We talked."

"Tell me what he looks like, Miguel," she said impatiently.

"A fine-looking man. A greater chief than Juh. He's handsome. Strong body, strong face. Stands straight. High cheekbones. Eyes set wide. I brought a gift horse for him from the Anglo *señora* whose son is a captive of Juh's. He accepted it."

Impatient again, she said: "You don't tell me half what's going on. They're saying around the plaza that your Anglo friend and the pretty *señora* from back East have asked for volunteers to rescue her son from Chief Juh. And each volunteer will be paid five hundred dollars?" Her eyes enlarged as she said the amount.

"True."

"That horses and pack mules and guns and supplies will be furnished them? That you will go into the Burro Mountains where Juh is camped?" Everything was a question.

"Yes."

"Yet you tell me none of this. And they're saying it is very dangerous? That Juh tortures captives? . . . is the cruelest Apache?"

Miguel nodded.

"They say you may all be killed?"

"Who knows?"

"Then why are you going, Miguel?"

To her slack-mouthed surprise, he smiled back at her. "Because I have to . . . because it is part of Ussen's plan for me."

She stared at him. "And you say you are not Apache?"

His answer was to leave her and go to his bed to drink. It was useless to talk about such things. He would drink and sleep, hoping his strength would return. No matter, he would

146

be at the hotel in the morning, guided by his looming sense of fate, which had first struck him so forcibly and clearly, thinking of his little mother as he rode toward the stronghold from the stage station.

He needed rest. Except sleep evaded him. His restless mind kept jumping to Juh. Always it was Juh, The Monster, who had killed many White Eyes and Mexicans, the one who tortured prisoners and threw little babies into patches of cactus.

He finished another beer from the several María had left on the table. María, that good woman, who understood men and their needs. He must leave her what money he had before the volunteers left, money the Anglo *señora* had given him, leaving the money, if it happened that he didn't come back. Strangely, however, that worried him not. Why worry about something that was already destined, whatever that might be. His awareness of Ussen's will had taken hold of him and would not let go. *The mystery of Ussen,* he thought, fascinated, trusting.

He drifted off to sleep, awaking cold in the desert night and finding María pulling a blanket over him and silently slipping out of the room. That good woman. Although he didn't love her, he understood and appreciated her. He hadn't described to her in detail about killing Santos, when he could have bragged. Looking back, it seemed less important now after his old enemy's cruel menace of many years no longer hung over him. He was fully awake now.

He had seen Juh up close only once, while as a mature warrior with a *Tsoka-ne-nde* raiding party in Sonora. Juh like a hunk of stone. No visible feeling in his inscrutable face. No true welcome for his kinsmen. Fat and violent-looking. Great, broad face. Strong nose. Black eyes like knives. Thin mouth like a slash.

The dark image sent a wave of fear and dread through Miguel. An honest fear. He knew that he was not a coward. He'd proved his bravery, when he killed the three White Eyes, two in hand-to-hand struggle, and his cool bravery as the noted Horse Stealer. But a brave man admitted fear, when faced with danger, only a fool denied it. Part of his fear was concern for the White Eye boy. Was he still alive? Had Juh's *Nde-nda-i* run into another fight after wiping out the boy's escort at Cow Spring? Maybe soldiers scouting out of Fort Bowie? They often did that. If so, and the Enemy People had lost warriors, the boy might have been murdered right there. The White Eyes called it eye-for-an-eye, that kind of killing. The Apaches called it revenge. A simple thing.

These thoughts stayed with him, whipping through his mind until he deliberately blocked them out. There was so much hanging on chance. Nothing was more dear than a boy's mother. Now a surprising and unsettling sensation of doubt entered his mind. A haunting qualm. Would Ussen protect and guide him long enough to accomplish this thing? He weighed that back and forth: the long desert ride, the questionable reliability of some of the noisy, swaggering White Eye volunteers, hoping that Juh hadn't moved his meat camp in the Burros, and, finally, facing Juh himself and bargaining with him.

Afterward, a gradual sense of comfort stole over Miguel. Yes, Ussen would protect and guide him long enough. Wasn't that part of the plan? At least guide him? From there, the danger, it was unknown.

He slept on that understanding, calm and determined.

Chapter Thirteen

Jesse counted fourteen left of the volunteers still milling around next morning after three more had dropped out from those listed, two saying they were going on to California, the other that he had a job on a ranch. In all, Jesse decided, those going shaped up no better or no worse than he had assessed yesterday.

"Now," he told them, "although we have listed your names, we'd like every man to come forward and on the muster roll, opposite your name, state where you're from, your next of kin, and where they live."

Cal Truett played him a sly look. "You mean, so you can send word back if the Apaches happen to put an arrow through a feller?"

"By that, you'd have to assume there'd be somebody left to send word," Jesse said, smiling back at him.

A volunteer Jesse remembered as Tom Powers asked: "Do we have to put all that down, Captain? I ran off from home, when I was thirteen. A cruel stepfather, who laid on leather. If the Apaches get me, nobody back there would give a hoot. I figure my dear old mother's long gone by now, God rest her sufferin' soul. Maybe I've got an uncle left. Maybe not."

"I understand," Jesse replied. "Do as you wish, men. But we'd like to have as complete a roll as possible, so we'll know who you are. I promise you there'll be no strangers among us when this is over."

Mrs. Lattimore cheerfully assisted those who needed it. Some told her they could barely write their own names.

"Some of you men will want to take your own rifles and side arms," Jesse continued. "We'll furnish you ammunition. One hundred rounds per rifle or carbine, fifty for side arms. Let us know after we finish the roll. Otherwise, we'll buy weapons locally."

Then a volunteer raised this question: "What if a man gets killed, but the boy is rescued, and the outfit makes it back here?"

Jesse hadn't thought of that. Mrs. Lattimore answered at once. "The money, which is now on deposit here, would be sent to the man's next of kin, if so desired. That is only fair and all the more reason for knowing the next of kin. However, I hope that would not be the case." Speaking in her pleasant and sincere voice, looking up and about, she included them all, and in that moment Jesse thought each man must have felt that her words were meant especially for him.

"Thank you, ma'am," one said.

As she returned to assisting, Jesse said: "There must be some good Army carbines available locally this close to Fort Bowie." This drew forth understanding grins, Army weapons being almost equivalent of legal tender on the frontier. "After we finish up here shortly, we'll all go to the plaza and see about additional weapons, and outfit you for clothes and footgear. This afternoon we'll start getting you mounted."

As it turned out, none needed hand guns, only ammunition. Since they'd be mounted, all preferred carbines to rifles for easier handling, except Hardin, the ex-buffalo hunter. A tour of stores produced a variety of carbines, a few Sharpses, and some hard-used Maynards, Burnsides, and Ballards, obvious castoffs from the Civil War, but no coveted Spencers.

There was a good deal of laughter and joshing as the volunteers, not knowing their sizes, tried on trousers, shirts, jackets, boots, and shoes and hats, keeping the obliging Mexican clerks hopping. When dressed, some looked more like rube farmers in town on Saturday than riders.

"They need just about everything a man can put on, including underwear," Jesse remarked to Mrs. Lattimore. "Some even need blankets. I told the clerks to outfit them in whatever they ask for. It's going to cost you a pretty penny."

"It doesn't matter," she said. "Cost is no concern. Rutherford can afford it. While I have an unlimited letter of credit from the biggest bank in Philadelphia, I'm afraid I'd be at a loss without dear *Señor* Murillo. He's so helpful and kind. He actually is a one-man bank. He has surprising resources and connections himself back East and in California."

Again Jesse wondered why her husband hadn't accompanied her across hundreds of miles of travel, much of it dangerous, instead of sending a pompous attorney.

As if her thoughts moved in the same general direction as his, she said, almost offhandedly: "I heard from Rutherford today. He's coming out here. He's well on his way by now." No gladness in her voice, no anticipation, just concern. "I'd rather he not come. He's more at ease in an office or talking politics." She looked away, her bright mood of the day overcast, and seemed suddenly preoccupied.

Whatever her inner feelings, he figured, Rutherford Lattimore's wealth was making this expensive venture possible. Some men would forbid it as an impossible quest, which it would be without Miguel, even if it was still a huge gamble. Another thought took root. Maybe Susan Lattimore had forced the issue and said she was coming out to search for her only son, or else. Whatever that *else* might have meant, he admired her grit.

Then, in a tone of turning to more immediate matters, she

asked: "How are we coming along in the ordnance depart-ment, Captain?"

"It's hard to find ammunition enough for some of the older model carbines. So we'll go with what we can match. I tried to talk our buffalo hunter into taking a carbine, but he said, no. He's used to the Big Fifty and can fire from the saddle, if he has to, though he used reststicks when hunting buffalo. However, he did take a Colt Army Forty-Four for a side arm."

A pleased expression touched her face, a remembering. "I still have my father's very own Colt Army Forty-Four," she said. "Carried it in my purse on the way out . . . just in case. I'm not a bad shot. Also, a handy supply of factory-made cloth cartridges and percussion caps."

He had to smile at her, letting her see his unspoken admi-ration before he went over to a gun clerk, locked in animated conversation with Tom Powers over the virtues of what looked like an old Gallagher carbine of such vintage Jesse was certain it wasn't battle-worthy.

"Show us another carbine," Jesse told the clerk. "I'm afraid of this museum piece."

"Very good gun, *señor*," the clerk insisted.

"Believe not," Jesse said, convinced the man was trying to get rid of the worst of the lot first. "Let's see that Sharps."

He examined the Sharps closely. Although worn, it looked as if it could stand muster. He nodded to the clerk and handed the carbine to Powers, who said: "Never fired any-thing much but shotguns."

From there he found Miguel with his shopping finished, holding a small bundle of clothing, including a blanket.

"This all you're going to take?" Jesse asked.

"Enough. As before, I will dress like an Apache. At night I will need the new blanket with my old one."

"You could use a jacket at night as well." Jesse picked one from a stack, shook it out for size, and handed it to Miguel. "Take this. How about boots and shoes?"

"I prefer moccasins."

"You're better today, *amigo*. You looked worn out, when we rode in. Not that you ever held back."

Miguel agreed with a nod. "I will do this thing, *señor*."

Jesse left him to check on others.

Murillo had arranged for horse and mule traders to hold their stock in the big corral behind the hotel for inspection.

There they are, like vultures set to swoop in for what they think will be easy pickin's, Jesse smiled to himself. *Only they don't know this little lady has the trained eye of a cavalry remount officer and can walk away from an over-priced horse and never look back. So be on the lookout, you daylight equine burglars.*

After he had informed them of their needs, he said — "Missus Lattimore will have the final say." — to which the traders to a man swept off sombreros and flashed broad smiles. The trader from whom she had purchased her dark bay wasn't among them. *Scared off,* Jesse thought.

"We might start with the price range of your mounts," she began.

A trader stepped out as the spokesman, a sharp-eyed Anglo, jaws working, brushing at a luxuriant handlebar mustache over a whiskery chin stained rusty-brown. "Yes, ma'am, I know we can run out some right good mounts for around, say," — cocking a bloodshot eye at the sun — "two hundred dollars. I. . . ."

"Stop right there, sir. I'm not looking for Kentucky Thoroughbreds or many-gaited saddlers. Just good, solid mounts that can go a distance of ground, preferably short-coupled horses, which are better suited to mountains and rough country than the longer-coupled type. Likewise, mounts no younger than five or six, and none too broken to ride."

Unruffled, he smiled like a tomcat. "You bet, ma'am. An' we'll do our best to rock back and forth with you on prices."

He signaled and a Mexican youth led out a bay, brushed and curried. Not a bad-looking individual at first glance, but a second look was enough for Jesse.

She spoke before he could. "Take the horse away, sir."

"Why, ma'am, he's in top shape, ready for the saddle."

She spoke more sharply. "Sir, this horse is pointing a toe."

"Pointing a toe?" He assumed a bewildered look.

This bird is a bare-faced road agent, Jesse thought. *He should be masked and holding a six-gun on us.*

"He's pointing a toe," she explained flatly, "to ease the weight of his body, which is an indication of lameness. A sound horse shifts its weight from one hind foot to the other . . . not a forefoot on its toe or holding a forefoot forward."

"Take 'im back," the trader said gruffly.

The next horse was pigeon-toed. She then pointed out that this defect causes a horse to cut himself with his forefeet. She was fast losing patience, and, when the next horse was cow-hocked, she exploded on the hapless trader. "Sir, you insult my intelligence. No more of these slippery deals!"

He ducked his head, trying to appear hurt. "Why, ma'am, I just want you to see what-all we have."

"We want mounts, not something that will go lame after half a day's ride." She turned to the other traders. "Surely, you gentlemen have better horses than the crowbait just shown me?"

Jesse and Murillo weren't the only ones smiling as she finished.

After a short delay, better horses were brought out. While Jesse checked teeth for age, she studied each mount's conformation. When a question arose, she and Jesse would confer.

Back and forth that went. Prices varied, from bold-faced rob-bery of a hundred and a half to more reasonable figures, the sales then ranging around a hundred dollars for the superior individuals to as low as seventy. No horses over eight years old were taken. As the dickering progressed faster, she would look at Jesse, and he would nod or shake his head, no. Murillo helped her keep track of the purchases.

They were making good progress, when a good-looking dun with many brands was presented.

"How much?" she asked.

"Will make you an extra good price, ma'am," said the first trader, who had held off after being rebuffed earlier. "I'll let him go for seventy dollars. Dirt cheap for a good mount."

Jesse gave a negative shake of his head and didn't even step over to determine the horse's age. She crossed over to him.

"Why, Captain? He looks good."

"Did you notice the many brands on him?"

"Yes . . . but?"

"That horse has changed hands more times than a bogus greenback. Something's wrong."

She looked at the horse again. "How can we know?"

"I'll ride him out a way. Furthermore, I read a near smirk on the face of our fast-dealing friend. He wants to get rid of this horse."

She turned to the trader. "We want to try the horse out first. Please have him saddled."

She got a surprised look from the trader, but, nonetheless, the dun was saddled. Jesse mounted and took off. A short dis-tance and the dun wanted to run. Jesse drew rein, but the dun hardly responded. It happened again, when Jesse reined still harder. Deciding not to fight the horse, Jesse let him go a way. As they headed back at a trot, he noticed the horse largely ignored the bit.

"This is a hard-mouthed horse," Jesse said aloud, dismounting. "He cold-jawed on me, Missus Lattimore. I think we'd better ride out all these horses before you finalize the sales."

She agreed.

"Who'll volunteer to ride?" Jesse asked.

Genial Cal Truett stepped out as Juan López hesitated. "I rode some salty ones back on the farm. Young work stock."

The first two mounts behaved well enough. A blue roan was next. As Truett settled himself in the saddle after some difficulty mounting, the roan dropped its head and started bucking. Truett virtually formed an arc as he was propelled from the saddle, landing with a loud thump that raised a little cloud of dust, his hat sailing off like a great leaf.

Laughter. Even Susan Lattimore smothered a laugh.

Apparently unhurt, Truett got up, chagrined, dusting himself off. "Reckon I'm a better farrier than a horse-breaker."

López was waiting, when the handlers roped the roan and brought him back, still wild to buck. While two Mexican youths snubbed the roan's head, López leaped to the saddle. The snubbers stepped free, and the roan slammed into the same jolting act, but López seemed to expect every jump, And when the horse switched ends, bellowing, López was ready and spurred and rode the horse out, forcing him to buck and run until he quit. Riding back, the young man said: "I like this horse, *señora*. He has spirit. Is tough. Just needs riding. May I have him?"

"He's all yours," she said, delighted. "Thanks for riding him."

As the day wore on and all the traders saw they were dealing with people who knew how to judge horseflesh, they quit trying to pawn off unsound stock. Volunteers tried all the horses. With the exception of one bucker, which López had to ride after it dumped a willing, but untutored, Enoch Tatum, the rest of the mounts offered for sale were already broken for riding.

It was past five o'clock when the last horse was selected, plus four pack mules.

Yet they were still lacking a stallion for Chief Juh. Murillo said he would ask the traders to show their best stallions in the morning. Only two said they had studs.

Forthwith, they all trooped to the hotel to complete the day's transactions. Afterward, the three sat down to go over the final muster roll. The volunteers were to report back early in the morning to be assigned mounts and make another trip to the plaza for horse furniture, not forgetting picket pins and lariats.

Susan Lattimore was a little downcast. "Fourteen volunteers," she said to Jesse. "I thought more would sign up."

"I had expected a few more. Not many. Then three dropped out this morning."

"Do you think the fourteen will be all right?"

He didn't want to disappoint her. At the same time he must be honest with her. "Depends on what we run up against. At least, these men have had time to decide whether they really want to go or not. Too, there's a core of veterans among them. Men who've been under fire. I tell you, Missus Lattimore, I'd rather have three men than twenty-five hanger-ons just going along for the ride, figuring to shoot a passel of redskins and collect their five hundred."

His words encouraged her. It showed in her face. "I want to thank you, Captain, and you, Miguel, again, for all you've done and are still doing. I feel so grateful."

Both men only smiled back at her, both wishing to help her. How could you not, this appealing Eastern lady?

"Let's go over the roll one more time," Jesse said, and he began to read them off. "Cal Truett, our amiable farrier. Ben Hardin, Union veteran and former buffalo hunter, who's taking his Big Fifty along. And young Juan López, our bronc' rider. Glad you spoke up for him, Miguel. And Jeff Donaldson. Another ex-Confederate. A tight-lipped man. I believe he'll do in a pinch. And William Brakebill. We all feel sorry for the man. Rarin' to fight Apaches. May have to keep an eye on him. Nick Crider, big talker. Hope he can back it up. Enoch Tatum, our ex-preacher, a willing man. Said he's always in good humor. We can use that." Jesse paused, frowning. "Jason Long and Henry Webb. They told less about themselves than anybody. I have a feeling they run together, though nothing was said. And Gabe Jackson. Believe he's all right. Any slave who has the courage to run away and make a life for himself is a man. Tom Powers, who ran away from home in Indiana as a boy. Seems reliable. Now we come to Theodore Shelby. Very open about his feelings as an Abolitionist. Understand that. The last two men, John Shaw and Dave Wallace, are nondescript. More of the faceless drifters headed for the golden climes of California." Thoughtfully, he added: "Few of these men put down any kin. Guess I would do the same."

She looked at him in concern. "You have no family at all?"

"A sister in Lexington, Kentucky. A brother in Corinth. I don't consider them family, and they don't consider me family. I was never forgiven for serving out West as a galvanized Yankee in order to get out of a Yankee prison where men were dying like flies. My father disowned me. My brother, who never fired a shot in the war, always had a soft staff job back in general headquarters somewhere, well beyond the fighting. I'm sure he's sounded off about the terrible dishonor I brought upon the family escutcheon, suh. I don't know why I'm suddenly telling you this boring tale of family history." He smiled ruefully as he went on, needfully for himself. "But I do have one friend back in Tennessee. The old family lawyer. We have an agreement. I write and let him know where I am. He understands."

"I'm sorry," she said, eyes intent on his face.

"The war divided many families, mine indirectly, you might say. Ben Hardin's another, back in Missouri. I've gotten over it. I've accepted it."

"The war has forced many of us to accept changes," she said, and he knew she was thinking of the colonel. "No matter the loss, there has to be some forgiveness." She was still watching his face. "What would you do if your sister and brother entered this room and, after a moment's hesitation, came toward you?"

He avoided her eyes, looking away, startled, lost for words. After a time, he said: "I . . . believe . . . I would stand and hold out my hand."

"You see," she said softly, gladly, "someone has to take the first step."

He said nothing more, surprised at his response to her insight, which told him that sometimes a man didn't know himself.

For a further pause the three shared the reasoning silence. Until Jesse said: "Besides the stallion, let's get everything settled tomorrow, including supplies. Each man has to know his mount and saddle up and ride him out. Also how to pack mules. That will give us some semblance of order before we leave. We should pull out day after tomorrow . . . at sunrise."

She agreed. Miguel nodded.

They parted then. She looked tired but relieved, that dark

head high. It was as if he could read her mind: *At last, they will go find Jimmy. I'm so grateful.* And he thought: *If only we could be halfway sure of that, even with Miguel.*

Jesse went for tequila on the patio. Sipping, looking at the muster roll again, he mulled over those who hadn't been forthcoming. Likely, some were deserters. Army officers in the West hated and detested deserters, Jesse recalled, and enlisted men despised them for the simple reason desertions left an outfit short in a pinch, when every man was needed. Likely, a few were criminals who had left their true names back in the States.

So be it, he decided. You took what you got. Everything will even out on the trail. Common danger and purpose make a good leveler.

Next morning the trader insisted the dark chestnut stallion was a "pure saddle-bred," once owned by an officer at Fort Bowie, who had sold it to a local merchant, who had died, and the man's widow, not liking that much horse, had sold it to the trader.

"He's yours, ma'am, for only five hundred dollars."

"He may be what the man says," she said aside to Jesse and Murillo, "but he's not impressive-looking enough. Doesn't stand out. Neither do I like the price. I want a flashy-looking horse, whether he's purebred or not. That wouldn't matter to Juh, would it?"

Neither man argued the point.

There was only one other stallion left for sale in all of Tucson, the next trader informed her, and this was it. "This fine bay Morgan. Comes straight down the ladder from Justin Morgan himself back East. I can let you have him for six hundred, and that's givin' him away."

She smiled at the man without comment and turned to

160

her friends. "These are both good horses, but not what I want. A special horse."

"Do you have to have a stallion?" Murillo asked.

"No. I just thought a stallion would look more striking, though realizing he'd be much harder to handle getting him there."

"You mean color, *señora*. It is color more than blood you are thinking of?"

"Why, yes, if the horse stands out. One as striking as the black gelding for Cochise."

"Don't give up. I am thinking about an extra nice gelding."

Murillo strolled over to the first trader and began talking. The trader continued to shake his head. After a while, he seemed to give ground and, leaving his stallion in charge of others, went outside the corral and returned leading a well-muscled buckskin Quarter horse.

"There," she exclaimed instantly to Jesse, "is what I want!"

"Let's rock back and forth before you take him," Jesse cautioned.

"This is the trader's favorite riding mount, a gentle gelding," Murillo said. "I've noticed him riding the buckskin around town. He's very proud of the horse. And because you want the horse, *señora*, you can bet he will ask more than the horse is worth."

"What is the trader's name?" she asked.

"*Señor* Blair. I don't know him well. They say he's from Texas."

A true buckskin, Jesse observed, a durable color for the Southwestern sun, as they watched the trader lead the horse up. No smuttiness in color, this horse, with black points that didn't extend above the knees. Black feet. Black eyes. Black mane and tail. A black stripe down the spine from the mane to the tail. Straight legs. Good conformation. Short back. A gaited horse? No matter. He had the looks. A striking, handsome animal. A walking picture.

"That's a fine-looking horse," she said. "How much do you want for him, *Señor* Blair?"

"He's my favorite. Can't let him go for less than a thousand."

"Oh, my. I believe you'd better take him back."

"Well, now, ma'am, I might whittle a little on that."

"How much, sir?"

"Say, fifty dollars."

"Afraid you're whittling with a dull knife, sir."

All the men laughed, including Blair, who pursed his mouth and said: "Well, ma'am, I might sharpen my knife a little. Come down to around nine hundred."

"You may have sharpened your knife, but I believe you're whittling on ironwood."

Looking more agreeable, he said suddenly: "Ma'am, I'll whittle on soft pine. The horse is yours for only eight hundred."

She glanced at Jesse, who gave her a barely noticeable, no.

"I won't pay that much," she told the trader, mixing a compelling smile. "As a matter of interest, how old is your buckskin?"

Perhaps sensing that she was about to take his offer, he replied obligingly: "This fine individual is only six."

Here we go again, Jesse thought.

"May I look at the horse's mouth, sir?" she asked sweetly, and he replied: "Certainly, ma'am."

"On second thought," she said, "I believe I should ask Captain Wilder to do that for me. He's more informed, a vet-

162

eran horseman from Tennessee. Do you mind, Captain Wilder?"

"Be glad to, Missus Lattimore." They were being very correct.

Going forth, Jesse slowly opened the buckskin's mouth and studied the teeth, peering up and down and sideways. The examination took a while. Stepping back, frowning, he said: "The upper corner teeth have one cup left. However, the corner teeth are smooth. I also studied the shaft, or length, of the teeth."

"Exactly what are cups, Captain?" she asked, although he knew she knew.

"Cups," he said instructively, "are black spots in teeth from three years to nine. I don't like to counter what Mister Blair said, but this horse is nine years old."

She uttered a surprised — "Oh." — and Blair coughed, quickly salvaging: "I've had this buckskin for two years. Bought him off a travelin' horse trader who claimed he was four. I liked the horse so much after I rode him in the runnin' walk, I never questioned his age. Didn't matter. That's gospel truth."

Which makes it all the more suspect, coming from a trader, Jesse thought.

"I had hoped for a younger horse," she said, looking downcast.

Apparently sensing that he was about to lose the sale, the trader said: "Ma'am, you'll have to take my word that I *understood* this horse was four, when I bought him. But if this gentleman says he's nine, then he's a nine. I won't argue the point."

She remained silent, waiting.

"Ma'am, you must admit he's a fine-looking individual."

"Yes, but. . . ."

"He's yours for only seven hundred, and remember this is my favorite riding horse."

"But . . . ?"

"Six-fifty, ma'am."

"But he's nine, *Señor* Blair."

Blair was beginning to sweat. He wiped his face and forehead with a bandanna. "He's yours for six hundred, ma'am, and, if you don't take him for that, I'll lead him away."

Catching Jesse's quick nod, she appeared to consider a moment, smiled engagingly, and, seeming to give in, said: "I will take the buckskin, sir . . . for five-fifty."

"Take him!" Blair said, throwing up his hands in despair.

After the deal was closed and the traders had gone, they all stood around admiring the buckskin. "I believe you got the right horse," Jesse said. "He fills the eye. He looks sound."

"What do you think, Miguel?" she asked.

"Juh will like this horse, *señora*." Nodding, nodding. "He will want the horse. I know. Any Apache would."

On the plaza, after more bickering, they completed buying horse furniture and pack saddles and supplies to be delivered at the hotel. As they passed Luis Vega's shop, the silver-mounted, hand-tooled Mexican saddle in the window caught her eye. Draped over it was a silver-studded bridle. She turned in immediately. Jesse made the introductions.

Family-man Vega, and loving father of his brood, could not have been more gracious. Bowing: "*Señora,* my heart goes out to you. I pray every day that your little one will be returned to you."

"Thank you, *señor*. You are most kind. That is truly a beautiful saddle and bridle in the window. You made them here?"

"Oh, yes, *señora*."

"I think these would help set off the horse even more," she

said, bringing her enthusiasm to bear on Jesse and Miguel.

Explaining for Vega's benefit, Jesse said: "Missus Lattimore has just bought a handsome buckskin saddler as a gift for Chief Juh, hoping he will release her son. I agree that this outfit will make the horse stand out even more."

"Ah," Vega said, "a beautiful buckskin. You don't see many."

"I know you will make her a good price, Luis."

"Don't I always, *amigo* Jesse? Why I am always poor," — spreading his hands and rolling his eyes as he spoke, smiling big — "the saddle took a long, long time. I cannot sell it for less than four hundred American dollars, and the bridle is priced at one hundred fifty. If you will take the saddle at that fair price, *señora,* I will give you the bridle?"

"How could I refuse?" she answered. "I will take the beautiful saddle, *Señor* Vega. And the bridle is a fine piece of work to go with the saddle. I thank you very much. You are so generous and kind."

Vega's smile was like sunlight. "Because I understand and want to help. Now, saddle and bridle are yours, *señora*. I am proud that you will accept them for this good purpose."

She held out her hand, which he accepted with an Old World bow.

For this last evening, Mrs. Lattimore invited Jesse and Miguel to have an early dinner with her. Miguel declined, pleading many things to do. Jesse could have said the same, thinking of many details, but felt he could not. She shouldn't be left alone tonight on the eve of the outfit's departure.

She wore the same beige-colored dress he remembered and greeted him warmly. Details, details. They went over them, and he assured her they would be looked after.

"We need order," he said over wine. "That will come fast

on the trail as we go along, out of necessity. Reliable men soon show up."

"This is such a tremendous undertaking," she said somberly. "So dangerous. So unbelievable that it's even happening. Going off into the mountains to find a fierce Apache chief, holding Jimmy. It's like an Arthurian quest. So noble, really." Her voice broke. He thought she might cry a little; instead, she smiled at him with glistening eyes. "I'm so grateful to all of you. Every man."

"In a way, it is remarkable that we could put the outfit together on such short notice. But don't credit it all to the nobility of man. It's mainly the mighty good money, for which you can't blame them. They also realize the risk."

"They are noble . . . every man . . . to take the risk."

"I won't belabor the point," he said cheerfully. "I respect any man who does his duty. I've seen men face pure hell. Sometimes you'll be surprised who stands up. Not the blowhard. Not the camp braggart. Often it's the quiet ones you want beside you. On the other hand, I've seen green boys turn and skedaddle at the first terrifying battle sounds, then a little later form and go back. A whole company of us did that at Shiloh. We'd never shot at anybody before. It was embarrassing to run. We hung our heads, looked at each other, then reformed for another charge."

It had been a long day, and the dinner soon ended.

When he escorted her to her quarters and they paused, he said: "We'll try to leave by early daylight. However, I doubt we can get off that early."

"How will you march?"

"Column of twos. Miguel out front as scout."

"I'll see you off," she said. "I don't know what to say."

"Whatever comes to your mind. Why not just wave us off?"

"I'm so grateful to everyone."

Seeing her there, looking so terribly alone at that moment, yet so resolute, he had the impulse to hold her and give her courage. Now for her the wearisome waiting and not knowing and hoping. He thought that, but dashed the inclination; it would only weaken her, and he didn't want a weeping woman on his hands, even a very attractive one like her. Another moment. But, to hell with that, and he took her in his arms and held her, and she held onto him for what seemed like the longest time. When they mutually broke the embrace, he kissed her tenderly on the forehead, as one might console a troubled child.

She looked at him, wide-eyed. "Only that, Captain?" — and kissed him fully on the lips, and he kissed her back and held her briefly. The physical contact was unnerving, and he was surprised at himself and her.

Stepping suddenly away, she said: "See you in the morning. . . . Good night."

"Good night."

He was still standing, dumbfounded at himself, when she entered the room without looking back.

He paced the patio until his head cleared, and presently, as always at a time like this before another venture, he went to his room and by candlelight wrote a letter to B. L. Sawyer, the trusted family attorney back in Tennessee who had urged Jesse to contest the will. Jesse had refused. Be damned if he'd give up his only family connection and friend back there!

Dear Mr. Sawyer:

   Sir, I hope this finds you well. At this time of year the leaves must be turning scarlet and gold and your buggy horse eager to take you on a pleasant ride.

As he penned the words, he could see again the rolling hills of home, ablaze in their vestments of autumn.

I am writing this from Tucson, Arizona Territory, where I came after the special mission as a scout into the Mexican state of Sonora for a U.S. Army detachment which I wrote you about. All I can tell you is that our mission was difficult but successful, and the red horse and I returned in good health.

I thought I would rest here. But an Eastern lady's little son is being held by Apaches. With volunteers and a guide, we are headed for the Burro Mountains, back in New Mexico Territory, some hundred and fifty miles. I hope this is my last undertaking of this nature. I need peace of mind.

Again, sir, I wish you well and good fortune. I often think of your kindness in my behalf.

Sincerely, your friend,
Jesse Alden Wilder

Miguel drank some beer, but not enough to get drunk. At supper with María, he ate and said little.

"You are very quiet, Miguel," she said, sounding worried. "Are you sick?"

"I am not sick."

"You must be thinking about tomorrow."

"I'm just resting."

"I've fixed you a pack of food to take with you in the morning."

"*Gracias*. You are always kind."

And she hasn't asked for one centavo, he thought. Well, he would leave her his remaining money, but he wouldn't tell

168

her now. It would be a surprise for her in the morning. More money than she had seen in a long time.

"You say nice things, Miguel."

He smiled. "Only the truth."

"You are much kinder than most men."

"Listen to me," he said, taking her hand. "Don't listen to what the fat *padre* says to you about hell. Say nothing back to him. Just say your prayers to Ussen, and Ussen will listen and understand and guide you."

She stiffened. "You say Ussen again. You mean God?"

"They are both the same. White Eyes and *mejicanos* say God. Apaches say Ussen."

She teased him with a look. "You are still Apache, Miguel. You think like one."

"Remember this," he countered, ignoring the last. "Ussen, or God, is everywhere. In the mountains. In the sky. In the streams that sing. Not only in the fat *padre's* Church."

"Oh, Miguel. You worry me. I hope God won't punish you."

He smiled again. "He won't for what I said about the fat *padre,* because the *padre* has no understanding or forgiveness. All he can talk about is sin. The Church needs a new *padre,* a skinny one to start. A *padre* who knows about hunger and pain and sorrow, and forgiveness."

He left her reflecting on that and went to bed.

Sleep came only now and then. In between he prayed fervently to Ussen. *Let me be brave. Let me be wise. When to go ahead. When to go there. When to wait. Give me this power. Let us find the White Eye* señora's *little boy and take him to her to hold as my dear little Mexican mother held me on the cruel walk to the stronghold many years ago.*

Gradually, a feeling of ease settled over him and he fell into a deep sleep.

He was up before dawn, feeling rested, dressing quietly. María was in the other room. He smiled as he left all his money on the table by the bed, imagining her surprise. His own surprise awaited him, when he found the food sack by the door, which told him that she had known he would leave early.

Dawn was breaking now. Leaving the house, he walked a way and stopped, looking back at the little house with the mesquite in front. And, looking, he sensed that he would not see María again.

Chapter Fourteen

After the confusion with untrained horses and some of the men not used to handling stock and the pack mules, displaying the obstinacy of their breed, Jesse decided the outfit was as organized at this point as could be expected. The settling down and order would soon come on the trail. A day's hard march could work wonders. He looked around, expecting Susan Lattimore at any moment. She should have been here by now or earlier. With her background and understanding, it was unlike her to delay them. Certainly she would see them off.

"What's holdin' us up?" a volunteer muttered.

Minutes passed.

They were formed behind the hotel. As early as the hour was, not long after dawn, some townsmen had gathered to watch the departure.

He was about to go to the hotel and ask about her when, suddenly, he saw her, walking rapidly. His jaw fell. Instead of a dress, she appeared much as she had the day they'd gone riding: brown boots, blue denim riding skirt, a man's gray flannel shirt, a light blue scarf at her neck, gloves, and the sensible, wide-brimmed hat.

So she was going to ride out a little way with them, he decided. Well, he would demand that she not go far.

She came up to him and said firmly, in that pleasant way she had: "I'm going with you into the mountains, Captain."

He'd been so intent on her face and what she was saying that he just now noticed the gun belt, nearly hidden by the folds of her oversize trooper's shirt, and the holstered Army revolver.

"You what?"

"I'm going with you. I cannot in conscience have all of you go on such a perilous mission while I stay behind. I won't have it."

Voices in the column grew deadly still.

"Look, Missus Lattimore. This is no place for a woman."

"For a woman, you say." Turning away, she went straight toward the low adobe wall behind the hotel where the drunks practiced shooting. Three bottles lined the wall. She drew the revolver with a smooth motion, eared back the hammer, took quick aim, and fired. A bottle burst. Earing the hammer back again, she broke a second bottle, and even faster the third.

There was a ripple of applause and voices.

"I understand how you feel," Jesse said. "But. . . ."

Before he could protest further, she faced away and called: "*Señor* Murillo, bring up my horse, please."

In an instant Murillo appeared around a corner of the hotel, leading her dark bay, saddled and packed. They had planned this since yesterday, Jesse concluded, kept the horse away from the corral so he wouldn't know.

He confronted her. "Do you realize what you're getting into? You could be killed, not to mention the hardships you'll undergo."

"I do. For that reason I've made arrangements with *Señor* Murillo as my banker to pay the men in full, if I fail to return. In fact, the funds are available now."

"I don't like this at all, Missus Lattimore. It's too dangerous. More so for a woman."

"I believe I just demonstrated that I can shoot as well as any man. And I've been riding since I was a child."

"And a better shot you are, ma'am, than a lot of men. It's

172

not that. It's just that it will be much tougher for a woman. The camping. The food. The heat, the dust. Lack of water. Long hours in the saddle. Everything. I'm totally against this."

She merely smiled, a bright little smile of finality. "I shall have to ignore your well-meant Southern gallantry, Captain, although I respect it. Are you ready to mount up, sir?"

"We are." She was going, hell or high water, and there was no way in God's world he could stop her, other than backing out himself at this final moment, which he couldn't do. He'd come too far. Stirred up the whole thing through Miguel. And he said in resignation: "I know I could never forgive myself, if anything happened to you."

That seemed to dent her resolve: he saw it flick across her eyes, saw the full ripe lips stir, saw it vanish, controlled, before she turned to mount. On instinct he started to give her a hand up, but, as if anticipating him, she swiftly mounted on her own to ride side-saddle.

He mounted the red horse and rode to the head of the column and shouted: "Prepare to mount!" A moment. "Mount. Form twos." A pause. "Foord, march!"

He'd given the commands hardly without thinking. Well, the sooner the outfit took on some order, the better. And for him, he felt this was just the beginning of a most painful and unfair responsibility.

As they moved out, he heard a man mutter: "Bad luck to have a woman along."

The man's words caused Jesse to ponder ahead. Would having a woman along influence a man's judgment? It could damned well happen to the detriment of the mission, if they held back for her safety, instead of acting.

They rode steadily. Jesse in the lead with Miguel was thinking to himself this would not be what the U.S. Cavalry called a "book" campaign, halting ten minutes of every hour, nooning for forty-five minutes, and making camp when there was still plenty of daylight left. He wanted the Burro Mountains before him within three days or earlier. Now and then Miguel would scout ahead. Looking back after an hour, Jesse noted that the dusty column was beginning to settle in and find itself. Susan Lattimore rode beside the once-Reverend Enoch Tatum. They were talking; Tatum was smiling constantly. As he'd said, he was a good-natured man. She would get plenty of attention and respect from these women-hungry men.

Young Juan López, who had asked for the assignment, led the handsome buckskin on a short halter rope. With the silver-mounted saddle glistening in the brassy sun, the gift horse stood out like a statue in a park.

Jason Long and Henry Webb rode side by side, Nick Crider in front of Long. Whenever Jesse happened to glance back, the three were conversing. Was Crider also part of the connection Jesse had figured between the first two? Ben Hardin sided Crider, but each ignored the other. It was interesting, Jesse thought from experience, how men thrown together would take an instant dislike for another. One small thing would do it: a sloppiness in camp or offishness or how another handled a horse or was careless with firearms. Then again you'd make friends you'd die for, men eager to share the pitiful little they had of tobacco, bacon, flour, even a thin blanket. One reason why in the Reb Army the men had cooked in groups. Common sense.

Thinking of this diverse command, if he might dare term it a "command," he wondered which man he might count on as an unofficial noncom, and yet not pick him out in front of the others. To do so could cause resentment. Just give the man certain duties. That should be determined by the time they reached the Burros, or sooner, if they ran into trouble.

At Miguel's direction he halted them at noon in a spring-fed little cañon. Thirty minutes later he had them in motion, and, as the punishing Arizona sun took over, the talk behind him died out to drivels. She was constantly on his mind. It gratified him that she seemed at ease, gazing off at the desert and mountains. He figured she was the sort of person who could put up a bold front, no matter her true feelings.

That evening they bivouacked on the inviting San Pedro where Jesse and Miguel had camped. After the watering detail, he pointed where the picket line was to be, and the volunteers unsaddled and fed mounts and mules, and a few men, like Hardin, let their mules roll, raising a raucous chorus of grunts and groans and squeals.

When Susan Lattimore started to picket her horse, Jesse offered, saying: "Let me do that."

"Thank you, Captain, but I've done this many times."

"I'm not surprised . . . your father trained you. But I would like to help you."

She looked up at him. "I shouldn't accept help so long as I can do it myself."

He shrugged, and, as he walked off, he thought — *independent*. Well, that sure as hell beat a helpless female. Regardless, he was going to keep a close eye on her. He must. She was his responsibility.

While the men were gathering firewood, he told them to pack some back for the days ahead and to cook in groups to save fuel.

Gabe Jackson approached. "Suh, Ah'd like to cook fo' de nice lady. Reckon she'd let me?"

"Ask her."

When next Jesse looked her way, after feeding his own

stock, Jackson was making a fire for her, while she was carefully reloading her Colt Army .44, ramming home cloth cartridges with the loading lever, then placing percussion caps on the nipples on the back of the cylinder. It occurred to him again how well the colonel had trained his daughter.

Beginning to share a fire with Miguel and López, he noticed Hardin and Truett and Powers looking around, undecided. He stood up and waved them over, and they gladly joined. Good sign. Some white men, Jesse knew, wouldn't tolerate the company of a Mexican. The only volunteer cooking alone was Donaldson, who seemed not to mind.

"How'd the buckskin do today, Juan?" Jesse asked.

"He pulled hard at first, *señor*, but pretty soon he come along just fine. I rubbed him down good."

Not much was said after supper, while they sat on campstools and drank coffee. Before dark, Jesse posted the first two sentries and named others to stand watches. Men who didn't stand tonight would next night. He and Miguel would take the last watch. In Apache country the most dangerous time was at the crack of dawn. And he thought of the reliable old warning: "When the light is bad and the shooting is bad, the Apaches come jumping."

Once the bivouac had settled down, he went over to Susan Lattimore. Her fire, down to low coals, left her face in mystery.

"How are you this evening, ma'am?"

"I'm fine, Captain. Gabe Jackson insisted on cooking my supper. He's a very nice man. I'm afraid I'm being spoiled."

"No danger of that."

"How did we fare today?"

"Better than I had expected. We moved along. No grumblings when I set out sentries. That will come later. Men

176

on the march are going to grumble. It's normal. You expect it."

"How far have we come?"

"About fifty miles. Making that every day, we should see the Burros near the end of the third day. Wouldn't be wise to push any faster. We have to think of the horses."

"I agree, yes, we must. Will we go near Fort Bowie?"

"We'll go miles around Bowie. Steer clear of it. I don't want the military to know what we're about. They might even try to stop us, if they knew. Say we're stirrin' up the Apaches, as if they weren't already. Miguel is guiding us as straight as possible, but water determines how we go. He knows every spring and stream in this part of the country. Tomorrow morning the Dragoon Mountains will be on our right as we head northeast. So will Cochise's stronghold."

She seemed to reflect on what he'd said. "Thank you for telling me. It's good to know our location. I'm so thankful for everything."

"There is one thing," Jesse said. "I know you were brought up to be independent and self-reliant, and that's good. But if you need anything at all, let me know. Don't hold back. Now, sleep well."

"I shall. Thank you and good night."

All the men had put down their packs and gear at a distance so as to allow her some privacy. Jesse did likewise, yet where he could rise up and see her sleeping form. Last in his ears before sinking into sleep was the shuffle and snuffle of horses on the picket line. Miguel slept nearby.

Long after, feeling a cool wind rising off the desert, he pulled up his blanket. Thinking of her, he got up in stocking feet and slipped closer to where she lay. In the mottled light, she slept like a child, one arm outflung, face turned. Her blanket lay across her knees. She appeared to stir uncomfortably. Going over, leaning down, he gently spread the blanket across her shoulders. She stirred at the touch, but did not awaken, and he crept silently away.

Later in the night the *tink, tink* of bridle metal broke his light sleep. He sensed it was about time for Miguel and him to take the last watch. The way it worked, one man coming off watch would touch the next to come on. He sat up, head cocked, intent. After a little run of time, he heard it again, now with dull hoof sounds, but more distant. The sounds came from the west, then suddenly faded out. He needed no more. Hurriedly pulling on boots, he jumped up and looked for Miguel, who was already up.

"I think somebody's takin' off," Jesse said, and sought the sentries. He found only one, Dave Wallace. "Where's John Shaw?"

"Ain't he at the other end of camp?"

"He's not there. Didn't you hear a horse goin' off?"

"Not from here."

In disgust, Jesse roused Hardin and Truett to stand last watch, tersely explained, then saddled the red horse while Miguel saddled, and they rode off to the west.

It was still too dark to track, although it hardly mattered. Twice, halting to listen, they picked up hoofbeats.

Light was breaking, when they sighted the rider. Shaw was going hard, punishing his mount. Now and then he looked back.

"Keep that up, he'd kill his horse before he made Tucson," Jesse said disgustedly, and fired a warning shot.

Startled, Shaw glanced back and whipped and spurred harder.

Galloping, Jesse and Miguel began to gain. Seeing that, Shaw fired his carbine at them, missing wildly.

"The damn' fool," Jesse muttered as he and Miguel split

up to present smaller targets.

They played that game for a while.

Shaw's horse, although a steady animal, lacked the speed of the others. When within good carbine range, Jesse fired once over Shaw's head, thinking he would surrender. Instead, he got off more sporadic rounds with his single-shot carbine and punished his horse, which angered Jesse the more.

Jesse knew he could kill the man at this range, but didn't want to. They'd have to run him down. Luckily, Shaw wasn't much of a rider and certainly no marksman, yet just wild enough to be dangerous.

Closing in, Jesse bent low on his horse, and Miguel veered out, riding faster to cut Shaw off. The tactic confused Shaw. He swiveled his head back and forth, from rider to rider. Now he was fumbling with the carbine. Suddenly he threw up his hands and quit beating his horse.

"God damn you!" Jesse shouted, rushing up and seizing Shaw's carbine. "We could've killed you for deserting and should have."

Shaw just hung his head.

"Hand over your side arm and get off that poor horse," Jesse ordered. "Damn you, you've already cost us half a day's march." His withering disgust deepened. "I'm going to give you a choice. You can take two canteens and start on foot for Tucson, which you'd make only by the grace of God and then some. Or you can go back to the outfit. What'll it be?"

"I'll go back."

"Then march and lead your mount."

Shaw was a sallow-faced man with thin shoulders and shiftless eyes and a shuffling way of walking. Jesse severely questioned his judgment for ever taking the man. And Wallace was no better. Wallace had to have been aware, when

Shaw took his horse off the picket line. He would hear about that, when they got back.

They marched Shaw until he was dragging. But walking him meant losing time, and finally Jesse relented and told him to mount up.

By the time they reached the bivouac, the outfit had long been ready to move out.

Jesse didn't hesitate. "Hereafter," he told them, "deserter John Shaw will cut wood for all the detail, water the pack mules, and any other needed chores. He will go unarmed. He let us all down by deserting his post in Apache country and cost us half a day's march, when speed is important. And Dave Wallace, you are just about as guilty. You had to know what he was up to. Hereafter, you will be on probation, though you may keep your arms. One wrong move by either of you, and I'll shoot you on the spot. I don't think it's necessary to remind you men that both sides shot deserters in the war."

That was all. Nobody spoke. Some nodded.

Susan Lattimore was thoughtful and composed.

Gabe managed some leftover coffee for the three, after which the column trailed out in a column of twos.

For a time, Miguel took them the way he and Jesse had traveled, but once past the abandoned stage station at Dragoon Springs he angled sharply northeast, the outfit making good time despite the late start. Cloud cover masked the sun and made the day much cooler, and the horses responded.

Jesse, riding alone while Miguel scouted ahead, was surprised to find Susan Lattimore beside him.

"Well, good day," he said, pleasure in his voice.

She said earnestly: "I want to tell you that I'm glad you didn't shoot Mister Shaw. I realize what the penalty was in wartime. Even so, it was a terrible thing to do. Instead, why couldn't deserters have been imprisoned?"

"I suppose some were. Desertion was a problem and had to be dealt with. An example made. Later, it was a problem for the cavalry on the plains. I've been with a few details sent in pursuit of deserters with verbal orders to bring 'em back dead or alive."

"And . . . ?"

To her waiting relief, he said: "They always surrendered without a fight. But I know sometimes they were shot and brought back lashed across their saddles. Believe me, that made a lasting impression on anyone thinking of going over the hill. I didn't report that Shaw fired at us. Fortunately, he's a lousy shot. I could have shot him, but didn't want to. Been murder. This is not the U.S. cavalry." He said further: "If we were in the Burros, I'd have let him go. No time to give chase. He won't try this again. He was only going to quit us when he was close enough to make it back to Tucson."

"I see. May I ride here today?"

"You certainly may, Missus Lattimore. It's *your* command, you know. Not mine."

"Don't you think it's time you called me Susan?"

"Thank you. I'd like to. But in front of the men, I think I should address you as Missus Lattimore, or ma'am."

"I guess you're talking about proper respect?"

"I am. Look at it this way. If I called you Susan in front of the men, it would be comparable to calling a colonel by his first name. We are more of a military detachment than not. We have to have order, and proper respect comes first."

"I understand. Just don't call me 'colonel.' "

He laughed lightly, appreciating her sense of humor. For the first time, he felt less apprehensive about her coming.

Their arid way stretched out before them, distant mountains like islands in a sea of desert.

181

Powers was having trouble with a devilish pack mule whose load had slipped. Riding back, Jesse motioned for Hardin to come along. Hardin soon had the packs secure. Jesse left Powers and the Missouri mule man discussing the ways of the cantankerous hybrid, realizing he'd called on Hardin by instinct as one of his reliables.

Reining back to the column's point, he saw that Crider had preëmpted his place alongside Mrs. Lattimore, and Crider did not show the courtesy of dropping back, when Jesse approached. Although irked, Jesse said nothing for now and rode ahead to where Miguel was waiting, thinking little warning flags of possible future trouble were already beginning to fly.

"Can't make San Simon River tonight," Miguel told him, frowning. "Lost too much time this morning."

"What does that leave us?"

"Good spring in the hills other side the big *playa* we'll come to. Camp there."

"Good enough."

"Tomorrow night Doubtful Cañon."

Jesse knew he meant the Butterfield station at Stein's Peak, above the cañon, abandoned like others when the war started. Not long after he called the day's first halt.

It was late afternoon when they skirted the broad *playa,* which looked bone-dry. But Jesse was of no mind to cross it after Miguel had said the footing was treacherous, so they trailed around in the foothills of what Jesse thought would be the Dos Cabezas Mountains on a military map.

At the late halt, he had heard Donaldson and Shelby exchange quarrelsome words, broken off by the order to mount up. To quiet them, he told them to ride apart the rest of the day. They obeyed without argument.

He assumed the matter was over, when they broke to make

camp, but, after watering and feeding, he heard their sharp voices rising again, more heated than before, and suddenly saw them squaring off.

He stepped over at once and held up quieting hands, speaking in a calm voice. "Men . . . stand back. Mister Donaldson, Mister Shelby, if there's an issue, we can always talk about it later. Now, let's fix supper."

"There's plenty at issue here," Shelby said, unappeased, very erect. "The senseless war. The terrible toll. Upon us the terrible aftermath of the crippled and everlasting sorrow over lost ones. All started when the South captured Fort Sumter. An inexcusable act!"

His intense gray eyes seemed to emit sparks as he fixed his accusatory wrath on Donaldson, who glared back at him with equal force as he replied: "Suh, your voice is an echo of others, such as the black Republicans, who really started the war. Lincoln was about to reinforce Sumter. The South had no choice but to defend itself as a matter of honor." Despite his dark temper, his voice was controlled and yet mannerly, and he stood tall and cool-eyed and wore his rough clothing in a manner that denoted the extra care of a gentleman.

"Honor!" Shelby snarled, nearly shouting, his slight frame shaking. "Sittin' on the verandah in fancy clothes, sippin' juleps. Ridin' around on blooded horseflesh. Life made easy by the sweat of slaves in the fields clad in rags to cover their bleedin' backs from the whips of burly overseers who took little black girls to their quarters at night. You call that honor?"

Suddenly Donaldson lost his poise. "Suh, I call you out! At this moment! Now!" His right hand rested on his hand gun.

"And I accept!" Shelby shouted back, eyes wild. "What's holdin' you back, most honorable *suh!*"

Jesse rushed between them, a restraining hand extended toward each man. "Enough of this, men. No more. There'll be no calling anybody out. Mister Donaldson, you camp at that end of the bivouac. Mister Shelby, you camp over there. I forbid you to speak to each other again tonight or tomorrow."

When each antagonist let down and stood back a little, Jesse spoke in a quieter and personal way meant for each volunteer. "Keep in mind that we're a small outfit. Every man is important. Every man will be needed. Now, let's all get after some supper!" He stood between the two until they turned away and obeyed as ordered. *The god-damned war,* he thought. *Would it ever be over?*

Susan Lattimore stood aghast, hands clasped, in her eloquent eyes the shock at the undercurrent of explosive violence. Jesse would talk to her later. It was a suddenly still bivouac now. It took the others a while to go about preparing supper, but before long the eyes of fires began to blink through the fast-falling desert twilight.

After eating, Jesse cleaned his tin plate with sand and ashes, set out pickets, and stopped by Susan's fire, some ten paces from his own. She seemed content, sitting on a campstool, arms folded, gazing off into the gathering purple darkness.

"What a lovely evening," she said. "Please join me. The colors at sunset were like a benediction."

"I can't think of a better description." He hunkered down.

The shared moment of reflection held until she said: "May I ask the line of march for tomorrow, Captain?"

"We'll cross the San Simon Valley. A dusty ride. You'll need a bandanna and to ride up front. From the valley, we'll go into the Peloncillo Mountains through Doubtful Cañon up to the Butterfield station at Stein's Peak. Plenty of water there. This way is shorter than going around the lower end of the Peloncillos on a dry march. We'll camp at Stein's and reach the Burros next day."

"Is Doubtful as doubtful as it sounds?"

"The Apaches have ambushed stages and parties going through. But with Juh in the Burros and Cochise in his stronghold, we shouldn't have any trouble. Of course, we'll scout ahead. Miguel would soon know, if a war party was waiting. He senses and sees things a white man doesn't."

"What if there is a war party?"

"We wouldn't force it. We'd back up and go around." He looked away, then at her. "I know you were shocked when Donaldson and Shelby got into it. It was a close thing. I thought I had 'em quieted down after yesterday. I'm afraid it's far from over. Best we can do now is try to keep them separated."

"I sensed real hate in each man."

"Now," he said, somewhat bleakly, "you know what kicked off the war. Hotheads on both sides. Neither side felt it could back down. And once it started, nobody could stop it. The slaughter at Shiloh should have told both sides war wasn't worth the price."

"It must have been terrible."

"I don't think I can ever be as scared again as I was that first day in the woods, when we caught the Yankees by surprise, with the Minié balls buzzing like bees and the death shrieks of friends tearing at my ears. There's nothing in the world that will ever make me that afraid again. After our retreat to Corinth, we had time for the full impact of what we'd lost and suffered to sink in on us all. I remember how difficult it was trying to compose letters home to the families of friends . . . searching for words of comfort that seemed so hollow and lacking. But it had to be done. It was duty." He

185

ceased. "Well, enough of that. Sometimes, when I think of friends long gone, I wish the North had let the South go in peace."

"And then," she said thoughtfully, "the Union would have been broken, and we'd be like two countries in time of war, say, with England."

"And very likely the old differences would have continued to boil. The Abolitionists calling for the end of slavery, the Southern fire-eaters spouting honor over a jug of bourbon. In truth, the war had been simmering for years and had to be fought sooner or later. Question is, when will the old passions die?"

"The healing will come with time."

"But time is slow."

"Slow as it is, it will come."

"A lifetime, maybe." He looked directly at her, feeling her faith and assurance, and said with a short laugh: "We settled that issue, didn't we?" And came to his feet. "Good night."

"Good night, Jesse."

She had never spoken his name before, and it lodged in his mind, unexpected and warm-feeling, like their kiss. On second thought, both were easily explained. A common purpose plus a threat drew people closer together as it had in the war. No more than that. As he lay watching the stars glitter, he wondered about her and the husband who hadn't come with her. She seldom mentioned him; there was a strange silence there. Sometime, maybe, he'd tell her the story of sweet Ana and the ribbon in *El Soldado's* mane and what had happened in Mexico, fighting Maximilian's mercenaries. What had happened seemed long ago and yet at times startlingly near. Memories swamped him, drifting across his mind like ravels of clouds on a windy day, vanished, and he slept.

186

His wily demons, in hiding, returned that night with all their relentless fury, perhaps brought back by his earlier reference that evening to the bloody Shiloh woods. The dead in windrows. Boys killing boys again. The haunting faces. The never-ending roar of battle. And fateful Franklin. He was there, also. How familiar everything was. No wonder, He'd been there so many times before. Was Hood insane or just plain drunk, or both? Sending men against the entrenched Yankees time after time? The bloody hand-to-hand fighting around the Carter House, where the Johnny Rebs had broken the blue line, only to see it reform and fight back. Powder smoke like river fog. The hot scent of firing. Jesse screaming — *"Yee-haaa! Yee-haaa-haaa-haa!"* — as he jabbed and swung his musket, not time to reload. Just fight them! These bastard Yankee invaders, some of them foreigners, on sacred Southern soil. And then something smashed his head, and he fell off into utter darkness, as he had so many times. He lay there for a long time. And then a demon that hadn't tortured him in a while returned. Quite in order after Franklin and his capture there, and his recovery in a Nashville hospital, and after his aborted prison break at Camp Morton, Indiana. He was standing in the office of the camp commander, swearing allegiance to the United States as a volunteer in the Army of the West — that or die here in the stink and filth and brutality as his friends had, and as he nearly had in the attempted breakout. As he raised his hand and recited the oath, he discovered that he hated himself, and his eyes suddenly blurred, and the hard-marching years and the dim faces, forever gone, forever young, forever haunting, seemed to pass before him accusingly, and he felt like the lowest traitor.

He cried out, begging forgiveness, but no one heard him. Finally, faintly, he heard a far-off voice, a soft voice drawing nearer, calling his name, and he opened his eyes to abrupt reality.

Bending over him in the dim light, he recognized Susan Lattimore. He caught her pleasant scent. She reached for his hand and held it, murmuring: "You kept crying out. I thought you were terribly ill."

He was in a cold sweat. "Dreams . . . old war dreams. Sorry I woke you. I'm all right now."

"Are you sure?"

"Yes. Quite sure. They don't come as often as they used to. Thank you, Susan. Sorry."

She left him then, and he lay back, feeling an utter exhaustion and some embarrassment. It was always like that afterward. It was kind of her to come to him. This admirable Yankee woman. He had expected her to voice discomfort and weariness from the heat and the long hours in the saddle. But she had not once. She had grit. *Nothing stronger,* he thought, *than a mother's love for her lost son. God, what a gamble this is.* Well, in turn, he was going to see it to the end, as he knew Miguel would. He owed her that. For some time he had known that he cared for Susan Lattimore. At first, out of respect for Ana's dear memory, he had refused to admit it to himself — denied it. But it wouldn't go away, because it was true. As a man, he had even wondered what she would be like in bed. It had happened without his seeking it. He had even felt guilt, a kind of guilt associated with surviving a war in which all his boyhood friends had died, every last one. In no way did it diminish his love for Ana, who had died with their unborn child. Sometimes life was cruel as hell. Things happened. You yielded and became a victim, or you faced up and went on. But you didn't forget. How could you forget someone you'd dearly loved, and you would always love?

On that tangle of thoughts, he slept as if drugged.

Chapter Fifteen

On the morrow he offered no further apologies about last night, and she made no reference to it, as if she understood. The insight warmed him, and he felt at ease.

Entering the broad expanse of the San Simon Valley, the column raised banners of reddish dust, and he placed her with him and Miguel. As before, she was a pleasant riding companion, her avid attention sweeping left and right. Once she said: "The grass looks so good. I thought desert was all sand."

"I guess it would be correct to call this grassy country desert plains. Our mounts grazed well last night on picket."

Deeper into the morning, he pointed out for her the Peloncillo Mountains, barren and craggy, on their left, and on their right the massive uplift of the Chiricahuas. Something caught her interest there. She kept staring, in sudden excitement. She turned to him and pointed: "Isn't that a face there, on the very top? An Indian face?"

"You have a good eye. I've heard it called Cochise's Head."

"I believe," she said, still looking, "he has a Roman nose."

Miguel had heard. He was nodding.

Jesse asked him: "Would you say the head looks like Cochise?"

"Enough," he said, grinning. "Cochise good-looking man."

"It's a magnificent sculpture," she exclaimed, looking

again, and asked Miguel: "May I ask how you felt when you saw Cochise?"

"Great respect. All Apaches respect Cochise."

"I'm so glad he accepted the horse and grateful for what he told you, Miguel, and again for what you are doing." She was so earnest and appealing.

He smiled back at her with all his understanding, this brave mother of the little White Eye captive, as he was once a captive.

Looking back, Jesse saw that Donaldson and Shelby still rode apart as ordered. Jesse thought: *It's not over. It will flare up again. In a small outfit like this it's difficult to keep them separated by much.*

After an easy morning, Jesse halted them for half an hour at noon. There was no water, but the mounts and mules enjoyed the short grass. Only antelope, those phantoms of the desert, moved in the burnished distance, white rump patches bobbing. Some stood still, like sentinels, curiously watching. Donaldson and Shelby glared at each other, but no words. Later, their smoldering eyes seemed to say: *Later!* Jesse eyed Wallace and Shaw for a moment. He hadn't forgotten them. Coming in, they'd ridden side by side, sticking to themselves. Neither man was probably worth a damn in an Indian fight. Well, they'd better hump up. He'd shoot the first no-account bastard he saw running.

Several men spoke to Mrs. Lattimore during the halt. Crider lingered the longest, making a show of courtesy. She handled the attention with the gracious ease of a cavalryman's daughter, Jesse thought, proud of her poise.

For about the last third of their way across the valley they followed the ruts of the old Butterfield Trail before it veered off southwest to Fort Bowie in the Chiricahuas. Fortunately, Jesse observed, nothing threatened their progress from that direction. No swallow-tailed troop guide coming.

Nothing disturbed their march to the shallow San Simon River. Before the clattering command could go in the water, Miguel coursed both banks like a hound, scanning for tracks.

"No fresh young pony tracks here," he reported to Jesse. "War party going into Doubtful would water here."

"Good, Miguel. We'll give the cañon a try."

When it was time to proceed, Jesse put Susan Lattimore back in the column's center beside Hardin, figuring the lead riders would draw the first fire in an ambush. In that event, they'd wheel out of there and take the longer route.

They trailed past the ruins of the San Simon station and strung out on the well-marked trail, virtually a road from the busy passage of stages before this foolish war with Cochise, Jesse reflected.

Holding to a column of twos, they started at a walk up the stony trail to Doubtful, the Peloncillos on the left now, open country on the right. Some distance onward the trail bent sharply into the beginning slopes of a rocky cañon, barren save for yuccas and catclaw brush and prickly pear clumps.

Miguel rode in advance at a trot. After several hundred yards, he halted, and Jesse did likewise, waiting for the outfit to close up. For what seemed an endless time Miguel observed the cañon walls. Jesse could see nothing unusual.

Clapping moccasined heels, Miguel rode ahead, and soon the walls grew steeper and the trail more winding, ideal for ambush, Jesse saw. Behind him the clatter of the column seemed unusually loud between these enclosing walls.

At the next bend, Miguel halted to look, his head high. He seemed to be sniffing for smells. Another short ride, another halt, working ahead in this careful manner.

Then, riding back to Jesse, he said — "Hold my horse, *amigo*." — and went bounding up the sloping cañon wall like a mountain goat. A short sprint and he pulled up, winded, in no condition for this. Chagrined, he looked down at Jesse and patted his chest. From there he took a much slower, zigzag course to the top. Hardly pausing to rest, he bent his gaze upcañon. He stayed there some minutes. Descending in easy rushes, he told Jesse: "Nothing moves. Looks quiet. But keep close watch. Go slow."

He mounted and rode ahead as before.

Presently, Jesse found stone-covered graves beside the trail. Farther on, a scattering of others. It was through here that the trail narrowed and twisted more sharply. Now there was the bullet-riddled wreckage of a stagecoach, the skeletons of its mules, and pieces of harness strewn by the wagon tongue.

Miguel hadn't stopped since his climb to the crest.

And then Jesse came to the place he remembered from not many months ago, more like yesterday, everything was so vivid. The parapets of stone and boulders were high on the cañon wall, stone laid on stone by human hand: a perfect ambush site. He saw again the Army ambulance halted, its mules shot dead, and the painted faces of the Apaches, firing down at the trapped Army detail, and his coming upon the ambush. After debating whether to get into this, climbing up to a place for a field of fire, he had emptied several tubes on the surprised attackers. Then, unnoticed until the last moment, an Apache slipped around behind him. Their hand-to-hand struggle had them rolling down through the brush and over rocks to the cañon floor, a knife at his throat. There were figures rushing out from around the wagon. A blast. The Apache had recoiled. A Yankee major had stood over Jesse with a smoking revolver. A shouted warning and they had all run back to the wagon. The Apaches charged, broke, and it was over. One dead trooper. Two wounded. They retreated to the stage station at Stein's Peak. The major had been Emory Gordon, with an escort from Fort Bliss to Fort Bowie, on a hurry-up mission of which, as it turned out, even Gordon didn't know the purpose.

They had buried the trooper, and Jesse had accompanied the detail to Fort Bowie. Again the unexpected, as if fate pre-ordained it: Jesse going as scout for a platoon of U.S. cavalrymen disguised as miners, Major Gordon in charge. To go in uniform could cause an international incident, in view of Mexico's sensitivity about foreign troops below the border. Their mission: to free the daughter of the Sonoran governor held by a big band of *bandidos* terrorizing the countryside from a fortified *hacienda,* led by a cut-throat known as *El Tigre.* The troopers had freed the girl and her *duenna* after much fighting, not only the *hacienda bandidos,* but Apaches and other outlaw bands on the march into Sonora and out. Why had Jesse volunteered? It was uncanny how fate had intervened. Startling information at Bowie had it that deserters from Maximilian's mercenaries were bolstering *El Tigre*'s band. Deserters from the 6th Hussars and the 6th's raid on the Juárista camp had killed Ana and others. Jesse could never even the score. But, by going as scout, he could strike one more blow for Ana.

These pieces of action fled through his mind like flying particles. He thought of Major Gordon, one hell of a horse soldier. And he thought of the Irish troopers, ready for fight or frolic. He'd never served with tougher fighters. So. . . .

Miguel, halted in the middle of the trail, waving for the outfit to come on, broke his reflections. That meant they were through. Sighing, he brought them forward at a gallop.

The Butterfield station was a sun-blasted rectangle of stone ruins at the foot of barren Stein's Peak. Jesse led to the spring in the broad wash below the station, thinking of the wizened, wild-looking old miner in ragged clothing who had occupied the place when Jesse and the Army detail had camped there after the ambush. He'd generously shared deer jerky while babbling about the rich vein of gold in the Peloncillos he was bound to discover before long — why, he'd already found traces! There were no signs now of recent occupancy. Jesse hoped the Apaches hadn't caught him, digging for the yellow metal they said drove White Eyes crazy. The old fellow had either found his gold and made it out, or. . . .

Jesse fed from nosebags and picketed, figuring there was enough grain in the mule packs for another three or four days. After that, it would be slim pickings on sparse desert grass this time of year. By then their mission should have been decided. Nearby, Susan Lattimore fed and picketed her bay. Gabe Jackson was gathering mesquite for her supper fire. She had removed her hat and was standing by her horse, gazing around at the mountains, now, as he knew she would, facing the east where their destination lay. She was still standing there like that, a loose strand of dark hair playing across her forehead, her face softly maternal and lovely, forever hopeful, when he walked on.

All signs pointed to a restful bivouac after the hot and dusty ride across the San Simon Valley. The water was good and plentiful, an ever-flowing spring, and there was enough wood, if a man hustled for it. There were no mountains between Stein's and the Burros, which they should reach before sundown tomorrow. Going over the camp, Jesse had several men picket closer tonight to the ruins. This was no time to get careless. In event of an attack, the walls of the station, although crumbling in places, would be a formidable point of defense.

The bivouac seemed to settle down faster than usual, with

the cooking groups established by now. Jesse noticed Wallace and Shaw by themselves, for the simple reason that no others wished to share the fire of the two or invite them to theirs. Crider and Long and Webb cooked together again. Donaldson and Shelby camped at opposite ends of the bivouac, as ordered.

Jesse sought Miguel, speaking in Spanish. "Any suggestions, *señor?* I won't divide the watches till after supper."

"No fresh signs around the spring. Some old tracks. Many days old. Everything is quiet now with Cochise in his stronghold and Juh hunting winter meat."

"Doubtful Cañon had me worried today. Tomorrow will be an open march all the way to the Burros."

"Yes. I know where we'll camp."

"More good water, eh?"

"Good enough, *amigo.*"

The leaping cooking fires were tongues licking the crimson twilight. A cool wind rose out of Doubtful Cañon. Jesse was thinking of supper, when something bothered him. Something was missing. A few minutes ago, while checking the camp, he'd seen Donaldson and Shelby, each still alone, at their fires. But now, happening to look again, he didn't see either man. What the hell! Where were they?

At that moment rising partisan voices sounded from the direction of the spring. Jesse knew then what had happened. They'd gone for water and run into each other. He jerked around to rush down there and break it up.

"I shall take your insults no longer, suh." Donaldson's precise voice.

"I speak only the truth. You Rebs started the war at Sumter."

"Stop it!" Jesse yelled as he ran, around him the volunteers rearing up to look. "Stop it!"

195

The hot words continued to ring out.

"It was a matter of honor, suh. I demand an accounting now!"

"And you'll get it, honorable *suh!*"

Two shots crashed nearly together. Then another, and another, the second a bit slower. Then silence.

Running down to the spring, Jesse saw two shapes sprawled by the canteens they'd come to fill. Both men were groaning and writhing, still gripping their revolvers. Blooms of dirty white powder smoke hung over them like a shroud. Looking at their bloodstained shirts, he saw that both men had been deadly shots. He felt for their pain, but could not swallow his disgust. So senseless. *The war — the god-damned war*. And now the outfit was short two good men.

Theodore Shelby was dead by the time they could carry him to the bivouac. Jeff Donaldson was limp and scarcely breathing. They made a crude bed for him inside the station. When Jesse started to remove his shirt, the Southerner stopped him. "Don't bother . . . no use, suh. I'm done for . . . know it." He tried to smile. "One favor . . . though."

"Sure," Jesse said.

"Bottle good bourbon in m'pack . . . a drink."

Powers ran for the bottle, handed it to Jesse. While Tatum gently lifted Donaldson's head, Jesse tipped him a slow drink. He swallowed with effort, some of the whiskey trickling down. Susan Lattimore wiped his chin.

Donaldson seemed to rally after that, even asked for another drink, which he got. But refusing further aid, he murmured: "Another favor, suh. Later . . . appreciate . . . pen note to Missus Lucinda Donaldson . . . Galveston, Texas . . . that her wayward son has come to rest out West." The words, spoken fast, had tired him. "Thank you, suh. Now, gentleman . . . leave me the bottle an' go about your duties."

"We're not leaving you," Jesse said firmly, knowing he was going to bleed to death unless they acted fast. "We're going to bandage you and. . . ."

Donaldson made an absolute gesture of refusal and appeared to be sinking fast, yet rallied again, apparently stirred by inner thoughts. Jesse let him go for another moment.

"Mus' finish m'story. Served throughout th' war with Gen'ral Kirby . . . proudly, suh. Came home . . . cotton business. Fine . . . till carpetbaggers descended on us like locusts." His eyes brightened. "Proud to report, suh . . . I shot two dead in one day . . . in front of th' courthouse fo' ever'body to see. Was cheered. So I'm a fugitive . . . hunted by th' Yankee guv-mint. Proudly, suh."

Delaying no longer, Jesse and Tatum removed his bloodsoaked shirt. One look at the man's wounds and Jesse bit his lip. They tore his shirt into strips and made compresses and bandaged him as best they could. Tatum had quick, skilled hands. It looked to Jesse that the bullets had gone clean through. If they could stop the bleeding and Donaldson could hold on through the night, maybe he'd make it. *Tomorrow the old standby prickly pear poultice,* Jesse thought. Next, they brought his blankets and pack, made him comfortable, and left the bottle by his side.

"You men go finish supper," Jesse said. "Mister Hardin, set the pickets same as last night."

"I'll stay with you," Susan said.

Donaldson's strength was going fast. He reached for the bottle, couldn't get it up. Tatum was instantly there to help him sip. The sunken gray eyes conveyed gratefulness. Donaldson mumbled — "M'ultimate dishonor . . . shot by a lowdown Abolitionist." — and the ghost of a smile crossed his face. "Ah . . . th' irony of it all." He smiled again. "Spare

197

me . . . don' include that in the obituary."

Susan wiped his face again and felt of his forehead. His eyes followed her hand. "You're an angel on earth, ma'am . . . a true ministerin' angel. Been observin' you evah since Tucson . . . fine lady . . . well brought up . . . what we Southerners call a Thoroughbred."

"You must rest, Mister Donaldson. Save your strength. That way you'll be better tomorrow."

The dim smile again. "Hardly true . . . but I thank you, ma'am. Mus' always thank angels."

The mountain evening had turned quite cool, and she was busy making him more comfortable, rearranging the blanket around him, tucking it in, and making a softer pillow of his pack. When he struggled to speak, she put a quieting finger to his lips and felt his forehead.

There was plenty of help, and they laid a cheerful fire, which seemed to gladden the wounded man, despite his groaning. He had ceased talking so much. Tonight they would take turns watching him. At Jesse's suggestion Susan went to her supper. When she returned after a short time, he left and checked the pickets and had his own spare fare. There was scant camp talk tonight. The anticipation of a comfortable bivouac was gone.

When he returned to the station to take his turn, Donaldson was sleeping.

"He's resting much better," she whispered.

She left, and after a while Truett relieved Jesse.

Jesse walked the perimeter of the bivouac, spoke to the sentries, Webb and Brakebill, and saw to his stock. Both were good keepers, as the saying went, busy grazing the scant desert grass. The red horse, always wary, suddenly raised up and watched as he approached. Jesse stroked the blazed face and patted him. Chico, the mule, cared less for any petting and continued to graze while Jesse patted his neck. Going back to his pack, he sat down and smoked a pipeful.

Restless, troubled, detesting the senseless shootings, he got up and headed back to the station. Truett spoke just above a whisper: "He's hardly stirred, Captain. While ago, when I asked him if he wanted some whiskey, he just moaned . . . poor fellow. A wounded man's mighty low, indeed, when he turns down whiskey."

The rock station felt chilled. Seeing the fire was low, Jesse heaped on wood until it blazed. Donaldson's face was ashen. Jesse shook his head and drew the blanket back and examined the bandages. The compresses had mostly stopped the bleeding. The trouble was, the man had already lost so much blood and had to be badly torn up inside. Donaldson groaned, when Jesse settled the blanket around him. Jesse scowled, thinking he'd seen too many doubtful outcomes like this. It frustrated him that nothing more could be done. But Donaldson would not be left alone.

The night seemed to drag. Jesse stayed, feeding the fire now and then. Tatum relieved Truett.

"How's he doing?" Tatum asked.

"Reckon we'll know by morning," Jesse said.

Pacing the perimeter again, he found the sentries posted where they should be and all was well. A rough day lay ahead. He'd better grab a few hours' sleep while he could. Pulling off his boots, he flattened out and surrendered to established ways, shut out the vexing day, and was asleep in moments.

Some time later he felt a hand on his shoulder and heard Tatum say: "Sorry, Captain . . . Donaldson didn't make it."

He cursed and sat up, rubbing his forehead. In the station, he looked down at Donaldson and gently spread the blanket over his face, thinking what a needless waste of life. He and Shelby deserved far better than the extreme paths the war had brought upon them. Furthermore, the outfit would miss them.

After breakfast in the morning, they found a miner's pick in the ruins and attacked the flinty soil, soon forced to take turns. Then they wrapped Shelby and Donaldson in blankets and buried them deep as a precaution against varmints. Searching the mountainside and the rocky wash, they found flat slabs suitable for headstones, and Truett carved their names with care. Jesse had taken to addressing Tatum as Reverend Tatum, and now he asked him to conduct the services. As Tatum spoke the brief, solemn words about resurrection and the Lord giving and the Lord taking away, they all stood with bowed heads, while Susan Lattimore wept silently, dabbing at her eyes with a tiny white handkerchief.

When it was over, they mounted up and trailed eastward toward the Burro Mountains in a column of twos.

Chapter Sixteen

With two good men gone, Jesse was considering where the outfit stood as he rode along. Down in him a hard appraisal churned. Of the twelve left of the original fourteen volunteers, which ones could he count on? The threesome of Crider, Long, and Webb, and the deserter Shaw and his accomplice, Wallace, rose to his mind. Little things revealed much about a man on a tough march, whether he was worth a damn or cared not one whit about his comrades. None of these five had offered to sit with Donaldson, or hustle up wood to provide a little warmth and cheer for a dying man. None had offered to help dig the stony graves. Not one! That knowledge burned. He supposed they'd fight Apaches if jumped: that was pure survival. Fight . . . or slip off and run at the first big threat? By now they knew the trail back to Tucson. All they had to do was follow the tracks. Simple. All the other men had pitched in, including Gabe Jackson.

If Jesse survived this mission, he would write Mrs. Lucinda Donaldson. Shelby's personal things had yielded a letter from a sister back in Boston. Jesse would write their loved ones, as he had done after Shiloh. Thinking so, he corrected himself. He would, or the Reverend Tatum would. Another realization struck: if Jesse Wilder didn't survive, Susan Lattimore might not. He had to get her through this, whether they got the boy or not.

She worried him this morning. She had taken the two deaths hard. She seldom spoke and looked straight ahead through sad eyes, not scanning the great yawning distances of desert and mountains as usual. He'd better talk to her.

"Susan," he said gently. "Buck up. This is a new day. Much to do."

"I know . . . I know. I keep thinking of Donaldson and Shelby. I can't help feeling some guilt because I hired them."

"Don't! Neither man would let go of the past, the damned war. It killed them. Two good men. A terrible waste. I hate it. Too bad." Now he was showing his true feelings. Better stop it.

Her expression softened. "You say understanding things."

"I know how you feel. But we have to go on. I've had to do it many times, losing people. I believe the colonel would tell you the same."

"Yes. My mother died young. He raised me, and we went on together. He never remarried."

"I wonder," he said, looking at her with a sudden perception, "if you might resemble your mother?"

"It's strange that you should ask. My father said I was the image of her, which always made me feel happy and helped me overcome the loneliness of not having her."

"Then she was a very beautiful lady."

She flushed through the tan of her face. "Thank you for saying that about my mother."

Miguel had led them to the base of the humping Burros well before dark. His promised spring, below an outcrop of rocks, was as good as he'd said. Scattered mesquites served as cover between the bivouac and the mountains. Miguel was finishing going over the area looking for signs, when Jesse and Susan rode up.

"Old tracks again," he said, and gestured toward the mountains looming massively above them. "Juh that way." He was speaking more often in English now.

On the picket line Miguel drew Jesse aside. "All day we make big dust. If Juh had lookouts for pony soldiers, he saw us. So be ready before sunrise, *amigo*."

The oldest of warnings in Apache country. Jesse nodded. What a cruel turn of luck it would be, if Juh hit them before Miguel had a chance to parley with the chief. Therefore, he posted sentries with extra care. He and Miguel and Hardin and Brakebill would stand the last watch.

Susan Lattimore appeared unusually thoughtful this evening, which he read as an understandable aftermath of Stein's Peak. He made a point of lingering at her fire after supper, and, as they made small talk, he seemed to see the past in her expressive eyes, a recalling, perhaps a kind of somberness, in contrast to her customary bright spirits. He sensed this might be due to something other than Stein's Peak.

Neither said much for a while, just gazing at the cherry-red embers.

"How will you and Miguel go about this tomorrow?" she asked after a bit.

First, why alarm her about posting extra pickets? And so he said: "Juan López will go with us, leading the buckskin. Miguel says he knows where the hunting camp is. They'll be drying meat for winter. We won't try to sneak up, and we won't approach too early. He may want Juan and me to hang back, out of sight, while he rides up to the camp. If so, I'll make sure to keep him in carbine range."

"It's so dangerous. I'm afraid for you all."

"Nobody is promised a tomorrow, Susan. This is our only chance, and we have to take it. We owe it to Jimmy. You owe it to yourself, for all you're going through. If you didn't take it, you'd never forgive yourself. You'd be miserable the rest of your life." He had spoken gently, but forcibly.

"I know. We must do it. I'm so grateful. I'll be praying for you." She looked down at her hands, and, when she looked up at him, he saw the unusual and puzzling expression again. It had to be deep and troubling, and it made him wonder. Then she said, hesitating: "There is something I feel I ought to tell you before you go."

"What is it?" he asked, wanting to help her get it out.

"Rutherford is not Jimmy's father."

He was silent. Hardly anything surprised him any more, he'd seen so much.

"His father," she said, the words coming painfully slow, "died early in the war. Second Lieutenant James Gilmore Bryant. Killed at First Manassas. A terrible shock. The colonel, ever my tower of strength, helped me through it. Jim didn't know I was pregnant. But he'd always said, if we had a son, he didn't want him named James, Junior." She swallowed. "But since my father was also James, I decided to name Jimmy after both of them. We were so happy. We were married the day he graduated from West Point. We thought he'd be posted in the East. Then the war came."

"I'm very sorry," Jesse said, reaching for her hand, feeling a sadness for her. "More than I can say. You did exactly right with the name, honoring both good men."

"I just thought you should know."

"Not necessary. But I'm glad you did. It's thoughtful of you to tell me more about your family. I cherish families, torn as they are sometimes. And I do know this . . . if my blessed mother had been alive, when I went back home after mustering out of the Union Army out West, I know I would've been welcome in her home. She'd have understood . . . no matter what my stiff-necked father or my glorious brother, who never fired a shot in the war from his soft government job, thought about the stain on the family's esteemed honor."

He shut off the spilling bitterness and almost drew her to him, sensing that she would have come. But he just held onto her hand and comforted her. Her face at that moment in the soft glow of the fire drifted toward him, as understanding of him as he was of her, and inevitably their lips brushed, and he caught her faint lavender scent.

The moment ended as she drew back, saying: "I thought Jimmy needed a father. So I married Rutherford in 'Sixty-Three. I soon learned that sometimes stepfathers have little patience or understanding with children other than their own . . . the one element most needed in molding a new family." She sighed. "However, I must say that Rutherford has allowed me unlimited use of his considerable fortune."

This last, Jesse felt, was said as if she needed to remind herself.

"He's very busy with his law practice," she continued, "and they say he may run for Congress. He's very much in the public eye. Very correct about all things . . . careful about anything that might reflect unfavorably on him."

She was being honest and fair, and he guessed that just about summed up her relationship with Rutherford Lattimore in a marriage that had gone wrong from the start. She seemed to stray off again in unhappy abstraction. Seeing that, he said in a rather roundabout way: "I'm sure you've wondered about the red ribbon in the mane of my red horse. I want to tell you about it. My Mexican wife, Ana, wove it, and it will stay there in her memory till it weathers away and is no more." He hesitated to say more as she had hesitated.

She turned to him. "Tell me about Ana. I know she was dear to you. It will be good for you, Jesse."

He began, slowly. "I guess it started just before the Juáristas took San Juan de Río. I had this malaise. Guess it was from bad water. With Cullen Floyd, of Mississippi, another expatriate like myself, we had trained the Juáristas and decided they were ready to fight Maxmilian's mercenaries. Besides muzzleloaders, we now had a hundred or so Spencer rifles, and Father Alberto Garza's boys knew how to use them. Father Garza . . . one of the finest men I've ever known. A defrocked priest . . . raised a little army of peasants to fight his country's invaders. All he needed was somebody to train 'em. Cullen came along and began smuggling guns across the Río Grande for the *padre*. Then I met Cullen in El Paso and soon joined the cause. Cullen and I led a night raid on the Fort Bliss armory for the Spencers. Got chased to the river."

At that, she gave him a naughty look. At least, his story was breaking her solemn mood.

"I began to feel listless and feverish the day we took San Juan. The French Foreign Legion garrison came out to fight what they thought was a rag-tag bunch of peasants. Our trained boys fought with discipline and broke the legionnaires. Soon after, to my shock and anger, a squad of ours executed some prisoners . . . that was too much. I flew into a rage. Called them barbarians. The *padre* stopped any more of that. He hadn't ordered it. Seems the Legion had been executing prisoners, and our men were getting even. I told the *padre* I couldn't advise him any longer. I was burning up, sick in body and mind. All I wanted was to lie down in a cool place.

"Cullen helped me mount, but I remembered little for what seemed a long time. Once I fell from the saddle, and I remember my horse never left me. Now and then I heard voices calling me. When I woke up, I saw the faces of friends around me. Among them Cullen and Father Alberto and a pretty Mexican girl I'd never see before. When she spoke, I realized hers had been one of the voices calling me back whenever I had wanted to give up . . . as you called me back from my demons the other night. In the days ahead, she nursed me back to health, all arranged by Father Alberto. It made me wonder if maybe it was also a little plot of his in hopes of getting me to stay as an advisor. I grew to love Ana. She was pure Mexican Indian. Not one drop of Spanish in her. She even rode my horse, named him *El Soldado* . . . The Soldier, and wove a pretty ribbon in his mane."

He checked himself. Was he talking too much? Was he too wound up in himself? He feared so. But when he saw the waiting in her face, her expectancy, he went on.

"We made plans. Ana was pregnant. We'd go to El Paso and start a new life, at last away from war. Scouts reported a big camp of the Sixth Hussars south of ours, led by the notorious Colonel Dubray. Father Alberto wanted to attack. A small Juárista force would be left to guard the camp and their families. Cullen and the *padre* both knew I was taking Ana back to the States. Although they didn't ask me to go along, I said I'd think about it."

She clung to him throughout the night, while the feeling tore at him that he ought to go with the command this one last time. It was his duty, he told himself. Hadn't he helped train these Mexican Indian peasants, shaped them into fighting men? He was proud of them. At San Juan they had charged the French Legion like wild bulls, broken some of the best professional soldiers in Europe.

When morning came, he told her: "I've decided to go with the boys. This will be the last time. Then we'll go to El Paso. Cullen and the* padre *won't expect me to fight."* A lie for her sake. If a hot fight developed, he'd pitch in if needed.

He thought she would object. She said not one word. But behind the black Indian eyes he read dread and fear. "I know you go. I know last night. I no want you go. I'm afraid for you. But you go. You man. You fight for my* Méjico."

When the red horse was saddled, she regarded him for a long time without speaking. He kissed her again and again.

"Vaya con Dios," she said, her arms releasing him. "Go with God."

He mounted and rode out to where Cullen and the padre *were forming the Juáristas. When he looked back, Ana was still watching. He waved. She waved. The picture of her waving clung to his mind. But somehow he already felt a dark sense of foreboding.*

"Nevertheless, next morning I decided it was my duty to ride with our little army. It would be my farewell. Ana didn't want me to go. A villager had brought news of the Hussar camp. He would guide us. After a long march, we reached the vicinity where the attack was to form. Cullen and the *padre* both told me to stay out of the fight. Even so, I rode with Cullen in what was to be a cavalry attack, some of our poor peasants having acquired horses by now. Father Alberto was to lead our infantry in a pincers movement."

Jesse paused once more, gathering his thoughts, not wishing to drag out the fateful outcome. Susan Lattimore's eyes had not left his face.

"But the Hussars' camp was empty. Horse tracks led eastward. Where was the enemy going? It was strange. We followed hard upon the tracks. Now they shifted north. Something was very wrong. Now the tracks leading into the sierra could be headed only one place . . . our own encampment. Our guide had dropped out. We knew then he'd duped us, leading us toward the Hussars' camp, while the Hussar company headed for our mountain camp defended by one lone rifle company. We rode at a run. There was a distant volley, then another. Some sporadic firing. The Hussars were gone by the time we rushed up. The camp was in shambles. I found

Ana, dead, in our tent."

"Oh, how terrible, Jesse."

"Maybe, if I'd been there . . . ?"

"You can't blame yourself. My father used to say anything can happen in war, and most of it bad. Worse, when innocents like Ana suffer."

Overwhelmed with grief, he walked the woods. Walking, walking, head down, weeping. No end to his self-torture. It was the worst time of his life. Ever restless, he wandered to the corral. The red horse raised his head, mustang eyes alertly watching him. Poor, neglected, faithful, once-wild creature. In shame, Jesse led him to the stream and back, threw down mounds of hay. As the horse lowered his head to the feed, Jesse saw the red ribbon in the black mane. It was a sacred object now. She had woven it with loving hands. It would remain there until it wasted away, untouched. Her El Soldado! *Overcome, he threw his arms around the bent neck and wept into the black mane. And the horse quit feeding and nuzzled Jesse's arm, and Jesse thought of the solace noble animals give their masters.*

After the rosary and Mass for the victims, and the burials, Jesse returned to the silent tent. Her scent still lingered there, like a soft, sweet rain. He bowed his head, holding the crucifix the padre *had given him, knowing he could stay here no longer. This place, now so empty of laughter and love and hopes for the future.*

Cullen entered, laid a long arm around Jesse's shoulders, and set a bottle of tequila on the floor. He turned to leave. Instead, suddenly drawn back, he stared at Jesse with a shock not far from open-mouthed horror, his eyes sprung wide. He started to speak, but the horror seemed to lock his lips. He could only stare.

"What is it?" Jesse asked dully.

Cullen made an uncertain motion toward Jesse's head, looked off and down, unable to speak, shock still in his eyes.

Puzzled, Jesse rose. His head, his face? Cullen wouldn't look at him. Jesse moved to a tiny mirror, hanging on a tent pole, and glanced into it. He saw a stranger's face: lined and drawn, the embers of the burning eyes, the flesh of the sagging mouth warped in anguished bitterness — and the long, snow-white hair. My God, his hair! With a gasp of horror, he threw up a warding-off hand and slumped down on the cot.

"It's all right, Jesse. It's all right," Cullen said quickly. Cullen held out the tequila. "Drink this. That's an order."

Jesse drank, coughed.

"Now another. A long pull."

Jesse obeyed and put the bottle down. "Y'know, Cullen, I remember an instance where a man's hair turned white from fear in battle, but not this."

"This is worse. It's grief. You've lost everything . . . your world."

"I'm all right now, old friend. I understand."

"I'll look in on you, now and then," Cullen assured him, and left.

There was a rustling at the tent-flap, but he didn't look up. He didn't care. He felt like dying; he wanted to die. He heard a step, and then he felt a hand rest lightly on his bowed head. Still, he didn't look up. Another moment and he heard Father Alberto's healing voice.

"You have suffered so much, amigo Jesse. First, in your terrible American war. Now in ours. War comes from the freedom of choice which God gives man. And man suffers. But God understands. He is not without compassion. I felt the same bitterness as yours when Apaches killed my dear mother and father . . . my dear brothers and my one precious little sister, Lucía . . . my entire family. One day a happy family. The next, wiped out. Man's cruelty to man." Jesse sensed the padre was speaking slowly, selecting his words carefully. "But God understood my grief. He touched

210

me, as He touches you now through me . . . in love and compassion, which you will feel, I promise you. He will dry your tears. He will raise you up. He will not forsake you. He cannot heal your hurt now, but He can take away some of the pain."

Jesse felt the hand press down, now lift. In his ears a faint rustling, and the padre was gone.

Eyes closed, Jesse found himself drifting off into blessed sleep here in this hallowed place of memory.

These painful memories had flashed through his mind, every bit like a print on his memory. Susan Lattimore was waiting for him to continue, rapt in his telling, understanding when he paused. Her eyes seemed fixed on his white hair. He didn't explain. She did not ask why, but he sensed that she knew. Nor would he tell her that afterward he became known as *el soldado del palo blanco,* the Soldier of the White Hair.

"Until now," he resumed, "it had been mainly an impersonal war. Now that the enemy had taken to killing women and children, it became very personal. It was also a matter of duty and honor. We took the *Presidio* Montána, and we cut down Colonel Dubray and his staff, as they made their getaway out the back way, as they had at San Juan."

He himself had shot Dubray out of the saddle, but why relate it? It would sound like self-glorification. He didn't need that. In that bloody climax, he had felt no great elation. He had thought only of Ana and what had been. . . .

"News of our victories spread, and our army of patriots kept growing with volunteers. We skirmished almost daily with the retreating Red Trousers, as we called the enemy, driving them southward. As our boys marched through the dusty villages, pretty girls in white waved and tossed flowers.

There was plenty of beer and tequila. It was . . . '¡*Viva Méjico!* ¡*Viva* Juárez!' Cullen and I were made citizen generals, commissioned by no less than President Juárez . . . more of Father Alberto's influence and regard for others." He faltered. "I'm talking too much."

"Please go on. I think it's good for you to tell what all happened in Mexico. Also I want to hear it."

"I like to give credit where due. In this instance, Father Alberto. A haughty *hacendado* named Sedillo brought his cowed peasants to our army. A fair-weather patriot, he didn't join until he was certain the French faced defeat. Wasn't long till I stopped him from executing prisoners. Told him I'd shoot him if he didn't call back his men. I would have, and he knew it. But I'd insulted him in front of his men, made him back down. He'd lost face. He called me a *gringo* and swore revenge. Cullen warned me. Told me to stay armed.

"It happened just after we'd taken San Luis Potosí without firing a shot, the French retreating toward Querétaro. Cullen had gone into town with most of the army to celebrate. I was resting in my tent.

"I heard a shouted . . . 'Wake up, *gringo!*' It was Sedillo, pointing a rifle at me. I got up, no weapon in hand. He kept shouting. 'We Sedillos never forget an insult. You are going to die, *gringo*. Let's see if you can die like a man.' He spat his words at me and lifted the rifle higher.

"I was thinking of diving for the rifle, when there was a blast of gunfire. But I didn't feel anything. Sedillo dropped the rifle and collapsed at my feet. Then Father Alberto stepped from the open door of the tent, holding a smoking pistol. He'd heard the shouting. The pistol seemed awkward in his hand. I believe it was the first shot he'd ever fired, that man of peace gone to war to save his people. Always dressed in peasant white. Wouldn't let the boys call him general. Only *padre*. I remember he said something about Mexico not forsaking a friend. He asked me if I was all right. I said I was fine. His hand was shaking. I asked him if he wanted me to take the pistol, and he said . . . 'No, we still have a way to go.'

"We were sweeping everything before us, the boys eager to fight, the countryside now freed of pillaging. With the new recruits, there was much confusion. Some volunteers no older than ten or twelve carried machetes. One day Cullen halted our main column and scattered the recruits throughout the companies, instead of forming them as green outfits, saying, if this kept up, we'd be more like an armed mob than an army. It was time for the *padre* to take a hand again. Time for more order and discipline.

"Cullen formed the command in double-ranked company fronts for inspection, standing at order arms, and the three of us rode slowly down the line. Now and then Floyd would halt and point to a man and tell him to hold his rifle properly or to straighten up. We had drilled them hard in the manual of arms, formed them in squads, companies, and battalions, and marched them in columns of fours, with officers and noncoms. Many had never fired a gun till they joined up. By now, with what we'd captured, most men had rifles.

"As we halted, front and center, Father Alberto, astride the brown mule he always rode, addressed them. He had a beautiful speaking voice, genteel and musical, yet firm in tone. He told them to be brave and obey their officers, to love God and country and honor President Benito Juárez. Then, riding along the line, he blessed each company as the men bared their heads and kneeled. Front and center again, the Father raised his right arm and shouted . . . *'¡Viva Méjico!'* . . . and the boys shouted back the same. Then he shouted . . . *'¡Viva* Juárez!' . . . and they roared back the words. Inspired by the *padre,* each man and boy could have whipped wildcats

213

that day." Jesse looked at her. "Getting tired of all this?"

"It's a moving story, part of history. Please go on."

"Not much more to tell." He had experienced a feeling of relief at the summing up. Now a lessening, as he approached the end.

"On the road to Querétaro we ran into a large force of Red Trousers, drawn up to stop us. Cullen and I'd had our fill of massed infantry charges in our own war. So, first, we gave them canisters from our one fieldpiece, a captured Twelve-pounder Napoléon. Pretty soon they started to fall back in disorder, and Cullen and I mounted up, and away everybody charged. Cullen was hit early." He wouldn't tell her all of it.

Jesse eased Cullen off his horse to the ground, Cullen's face already ashen. "Long way from home, Jesse." A going-back in Cullen's eyes.

"Home is where we are, Cullen." Jesse took his hand. "I'm right here with you."

"Don't leave me." He was going fast. A sip from Jesse's canteen wouldn't go down.

"I won't. Hell, no! I'll get you some tequila from your pack."

A glint of mockery in Cullen's eyes. "Nevah . . . waste good liquor. Remember that, ol' Reb."

The tequila merely driveled away.

Suddenly Cullen strained to sit up, but fell back, coughing blood. "How'd the charge go?"

"The boys are drivin' 'em back. They're breaking. We're winning."

"One war we won . . . eh?"

"You bet!"

"Ah . . . that's good. Don't leave me, Jesse."

"I won't! You know I won't!"

★ ★ ★ ★ ★

"Cullen died in my arms. He was like a brother. Another so-called galvanized Yankee like me who'd worn the blue on the plains. Disowned by his father, who refused to ask him into the house when he went back to Mississippi. His mother was dead. No home to go back to . . . that hurt him more than anything. Father Alberto was there to administer Last Rites. I was glad for that. Cullen died among friends."

"How sad," she said.

"We used to talk about Southern pride. How it had probably cost more lives than Yankee bullets." He had tried to be objective in the narration, leaving out emotion, and he went on in the same level voice. "The war was really over. We moved on to Querétaro, where Maximilian, under siege, had surrendered and was held prisoner with two native generals. President Juárez was there. Maximilian's other forces had either surrendered or were retreating toward Vera Cruz to board transports."

He started to relate the climax, but was silent so long that she asked: "Wasn't Maximilian executed?"

"He was. He and the native generals. I was going to tell you how I tried to stop it, but I thought it would make me sound vainglorious."

"You aren't one bit. Believe me. Go on."

"I wanted to stop the eye-for-an-eye killing, more of the endless blood-letting. First indication I had of the coming executions was when Father Alberto said each prisoner's cell had a large crucifix and two silver candlesticks. A clear warning they must prepare for death. I told the *padre* I wanted to plead for their lives. He doubted the *presidente* would change his mind, but to try. He was pleased.

"After some delay, I was let in to see Juárez. Behind a plain wooden desk I saw this short, solidly built man in a plain,

215

dark suit. He had black, Indian eyes in a strong-boned face. The eyes bored into me. I saluted and began to feel intimidated. To my surprise, he spoke in a pleasant voice. Said he knew who I was from serving in the *padre's* army.

"Then he asked me . . . 'Why do you come here? Do you seek land or a post in my insolvent government?'

"I said I'd come to plead for the pardon of Maximilian and the two native generals. He reminded me they'd been found guilty by the courts."

Jesse fell silent, his mind sweeping back to that vivid scene. She didn't break in, and he could hear himself again imploring Juárez, the words echoing in his head.

"It's barbaric, sir, to execute prisoners. Méjico *must rise above that as a nation. The trials were hardly more than a mere formality, since the death penalty was fixed at the time of their arrest."*

Juárez stood, his black eyes like points. Although he couldn't stand more than a little over five feet in height, Jesse saw, he created the impression of a much larger man. His black hair, cut short, danced with the motion of his head as he spoke. "The execution of the invader and the two traitors is the law of Méjico, *written in a decree. Your plea is denied, General Wilder."*

"Sir," Jesse said, "with all due respect, I remind you that as bloody as was our American War Between the States, which the Yankees call the Civil War, neither side shot prisoners."

Instead of curtly cutting him off, Juárez had more the attitude of a patient listener.

Now Jesse's words came in a flood. "There's been so much killing, Señor Presidente, *that* Méjico *runs red. I've lost my beloved Indian wife and unborn son and my best friend in your war. What* Méjico *needs now, sir, is mercy and forgiveness to build on." He bit his lip, primed for an outburst.*

216

It did not come. Juárez considered him intently, yet without anger. In his low, inflexible voice, he said: "You are dismissed, General Wilder."

The scene dissolved as quickly as it had materialized, and Jesse said to her: "We talked on a short while. He never raised his voice. He told me my plea was denied. I tried again, even pointed out that in our American war, bitter as it was, neither side shot prisoners.

"No matter. He calmly dismissed me. I saluted, about-faced, and walked out to Father Alberto, waiting for me. He said . . . 'I know what the *presidente* said. But he heard a voice raised in forgiveness . . .' meaning *that* was a beginning, I guess. We waited in the hot sun for the end. It was about three o'clock, when we heard a volley crash . . . a single volley. I saw the *padre* flinch and close his eyes.

"We looked at each other. It was over for Father Alberto and for me as well. He spoke some kind words, and finally . . . '*Un abrazo, amigo.*'

"We embraced. I must say I looked at the great little man for the last time through damp eyes . . . hugged him hard once more. Then I mounted the red horse and rode north."

She seemed to let the words sink in, still in a listening posture.

"I hope I haven't burdened you with this lengthy recital of my history?" he said, meaning his words to be apologetic.

"Indeed not. Nor I you with mine. All you've been through has only made you stronger."

"I think we both needed a listener. Again, Susan, I'm mighty sorry about what happened back there. Now, try to sleep. Good night."

"Good night, Jesse."

217

★ ★ ★ ★ ★

His rest was broken. He kept thinking of her. He eased over to see about her. She was restless, too. After watching her some moments, he retraced his steps and lay down again. Dawn was just a few hours away, when he finally dropped off to sleep.

It seemed but a short time until he awoke at a touch to stand the last watch with the others. With four men alerted, Jesse figured they would not be overrun at dawn. Any surprise would be with the defenders, not the attackers.

Chapter Seventeen

Dawn passed without bronzed shapes, jumping and screeching, in the fooling first light. Jesse relaxed beside Miguel, while continuing to sweep the desert brush and scattered mesquites for movement. Not until Miguel nodded all clear did Jesse pass the word to fix breakfast.

Afterward, he called the outfit together. "Mister Hardin will be in charge while we're gone, second in command, of course, to Missus Lattimore. I urge you to be alert at all times, particularly at dawn, if we aren't back by then. In that event, we're taking dry rations for a day. Miguel believes he can find Juh's camp today. Juan López is going with us to handle the buckskin."

That was all. No questions asked.

However, Hardin came over while they saddled. "Any other suggestions, Captain?" Somehow the Missourian always reminded Jesse of a Daniel Boone type of frontiersman. Tall, square-shouldered, keen black eyes in the sharp-featured face, black hair to his shoulders.

"Well, yes, Sergeant. Keep a lookout on the mountains and all around. And always keep a sharp eye out for Missus Lattimore."

"You bet."

"Another thing. Should you see Indians in the distance, don't fire unless they threaten you. For all you know, they could be on an antelope hunt. We saw plenty comin' in. Stay quiet. You know, Ben, I didn't think to ask if you'd take this on. I just assumed you would. Your Army background. Time on the Texas plains as a hunter. I respect you as a man."

"Why, thanks, Captain." Somewhat embarrassed, he ran a big hand over his beard. "Man has to do the best he can when called on . . . that's all. An', believe me, nothin's been easy since 'Sixty-One."

"I know."

"So, good luck today."

"Thanks. Same here."

Susan Lattimore was waiting, when they were ready to leave. Jesse said cheerfully — "Don't worry, if we're not back by dark." — wanting to encourage her. The less he made of their departure the better.

The gratitude in her eyes covered them all, and she was smiling. "I'll pray for you. Good luck. Watch out for yourselves." She gave a little wave as they rode by.

The always-smiling López had curried and brushed the buckskin to perfection. Being a true buckskin, the gelding had the color of a tanned deerhide, set off with the black mane and tail and black hoofs and legs black up to the knees. The silver-mounted saddle and the silver-studded bridle glistened.

Miguel set a circling course to the west, around the base of the mountain towering above the camp. Sloping away below them stretched the undulating desert to the far-off Peloncillos, to their left as they climbed lay grassy plains where antelope played.

Miguel was dressed like an Apache except for the gray flannel shirt. During the night he'd slept little. Instead, he'd prayed to Ussen with all his heart. Prayed for power this day: to find the camp and approach it in such a way as not to cause alarm and without being fired on, first giving his coyote barks as the Chiricahuas' great Horse Stealer. Those calls were his. No other person was known by those signals; still, he realized, he was better known among Cochise's *Tsoka-ne-nde* and the eastern *Tci-he-nde,* the Red Paint People, than Juh's roaming *Nde-nda-i,* the Enemy People. Most of all he must be calm when he talked to Juh. He must not show fear, yet knowing he would feel fear before the cruelest of all Chiricahuas. And he must flatter the vain Juh; however, he would not call him the Great Chief. That honor belonged only to Cochise, and Juh knew it. Miguel had heard older Apaches say Cochise was the only person Juh feared, and that Juh was jealous of Cochise because he was the Great Chief. How should Miguel address Juh? — Mighty Chief? Most feared Apache warrior in all of *Méjico?* How *méjicanos* cowered at mere mention of his name? All that would be true. Lay it on thick, but not too thick; too much would not be convincing. And be careful to speak in a respectful voice without fear. And Juh would demand to know how Miguel knew to come here. How did Miguel learn Juh had a captive boy? How would he answer that? Another thought jarred him. He must convince Juh to take the gift in exchange for the boy. Suddenly his confidence was shaken. *Oh, kind Ussen help me. Give me strength, dear Ussen.*

He rode on in that uncertain state of mind for some distance, head down, vaguely aware of his surroundings, a dangerous lapse. And then suddenly, as it had happened that day riding toward Cochise's stronghold, he knew again why he had undertaken this most dangerous mission. Why it was revealed to him in such a stunning way. It was to honor his blessed little Mexican mother, his brave little mother, who loved children, who had saved his life on the terrible walk to the stronghold. So he, in turn, must be brave. He looked up gratefully at the turquoise sky. *Thank you, kind Ussen, for reminding me, for making me brave again.*

In the excitement of his elation, he turned and waved at Jesse and Juan, and they waved back and closed up.

★ ★ ★ ★ ★

Susan Lattimore watched the dragging sun. Time seemed to stand still. The bivouac was quiet. Some of the men played cards. Others lounged or repaired equipment. Gabe Jackson, who was so kind and helpful to her, was grooming his horse. Reverend Tatum was reading his Bible. Mr. Hardin and Mr. Powers were on guard, watching the mountains, watching the desert flat where dust devils danced. The outfit seemed so few now. In her mind she rode with Jesse, Miguel, and young López as she lifted a fervent, silent prayer to heaven for them. They were so brave, so noble to risk their lives for Jimmy. And her Jimmy. She prayed he was still alive. She must not think otherwise. What would he be doing now? Bound like a captive or playing with the Apache children? Jesse, who always tried to encourage her, had said Jimmy would be playing with the children. She could almost remember his exact words. *Eating what they ate. Sleeps in a wickiup. By now he's made friends.*

Today her mind also kept turning back to the colonel, a model for her as a parent. If he were alive, he'd be right here with her, telling her she was doing the right thing. That, or he'd be riding into the mountains with her friends. Growing up on Army posts, she'd had the necessary niceties a girl needed, thanks to her dutiful father, despite no mother after she was seven. He'd also brought her up as a boy. They had camped out, had fished, and there had always been horses to ride, beginning with her pony. They had enjoyed target practice together with Army revolvers. Her skill was soon evident, so he had encouraged her and bought her the Colt Army .44. His death had been a blow she still found difficult to accept. Having Jimmy was such a comfort, having someone to love and to envision his future. Rutherford had been very proper, when the colonel died. She thought he meant well. Only he

222

lacked human warmth. He probably loved her in his cool, aloof way. He had severely disciplined Jimmy. More than a whipping, close to a beating. It had been too much in her eyes, and they'd had words. The severe whipping had not been repeated, but the damage had been done. He didn't like children. Jimmy feared him. Perhaps Rutherford meant well. If he'd only let some warmth creep through, some understanding of others. She had been strongly considering the stigma of divorce, when Jimmy was captured. The trip's purpose had been to get him away from Rutherford.

She was brooding because she was afraid and uncertain. Her father used to say when that happened and you were unhappy, you should do something. Get out! Move! Busy yourself at something. Smiling to herself at the timely parental admonition, she led her dark bay to the spring. While he drank, she let herself enjoy this special place alive with twittering bird life. A surprising number of species for the desert, she thought. She could name a few.

Engrossed, she suddenly sensed that she was not alone. Jerking, she found Crider beside her.

"Oh," she said, "Mister Crider."

He touched the brim of his hat to her. "Call me Nick, ma'am."

She had no intention of calling him by his first name. She didn't like him. The man always made her uncomfortable, when he was nearby, beginning when he'd usurped a place beside her in the column. His pale eyes always seemed to be undressing her, as now.

"Be glad to water your mount for you anytime," he said, his gaze traveling up and down her.

"Thank you," she said, drawing her mount around. "But I still like to look after my own horse."

She turned to go, holding the reins. He stepped along

beside her, his pitted face closer than necessary. "Been aimin' to tell you, ma'am, you can always depend on Nick Crider." He struck that exaggerated military posture of his interview at the hotel.

"That is good to know," she replied, walking on. "I'm sure that can be said of all the volunteers."

He still persisted, keeping up with her. "Wouldn't be too sure uh that, ma'am. No tellin' what some of these fellers'd do in a showdown. If this mission don't pan out, most of 'em'd take off like a scalded cat."

"I have to disagree with you, Mister Crider. I'm expecting our mission to succeed. I can't afford to think otherwise."

He made a disparaging noise in his throat. "It's got about as much chance as a snowball in hell."

"I wouldn't be here, if I thought that. Neither would Captain Wilder nor Miguel."

"Captain Wilder . . . what's he know about Apaches? Or that runty little Mexican?"

"They know the country. Miguel grew up as a Chiricahua with Cochise's band."

"Still mighty chancy, if you ask me."

"Of course, it's chancy . . . but it is a chance. The only one we have." It infuriated her that he must remind her of the mission's hazards. "If you feel you have to bring that up at this time, why did you volunteer?"

"The money, for one thing. And Nick Crider fears no man. That means the whole Apache tribe. Why I said you can always. . . ."

"Good day, Mister Crider," she said crisply, cutting him off. She could feel his eyes stripping her naked as she led her mount away.

It took a while for her anger to cool. Again, do something! She found a copy of Tennyson's IDYLLS OF THE KING in her pack and forced herself to sit in the shade of a mesquite and start reading, even though her thoughts were ever on the three riding into the Burros. By this hour they should be some miles away, perhaps approaching Juh's camp.

Glancing up, she saw Hardin walk up to Crider and speak. Whatever was said, it was brief. Crider sneered. Hardin spoke again, then left. Crider looked after him, jaws working.

A little later Hardin crossed over to her. "Ma'am," he said, awkwardly removing his hat, "want to say . . . if any of the boys bother you in any way, you just let me know. It will not happen again, I promise you."

"Oh, thank you, Mister Hardin. It's very considerate of you. But no one has bothered me. I'm sure no one will. I'm quite all right." She gave him a reassuring smile.

His hawk-like features said he wasn't convinced. "Well, I just happened to see Crider go over to you at the spring, an' I thought you looked just a little upset . . . maybe somethin' he said."

Thinking of the need for harmony in the small force, she wanted to convince him that all was well. "We had a short conversation about our mission. It happens I'm more hopeful than he is. That was all."

"I see," he said, although not quite certain. "Just remember you don't have to take anything off anybody. No rough talk."

"Thank you very much, Mister Hardin. I'll remember."

They were still climbing steadily, the horses grunting at the steep grade. About them were thick stands of juniper and oak. Deer country, Jesse observed. Plenty to browse on. Not high enough for pines, but cool after the desert.

Jesse figured they'd been at this about three hours, when, catching the pleasant scent of juniper smoke on the wind,

Miguel signaled a halt.

"Maybe you better stay here," he said to them, reining back. "Camp's in the next big cañon over." He started off.

"Wait," Jesse cautioned. "I want to keep you in carbine range, if you need help. I'll leave my horse here and follow you on foot, staying under cover. What do you think?"

Miguel pondered that in his deliberate way and nodded approval, adding: "Juan, be where you can see me. When I wave, bring the buckskin down to where *Señor* Wilder will be. I'll wave again, if I want the horse led down to show Juh." He pondered again. "Maybe *Señor* Wilder better stay under-cover, if you bring horse down." Nodding to both, he rode off.

Jesse dismounted, tied the red horse in the shade, and drew the Spencer, leaving the Quickloader tied on the saddle, hoping it wouldn't be needed today. If so, it was all over. He had shells in his pocket. Waving at Juan, he followed Miguel at a walk.

It wasn't long until he saw that Miguel was following a trail that curved in from the east. Wood smoke smell came stronger as they moved downslope. After a brief interval, Miguel pointed for Jesse to post himself along here. When Jesse looked, he saw grazing horses and brush wickiups scattered on the floor of a wide cañon about three hundred yards away, and the silver ribbon of a running stream. When Miguel disappeared in the lower woods, he knew that he had to go on farther to keep him in sight. Thus, he began working down, keeping low.

The timbered mountains, the beckoning cañon with the running stream, fed by the ever-flowing Sweet Spring — Miguel remembered the place so well. What more could an Apache want? — many fat deer for the taking, good water, plenty wood, and pony grass.

Knowing that in this time of war it would be dangerous to ride suddenly into camp without warning, he did what any Apache would. He signaled first. Even the great chief would do that. It was also the courteous thing.

He dismounted and, facing the camp, raised his face to the sky and barked like a coyote. Three times he barked, the signal of the Horse Stealer, the Chiricahuas' most noted thief. He knew the barks would cause more than casual attention because, generally, coyotes didn't bark until after dark.

He led his horse on a way and waited, in plain sight. After a short time, he gave the signal again. Movement now in the camp. He thought: *they must feel secure in this remote place. No guards.* Still, he would not ride in boldly. The *Nde-nda-i* were touchy people, quick to anger, to take affront. Cochise had not liked to camp with them. They were also thieves, sneaking blankets and clothing from the more prosperous *Tsoka-ne-nde,* and there had been fights.

At last, somebody was coming toward him. An older fat man climbed slowly up the gentle slope, eyes searching. Miguel waved, waiting, and the man walked up to him, panting from the climb.

"I gave my signal so you would know I'm the Horse Stealer of the *Tsoka-ne-nde,*" Miguel said courteously.

"I've heard of you," the man said, not impressed. "What do you want?"

Miguel didn't know him, knew none of the Enemy People by sight except Juh. Some years had passed since he'd seen them. This man was not friendly, not that Miguel had expected him to be. They were all like that. "I want to see Chief Juh."

"Why?"

"I have a gift for the chief." He wasn't going to say why he

227

was here for fear Juh wouldn't see him. This way, mentioning the gift, should bring him out. The *Nde-nda-i* were known to be greedy, besides being extra cruel. He wondered what made them so mean and suspicious, unless it was the example of their chief, and their hard way of living, often in need, constantly raiding to survive. Their main camp in the Sierra Madre was not rich in game and plant food.

"What is this gift?"

"I would rather tell the chief, when I see him. I know he will like it very much." When the fat Apache didn't speak, Miguel asked: "Will you tell the chief?"

"I will." He drew himself up, a big-chested man with a thick neck and a hanging belly, a haughty man. "I am Gómez, Juh's first war leader. Wait here, Horse Stealer."

Miguel nodded back courteously, impressed, which must have shone in his eyes, because Gómez's heavy features broke into a satisfied smile as he turned downhill.

Miguel watched Gómez enter a wickiup on the other side of the stream where horses grazed. Horses of many colors. From here his experienced eyes told him they looked like good horses, larger than the usual hard-used Apache animals, lean with ribs showing. These were either stolen from *mejicano* soldiers or from ambushed wagon trains. Maybe a few cavalry mounts. Some long-limbed, racy-looking horses.

He sensed that he was in for a wait. Juh would not rush up here, even knowing of the Horse Stealer, and even eager for the unknown gift. He had survived years of warfare because he was cautious.

Some children played in the stream, laughing and splashing. But no White Eye boy among them. A bad sign. Yet he also could hear children's voices at the other end of the meat camp. Trees blocked his view. Maybe the boy was there. He could see people moving about, mainly women tending strips of meat on drying racks. They also would be tanning. Weather like this was best for tanning. Men would be gambling or working on weapons. It dawned on him that this was a comfortable, well-fed camp, better than what the *Nde-nda-i* were used to in the Sierra Madre. Since he couldn't see all the camp, he wondered how many warriors it held. He estimated at least thirty. Maybe forty. Apaches would call a camp this big a *rancheria,* or village.

Time lagged. The glaring eye of the sun climbed, and suddenly the earlier coolness vanished. Miguel was becoming worried, when, abruptly, Gómez and another man left the wickiup. A man bigger than Gómez. It was Juh. He looked heavier than when Miguel remembered him some years ago.

Fear began to build in Miguel, as they approached. He felt himself stiffen. But he must not show fear, and he forced himself to think of what he must say and how to say it. *Ussen guide me.* He took a deep breath. He had been sitting against a rock while waiting. Now he stood, unarmed, head high, his carbine on his saddle, knowing he must not show a weapon other than the knife at his belt, essential to every Apache.

Juh stopped. He was dressed like any Apache — thick chest bared this warm time of day, long breechcloth wrapped around his waist that fell over a potbelly as far as his knees in front, and moccasins with uppers that reached almost to his knees, plain headband and hair below his shoulders — except he was not just any Apache. He was Juh, proud chief of the Enemy People, feared as no other Apache was feared for his ferocity. A long knife in a beaded sheath hung at his belt.

He studied Miguel through narrowed eyes. "I remember you, Horse Stealer, born a low *mejicano.* Raised by the *Tsoka-ne-nde,* who taught you to be a man and how to steal many horses." He chopped off his talk, still studying. He had

229

a strong, broad face and piercing eyes. A straight, rigid mouth like a slit.

Miguel smiled. "I'm glad you remember me, Mighty Chief."

"You say you bring me a gift. I've fought the *mejicanos* too long to be fooled with a gift. Give Apache a jug of mescal . . . get 'im drunk . . . kill 'im." The flinty eyes flung suspicion. "What do you want?"

"I'm trying to help a *pindah* woman who is looking for her only son. A little boy with yellow hair made captive in a fight at Cow Spring stage station not long ago. His name is Jimmy. She is a good woman. I said I would help her. She has sent a beautiful gift for you."

Juh made a flinging-away gesture. "You say you are trying to help a *pindah* woman find her son. How can this be, when Cochise is fighting a war with the *pindahs?*"

"I left Cochise a few years ago. My mother died. My wife died. I have no children. I went to Tucson."

"Tucson? Why didn't you go to *Méjico?*"

"I did . . . back to Bavispe, where I was born. They said I'd been gone too long. Said I was Apache. They turned their backs and walked away. Didn't trust me."

What Miguel thought must be a rare laugh broke from Juh's throat. "Called an Apache should have made you proud."

Miguel shrugged, managing a self-pitying grin. Juh was feeling him out, torturing him in a way. He must stay calm and swing the talk around to where Juh, always suspicious, always wary, would trust him enough to reveal he had the boy, and then to accept the gift.

Juh asked: "How did you find my *ranchería?*"

"Mighty Chief, you forget that I've hunted deer in these mountains with Cochise's people many times. There is a fine

230

spring in the cañon called the Sweet Spring. I hope the hunting is as good as I remember it."

He couldn't tell by Juh's inflexible face whether it was or not. Juh's voice dropped a notch, low and menacing. "How did you know to come here, looking for a captive *pindah*? Why didn't you go to the stronghold?"

"I did. Cochise reminded me he never took *pindah* captives."

"You grew up a *Tsoka-ne-nde*. You knew that. Why go there?"

Dangerous footing, Miguel sensed, and he replied: "It's been five years since I rode with Cochise. Since he's at war now, I thought he might have a few captives . . . *pindah* children taken from wagon trains."

"Did Cochise tell you to come here?"

"He told me nothing except he had no captives." He was not going to involve the Great Chief in this, even if he had, reluctantly, given Miguel this lead. To do so now would only make the jealous Juh angry, which could very well ruin the parley. In what he felt was a reasonable tone, Miguel went on. "I knew that often your people hunted here this time of year."

"Why not ask the Red Paint People on the Mimbres River?"

"They are farther away. Another reason, Mighty Chief, is this . . . there was one survivor in the Cow Spring fight. He saw Apaches take the boy and ride toward the Burro Mountains." Partly a lie flashing into his mind, that about Apaches riding for the Burros, but it had the instant effect of the truth as Juh's impassive face changed to a snarl, and he grabbed Miguel by his shirt front and lifted him up to his tiptoes. "You're lying, *méjicano!* You may be called the Horse Stealer, but a *méjicano's* always a *méjicano* to me!"

231

* * * * *

On the timbered slope, Jesse brought the Spencer up and drew a bead on Juh's big shape, ready to fire if Juh tried to knife Miguel, then lowered the carbine when Juh unexpectedly released Miguel.

Miguel pulled down his shirt, chest pounding inside like a drum. He'd never seen such brutal hatred. Never felt such fear. Never felt such strength in a man. Before he could speak, Juh demanded: "How did you find this out?"

"A party of *pindahs* came by, found the survivor, a *pindah* soldier. Took him to Fort Bowie . . . that is how it is known in Tucson, Mighty Chief."

As suddenly as he had erupted, Juh grinned and asked: "Where is this gift, and what is it? Is it worthy of the Mighty Chief?" And Miguel realized Juh had just been playing with him, like a cat with a mouse. More torture. Yet, for the first time, he felt a little ease.

"I will show you," Miguel said, and turned and waved.

In a held breath, he watched Juan appear, leading the buckskin. He rode down to about where Jesse was posted and halted, holding the buckskin broadside for a better view from below. Jesse was not in sight.

Ah, how the buckskin stood out against the green timber, and how proudly young Juan displayed the horse. *The deerhide horse,* Miguel thought. And the silver ornaments on the new Mexican saddle and the bridle sparkled in the sun.

Juh's eyes betrayed him at once. He wanted the horse and saddle. The hungry desire of a born horseman.

Now, Miguel knew, *the time had come.* He must not grovel. Ussen had guided him up to this moment. He had something to bargain for the little boy. And he said, speaking with care in a casual tone: "So you have the little yel-

232

low-haired *pindah* boy, Mighty Chief?"

"Did I say?" Juh snarled, whirling on him.

"You did not. But from what the survivor said. . . ."

"Then . . . if I tell you I have no *pindah* captive?"

"Then I would believe you." Miguel sensed he was being tortured again.

"What would you do?"

"Ride to the Red Paint country."

"What if I killed you and the *mejícano* up there and took the buckskin?"

"That would be up to Ussen to decide," Miguel answered and meant it.

Upon that, Juh seemed to relax. Another longing look at the buckskin and he said: "Come back here tomorrow, *méjicano*, before the sun gets high, and I will talk to you again. Camp tonight where Water Flows Over the Cliff."

Miguel nodded that he would, noting that Juh no longer called him by his honored name of Horse Stealer. Well, it didn't matter now.

As Juh strode away, Gómez threw Miguel a look of utter contempt and jeered — "You're nothing but a low-bred *méjicano*, lower than a snake's belly." — and followed his chief.

Miguel kept his face straight, boiling inside. How he'd enjoy putting a knife into that fat belly! And wishing that, it occurred to him that his upbringing as an Apache had taught him to hate his enemies and thirst for action. In one way, it was not a bad path to take. It made you a man.

Absolute certitude raced through him, as he watched them reach the cañon floor: *Juh has the boy. But he is suspicious and distrustful, like always. He may kill me and Juan and take the buckskin. Tonight he will have us watched.* Mounting, he thought further — *It is up to Ussen.* — and, somehow, he felt a sense of relief. It was out of his hands.

In a few words, he told his friends what had happened, while Jesse stayed hidden nearby.

"Does he have the boy?" Jesse asked.

"He wouldn't say yes or no. He . . . what you White Eyes say . . . beat around the bush. I think he has the boy. I'm sure of it. Let's ride on where Water Flows Over the Cliff and camp. It's not far. Better to talk more there. Don't show yourself, *amigo* Jesse. We must not let Juh know we are three."

Gazing back over his shoulder as he rode up the long, timbered slope, Miguel saw Juh, standing in front of his wickiup, watching this way. *He wants the buckskin. He craves it. Tomorrow he will have it. But how will he go about it?*

Again, Miguel reflected, it was up to Ussen.

Chapter Eighteen

Miguel took them eastward along the spine of the mountain. Before much time had passed, they came to a stubborn stand of junipers amid a scatter of boulders, and there murmured a hidden little gem of a spring that dashed, sparkling over a reddish cliff.

Ideal for defense, Jesse saw and, guarding their horses, thought old habits in the field never changed. They watered the horses, picketed behind boulders and fed from nosebags, then ate dry rations and rested and talked while the rest of the afternoon spent itself.

"Why do you think Juh is putting us off?" Jesse asked Miguel.

"He wants time to think about this."

"Can we trust him?"

"No farther than we can see him."

Jesse grunted a short laugh. "I don't trust him that far. If he has the boy, he could have made the swap today."

"He's being very careful. That's why he's lived so long as a raider. He probably had scouts follow us here."

Jesse frowned. "I hope he didn't have our tracks followed back to our camp at the foot of the mountains."

"Too far. All he's thinking about is the handsome buckskin. He knows we're no threat to him because we want the boy."

"He could overrun us in the morning with fifteen or twenty men. But we'd make him pay."

"Two things give me hope. He could have taken the buckskin without giving up the boy." He fell silent.

"What's the other one?" Jesse asked.

"That he didn't murder us all."

"Just the same, let's all be on guard before first light in the morning. If he tries to take us, it's going to cost him."

The remainder of the day passed with increasing slowness. Before dusk Jesse bunched the horses behind boulders for protection, which would enable the three men to concentrate their field of fire. He assured Miguel and Juan the buckskin was going to be one damned expensive piece of horseflesh, if Juh charged in here. "If they come, look for Juh. Shoot the bastard first, if possible. Does Juh always lead the charge?" he asked Miguel.

"I don't know. I was never on a raid with Juh."

"What do Apaches say?"

"If not in front, close to the front. He is fearless."

"Good," Jesse concluded. "In the half light, it's hard to make out a face, so just shoot at the first big belly we see. He's got a big gut."

Young Juan's laugh broke the tension.

"The same goes for Gómez, who says he's Juh's first war leader," Miguel said. "He insulted me today, but I ignored him. I would like to kill him."

"Then we'd want to get them both. That would break their charge."

For an early supper they built up a juniper fire and made plenty of coffee, and, as the long evening enveloped them, they laid on pieces of oak for coals to last into the night. A nice campfire, Jesse thought, was like a needed cheerful companion on an uncertain night like this.

As they sat around the fire, Juan suddenly asked: "*Señor* Wilder, do you think we'll all be killed tomorrow?"

"Not if we shoot straight, and we will. This whole thing is

strange. He wants the buckskin. He has the boy, but wouldn't swap. If they don't jump us in the morning, Juh must be ready to deal. Do you think so, Miguel?"

"Yes, if they don't attack here. Yet, maybe attack closer to camp, when we come back before the sun is high, as he told me. Juh is very sly."

"Tell me something, Miguel. I've known for a long time that Apaches don't attack at night. Why is that?"

"Snakes come out at night, when it's cool . . . one reason. Can't see snakes in the dark. Step on snake, he bite you. You die painful death. But main reason . . . Apaches think, if they're killed at night, their spirits no go to Happy Place."

Nevertheless, they would stand watches. Juan, Miguel, Jesse in that order.

An uneasy night set in. Neither Jesse nor Miguel could sleep, while Juan watched. Around them the shrill cries of flitting night birds. And distant coyotes began to sing and nearby coyotes responded until they raised a high-wailing, drawn-out chorus. A good sign, Jesse told himself. In a way, they served as watchdogs. Coyotes would not bark this close, if Apaches prowled near the camp. When the *hoo-hoo* of owls joined in the serenade, he noticed that Miguel became restless at once, walking to the glow of the fire and back, and often changing position atop the boulder the three occupied overlooking the horses and camp. *Owl spirits, owl medicine,* Jesse mused. Whatever that meant. *Miguel, you are more Apache than you think. Thank God you are for all of us.*

He doubted that Susan Lattimore was getting any more rest at the bivouac. He dropped off to sleep with the owls still making medicine.

The three were waiting, when the first pearl-gray streaks smeared the eastern sky. *Not yet,* Jesse thought. *Not yet.*

The sky changed to a faint rose pink.

Not yet. Not quite. There was not a sound anywhere beyond the camp, not a single bird twitter.

Suddenly the rolling clouds parted, and golden sunlight burst upon the three.

Nothing happened.

Still, they waited, watching the east from where the attack would come. The defenders shaded their eyes against the blazing sunlight.

Nothing moved. Still, they waited. Juh was very sly. As the sun climbed and the opportune time for surprise had passed beyond all doubt, Miguel stood up, and Jesse said: "Let's make coffee."

Yet, even then, for a while, they took turns watching from the lookout boulder.

When it was time to saddle up and they rode out, Jesse knew they all felt a certain deliverance for the moment, only to be replaced by the stress of what Juh had in mind.

Once they reached the opening in the timber where they could see the *ranchería,* it was agreed that Jesse would dismount and cover as before. Then, with Juan leading the buckskin on a short halter rope, Miguel rode down to the meeting place.

Jesse, watching, was surprised, when after only a brief wait Juh and a little flaxen-haired boy came out of a wickiup. Gómez joined them immediately, and they started this way, now Gómez, instead of Juh, holding the boy's hand, more leading than holding, it looked. Juh strode in front. Jesse could hardly believe his eyes. The exchange he'd once thought virtually impossible was actually taking place!

Miguel's anticipation soared. And suddenly he felt humble and ashamed after the bad things he'd said about Juh. The chief had a soft heart, after all.

"Here is your *pindah* boy," Juh announced, and motioned Gómez to bring up the boy. The boy seemed bewildered and hung back. Gómez had to pull him forward.

"Thank you, Mighty Chief," Miguel said, playing the flattering game to the fullest, except that now he meant every word. "Here is your beautiful buckskin horse, a gift from the little *pindah* boy's mother. She will always be grateful to you, Mighty Chief."

Juh accepted the buckskin's bridle with a lordly air that said Miguel was no more than an apprentice warrior serving his chief. Eyes bright with appreciation for handsome horse-flesh and gleaming new saddle and bridle, he led his gift away. Gómez, following his chief, left the boy standing there.

He was a pitiful sight: dirty-faced, barefooted, in ragged cloth pants and shirt. The *Nde-nda-i* had wasted no buckskin on this pathetic little *pindah*. Miguel's heart turned over with compassion.

The child drew back when Miguel held out his hand. But time was important now. *Get out of here!* Miguel smiled and, despite the boy's whimpering fright, picked him up and sat him on Juan's saddle in front, and they took off up the slope. Jesse left the timber to join them.

They rode fast to the crest, then headed back the way they had come the day before. No time for talk. They must make tracks from here as fast as they could, while Juh was still smitten with the buckskin. They galloped a distance, eased back, and settled down to a fast trot, Jesse riding rear guard. No riders followed. He was still amazed this had happened, furthermore without bloodshed, and that they'd even found the boy. It was almost too easy. He felt a great wash of gratitude.

Once he rode up and said — "Jimmy." — and the boy's blue eyes lit up a moment, but he didn't answer or show rec-

239

ognition. God, such a wretched-looking little kid. And so thin. However, he didn't look physically beaten. Just no spirit in him. And dirty. Yellow hair like hemp. Fear lurked in those hungry eyes, as if he was about to cry. A forlorn kid, neglected, of course. Those little arms like pipestems. It pained Jesse to look at him. And to think the sturdy Jimmy of the tintype had come to this state in barely two months. Susan would be shocked, but, oh, so happy.

On impulse, Jesse patted him and gave him a biscuit, and the boy wolfed it down, while the blue eyes thanked him over and over. Did he detect the bare hint of a smile? My God, didn't Apaches feed captive kids! They must, but remember he's a captive. It was odd that he hadn't spoken. Yet, Jesse could see that the shock of witnessing the bloody attack at Cow Spring, and your uncle killed before your eyes, then the shattering change to captivity from a protected home back East might scare a little white kid speechless until he felt safe again. And there'd been another shock back there, when he'd been handed over to strangers again. What would happen to him next? Poor kid!

They didn't halt until they reached the edge of the Burros and saw the antelope country rolling out below them, like a great dun-colored carpet. A streak of dust marked a west-bound stage under strong cavalry escort.

Jesse rode up to Miguel and said: "*Amigo,* you pulled it off. You were one brave *hombre* to go into Juh's camp and trade him out of the boy. I'm proud to know the man who faced both Cochise and Juh. I can't thank you enough. Missus Lattimore will go wild."

Miguel kept looking beyond them, a sort of reflective cast to his face. "Juh . . . very sly," he said thoughtfully, and rode on.

They dropped down to the flat, reined left, and made for

the camp among the distant mesquites. Jesse saw that Hardin had posted sentries. One waved. Looked like Tom Powers.

As they approached, Jesse told Juan: "You ride in first with the boy."

When they rode in, all the volunteers awaited them, Susan Lattimore in front. She shrieked, when she saw the boy, and came running. Juan halted, lifted the boy down into her reaching arms.

She kept hugging and kissing the boy's dirty face, murmuring his name over and over. And then, suddenly, she drew back, parted the dirty flaxen hair, stared into the small face, her eyes widening, her mouth falling open.

"He's not my Jimmy," she wailed, and covered her weeping face with both hands.

Chapter Nineteen

The men stood frozen, the only sounds her unbroken weeping. The boy looked more forlorn than ever, the fear in his eyes big again, and in it a haunting question. This nice woman who had just kissed and hugged him was crying. What was wrong? What was going to happen to him next?

Jesse and Miguel dismounted. Jesse dropped the reins and put an arm around her shoulders. "This boy hasn't said one word since Juh handed him over to us. He may have trouble talking. Miguel, will you talk to him in Apache? Jimmy may still be in Juh's camp."

Struggling, weeping, she found herself again. "Before we say anything to this poor child, let me clean him up and feed him. We'll talk to him then. He's so frightened."

She kissed him and patted him and took him by the hand and led him below to the spring and sat him on a flat rock where he could play with his feet in the running water. Hurrying back to her pack for soap, towel, and comb, she stripped off his rags, washed him all over, including his flaxen hair, combed it, and dried him. Another trip to the pack for scissors, and she cut his hair until he looked like a cute little boy again. She kissed him again and hugged him, and wrapped the towel around him. The tenderness smoothed away his fear. He was actually smiling by the time she had finished. She touched a forefinger to her chin in sudden thought. Facing the watchers, she asked: "Can one of you men spare a shirt and britches? I'll cut them down. I have needle and thread."

There was a scramble to contribute. She chose one blue shirt and a pair of gray pantaloons, each from a different man, and thanked them all. Dressing the lad, she rolled up the sleeves and the legs of the pants for now, a ludicrous fitting, but he was covered and clean. He'd have to go barefoot. Then she scooped him up in her arms and took him to her camp and sat him down on her bedroll while the volunteers crowded around. The boy was smiling almost continuously now. She combed his hair for an uncounted time and kissed him.

"Let me talk to him first," she said, and asked: "What is your name, sonny?"

Visibly, he tried to answer, tried to summon it. But it stuck somehow, and, when she repeated the question, he seemed to struggle again within himself and something like — "J. . . ." — blurted out.

"Is your name Jimmy?" she coaxed softly.

He frowned, shook his head in negation, but once more he appeared to understand. He just couldn't get it out. "J . . . ," he said again, and "Ja . . . Ja. . . ."

"Is your name Jamie?"

A light seemed to break across his scrawny face. He shook his head, yes, and said: "Jamie."

And she clapped her hands, and the men applauded.

"Where is your home, Jamie?"

Again, he stumbled. Something like — "Mmn. . . ." — came out. And that was as much as she could get out of him at the moment. She turned to Miguel in appeal. "Now see what you can do, please."

He said: "Maybe this little White Eye boy been captive long time. Forget White Eye talk. All he hear Apache. I'll talk to him."

243

Miguel kneeled and, smiling, spoke Apache to the boy in a kindly, questioning tone. Jamie brightened at once. He answered with a few words. Miguel spoke again. This time Jamie's reply flowed faster. There was no hesitation now, no fear, and the exchange quickened. Miguel would say something, and Jamie would answer. Jesse, catching some of the words, saw pain suddenly fill the appealing little face. All at once he started crying, then a torrent of tears. Susan patted him and kissed him, and gave him a biscuit. He took it eagerly, and his crying ceased while he ate.

Miguel waited until he had finished the biscuit, then they talked again, more briefly this time.

Some minutes had gone by when Miguel said to Susan: "He was captured on Mimbres River over in New Mexico long time ago. I guess three, four years ago. He remembers Juh's warriors came. The paint on their faces. He saw them kill his mother and father and brother . . . still sees that at night in his dreams."

"Oh, how terrible," Susan cried. "This poor child." She patted him and drew him to her.

"Besides Apache, he speaks some Spanish. Forgot most his White Eye or *pindah* talk. He was afraid all time Apaches kill him because he cries so much. They said his crying might give away their hiding place when chased by pony soldiers. He. . . ."

She broke in. "Ask him about Jimmy."

"Just have. Jimmy is with Juh's band."

"Oh, wonderful! Wonderful! Go on. Is he hurt?"

"No." However, Miguel seemed to be withholding something. "Don't like to tell you, *señora*, but Juh has adopted Jimmy as his son. Wants to raise him to fight *pindahs*."

"Oh, no!" Susan protested. She gasped and sank to her knees.

"I am very sorry, *señora*."

Jamie started crying as well.

"We're going back," Jesse said.

Brakebill made a fighting motion with his fists. "I say, let's hit the camp, ride in shootin'. Make the family-murderin' brutes pay!"

Others nodded the same and muttered.

Jesse, looking at them, said: "That would put Jimmy in danger. First, we have to know where he is in the camp. We didn't see another white boy. Once we locate the wickiup he's in, we can do something. Juh was the only person we saw come out of his wickiup."

Miguel held up a hand for quiet. "Jamie say old woman watch Jimmy all time. Follows him wherever he goes. They live in another wickiup. Juh won't let Jimmy run around much. Afraid he'll run off."

"What can we do?" Susan cried. "What if they break camp . . . go to Mexico?"

Miguel shook his head. "No . . . no. It's meat camp. Drying meat for when Ghost Face time comes. No *Méjico* now."

She looked somewhat relieved.

Jesse was focusing on which men to take and how many. He drew Hardin aside. "Besides Miguel and Juan, I want you and Powers to go. Take a spare carbine and your long-range buffalo rifle. May need that comin' back."

Hardin agreed, then hesitated. "Cap'n, I don't think it's wise to leave Crider here. He's got his eye on Missus Lattimore. I warned him once. Him and Long and Webb are thick as thieves. No tellin' what they might try."

"Glad you told me. I don't like the man, but I'll add him. He'd better not let us down. Let's get ready."

When he told the others who was going, he saw surprise

flicker across Crider's face. "Don't figger my mount's up to hard ridin' in the mountains. He was sore-legged up front comin' in."

"There are plenty of horses. Take Shelby's or Donaldson's. Be good to have a man along who fought at Brandy Station." Jesse was rubbing it in, and Crider knew it. He had a sour look, but said nothing.

"Mister Brakebill," Jesse said, "you will be in charge, second to Missus Lattimore, as Mister Hardin was. Set pickets tonight, as usual. Tomorrow morning saddle up and be ready early to ride. Be sure all canteens are full. Mister Truett, it will help if you'll check shoes on all mounts. As I told Mister Hardin, if you happen to see Indians hunting antelope, don't fire unless fired on. You may hear the boom of Hardin's buffalo gun before you see us. There'll be no more bivouacs after we tear out from here. Our destination . . . Fort Bowie. Now, men, let's pack up and get ready." As he finished, he realized he'd been assuming their second ride into the mountains also would be successful. But how else could a man think?

When they broke up, Gabe Jackson asked Jesse: "What can Ah do, Cap'n?"

"Look out for Missus Lattimore and the boy."

"Ah will, suh. You bet."

"Thanks, Gabe. And yourself, too."

When they formed to leave, she regarded them with eyes equally grateful and concerned. Her voice was tired as she said: "Good luck. I'm sorry it's necessary to go back, even for Jimmy. I cannot thank you enough. May the Lord watch over you."

Riding toward the Burros, Jesse saw that Crider was astride his own mount. So the sore-legged excuse jibed with what Hardin had told him.

"Tonight," Miguel said, "we camp where Water Flows Over the Cliff."

He took them a different way this time, a shortcut Jesse began to see, horse-grunting, up-and-down going.

Deepening shadows laced the timber, when they reached the spring. Miguel looked up at the sky, as if measuring the remaining daylight. "Go ahead camp, *amigo*," he told Jesse. "I better go and look." He reined away.

They watered and fed the horses, picketed behind boulders, and made a fire where it couldn't be seen from the trail.

"About how far is Juh's camp?" Hardin asked at supper.

"About three miles or so."

"Huh. That's close."

"What good would it do for the Mexican to ride off?" Crider said in a complaining tone. "Dark ain't far off."

"Miguel," Jesse said, pointedly speaking his name, "wants to be damned sure the *ranchería*'s still there, even though it's a meat camp, like he told Missus Lattimore. You never know for certain about Apaches. They can break camp and be gone in minutes. Juh spends more time in the Sierra Madre than he does on this side."

The moon was up, when Miguel clattered in. "No sign Juh's breaking camp. Some more *Nde-nda-i* just come in from *Méjico*. Big fires. Much talk. Much eat. Women makin' *tizwin*. Be big drunk tonight. No sign of Jimmy. But *tizwin* night no time for little boys." He was mixing English with Spanish tonight.

"Plenty of coffee left," Jesse said. "Better have it. First thing tomorrow set up watch on the camp."

"We'll find him," Miguel said, and started fixing some supper.

"Then?" Hardin asked Jesse.

"Ride in quietly and get 'im. Just two of us would make less commotion."

"Sounds crazy as hell to me," Crider said. "Good way to get shot."

"We have to ride in to get the boy," Hardin pointed out. "How else you figure to do it?"

Crider didn't answer.

They sat in silence until Miguel spoke up. "Be big heads tomorrow from *tizwin*. Sleep late. Good time to get Jimmy. Just hope."

The downcast way he'd said it struck Jesse as odd. "There's something else bothering you besides locating the boy, Miguel. What is it?"

"I heard men talking. Some people left for Mimbres River this afternoon, before *Nde-nda-i* come in from *Méjico*."

"You mean . . . you're afraid they took Jimmy with them?"

"Only Ussen knows. All this heavy on me. I keep remembering, when I was Jimmy's age, and my mother, when we walked from Bavispe to Cochise's stronghold, and the Apaches beat us when we lagged, and how hungry we got, and how she took care of me, my little *mejícana* mother. My heart is heavy tonight." He shook off the thought and spoke in a firmer voice. "But we must do this thing."

"We didn't get a good look at the rest of the camp first time," Jesse said. "It's strung out up the cañon."

"Not much I could see tonight. Much smoke. People movin' around. I could hear Juh's voice. He was drinkin' plenty. I could tell. He make big brag about his buckskin horse and his *pindah* son."

"That means he's still in camp, Miguel! Juh wouldn't send his *pindah* boy away now. Wouldn't he want to show him off?"

"Unless he think the boy safer on the Mimbres, if we send

248

pony soldiers back. Like I tell you, Juh is sly."

On that discouraging note, further discussion about tomorrow ceased. Hardin volunteered to stand first watch, and the star-studded night closed down with its haunting sounds.

Miguel couldn't sleep. He prayed to Ussen. *Pity me. Let me be brave. Let me be quick to see. Let us find the little White Eye boy, take him to his brave mother. Let our horses run fast. Let our guns shoot straight.*

On that imploring note, he drifted toward light sleep to the *peent!* of night birds and the rushing sound of wings and the eerie *hoo-hoo* of an owl unusually close, like a conversation. The owl was a medicine person. Miguel could thank his Apache upbringing for that knowledge. Medicine men wore owl-feather hats. Was hearing the owl person this close a good sign for tomorrow? Was Ussen talking to him through the owl person, trying to tell him something in His mysterious way? Miguel decided Ussen was, so it was a good sign. Ussen was saying everything would be all right. *Go ahead. Don't be afraid. Be brave. Have brave thoughts. You must do this thing, Miguel. It is good.*

Through the years of war Jesse Wilder had learned to take rest, when he could get it. Rolled in a soggy blanket by a muddy Tennessee road while artillery pieces clanked by a few feet away. Dozing in the saddle while the red horse trotted faithfully on in a column of ragged Juáristas. *Now,* he thought, *we've finally come to it.* It was difficult to plan ahead more than the little they had. Locate the boy, work around, and quietly ride in, hoping most Apaches would be sleeping off *tizwin.* Just two riders going in. Six would make a big clatter. He hoped he and Miguel could grab the boy without firing a shot. After that, pandemonium. After that, there was going to be one hell of a running fight.

An old physical and mental weariness smote him, a mixture of anticipation and dread. Sighing heavily, he stretched out and fell into a state between rest and sleep, unmindful of the night sounds. Miguel would wake him for the last watch.

They were stirring early, watering and feeding and making a fire. They drank much coffee, ate dry rations, and were in the saddle by good daylight.

Miguel led away along the trail, not halting until they were above the camp, about where the three had stopped the first day. As if feeling his way, he dropped down the timbered slope about a hundred yards, then angled right some distance. When he halted again, they were in an opening among the trees, and the entire camp lay sprawled before them in the gentle, stream-fed valley.

Little movement at this hour. Some smoke. A man left his wickiup to relieve himself. Across the stream two boys, no doubt novice warriors, herded the horse herd. Off to the volunteers' left Jesse made out Juh's wickiup. Nobody stirred there.

About an hour wasted by. The camp was beginning to stir itself. Voices. A few women started cooking fires outside wickiups. In another hour, Jesse worried, the place would be wide awake. He looked at Miguel, who shrugged and went on looking, his face tense, eyes flicking everywhere. Jesse tried to tell himself it was still a little early for children to be about, playing.

Minutes passed like lead weights. The chill of early morning burned away.

And then, suddenly, breaking the stillness, Jesse heard voices. The shrill voices of children. Three boys appeared, racing like colts for the stream. He leaned forward, hoping. But no blond-haired boy ran with them. They raced to the edge of the stream, laughing, jostling, now splashing.

A terrible knowing burst upon Jesse. *Jimmy's not here. They took him to the Mimbres.*

Upon that fear he saw a boy streak from a wickiup to join the others. A blond-haired boy. As Jesse looked, an old woman came out of the brush hut, watching the boys.

"There he is, Miguel!" Jesse said. "Let's go!" To the others: "Cover us. But no wild firing."

They rode quietly down the grassy slope, seeing only a few more adults besides those tending fires. Going at a trot now, crossing the campground. As they neared the stream, Miguel cut Jesse a look that meant: *You take the boy!*

Jesse rode up to the boys, playing in the water. Startled, they all stared at him in mute astonishment. "Jimmy!" Jesse said clearly, but not shouting. "Come here! We've come to take you to your mother. Hurry!"

Jimmy stood dumbfounded. In another moment, the Apache kids would be shouting and rousing the camp. Clapping heels, jumping the red horse into the water, Jesse reached down and swooped Jimmy to the saddle and cut away, heeling into a run. The kids were shouting now. As Jesse tore across the campground, Miguel beside him, he heard the old woman screaming alarm.

A man emerged from a wickiup, suddenly blocking the way. Jesse rode over him, the impact making a solid thud as the Apache cried out and rolled away. They were running free now.

They tore up the slope where the others waited. Glancing back, Jesse glimpsed warriors running for their horses. But something had to be said right here and now. "Jimmy, we're taking you to your mother. Understand? She's camped below the mountains."

Jimmy nodded, still in a state of wonderment.

"Hardin, you men are the rear guard. Let's go!"

They went at a hard gallop for a long spell, no sign of pursuit, Miguel in the lead. Jesse eased off to a fast trot, knowing a greater race was coming.

He was surprised to find Crider beside him.

"Get back there with the rear guard!" Jesse yelled.

Crider sent him an oblique look and dropped back, in no hurry.

Damn the man!

They rode like this for a time. The timber was thinning. In the distance, Jesse could see open country.

Hearing Hardin's yell, he looked behind and saw a knot of riders materializing. Catching Juan's eye, Jesse motioned him forward. "Take Jimmy for a while."

Reining back, he told them to start firing. More scare than effect, he thought, figuring the riders were beyond carbine range. He joined in with the Spencer. When nothing changed back there, he turned to Hardin. "Ben, it's time to unlimber your Big Fifty. Keep 'em at a distance. What's its range?"

"About a mile."

"Let's halt so you can sight your rifle."

Whereupon Hardin brought up the long-barreled Sharps. Adjusting the sights, he eared back the hammer, aimed, and fired. There was a monstrous boom as Hardin jerked from the recoil. Watching, Jesse saw a horse and rider go down. Hardin ejected, blew into the barrel, and punched in another long shell. His second shot knocked down another rider.

"Great shooting!" Jesse said. "They're falling back. Not that they'll quit. Let's go!"

They rode out of the timber to the downslope of the Burros. Jesse took one last look behind. Nothing in sight, but he knew they were back there, and they would be coming. Hardin's buffalo gun had bought precious time and distance.

Going at a gallop, they reached the flat and struck out for the bivouac. Looking back, Jesse saw the Apaches reach the crest, their horses making a display of many colors. At least thirty warriors.

When the bivouac came into view, Jesse told Hardin and Powers and Crider to stand by until the outfit was ready to move out.

Juan looked in question at Jesse. Should he take Jimmy to his mother, or should Miguel or Jesse? Jesse motioned for him to do it and be quick.

Susan Lattimore was waiting. This time she did not come running. Instead, perhaps remembering before, she waited, immobile, hands clasped, face set, waiting, hoping.

Just then, Jimmy waved. That broke her apart, and she ran to meet them, waving and shrieking his name. Juan handed down the wriggling boy. She took him in her arms, kissed him with rough gentleness, then buried her face in his mass of long, yellow hair. When she looked up after a moment, her face was streaming, and she kept thanking the riders, over and over. "Oh, thank you! Thank you! You brave and blessed men! I can never thank you enough! God bless you!" Then she kissed and hugged her boy again.

It was, Jesse thought, like witnessing a miracle. In all honesty, one he'd not dreamed quite possible, yet worth the try in view of the unusual circumstances, and Susan Lattimore. It could be credited to only one person, to the vision and bravery of one uncommon little man, himself virtually without a country, regarded as an outcast. Miguel was smiling at the reunion, his earth-brown face humble and gentle with memories.

These thoughts rushed through Jesse's mind. He rode on quickly. Brakebill hurried over. "We're ready, Cap. Heard the buffalo gun boom. Figured that was good news." His eyes glittered. "How I'd like to knock off some o' them murderin' bastards!"

Jesse thanked him. "We'll head for the stage station at Doubtful Cañon. Just water and a short rest. No bivouac . . . they'd slip around and ambush us in the cañon next day . . . keep goin' straight for Fort Bowie."

This had formed in his mind, piece by piece, coming back. No other way. Outnumbered, they couldn't make a stand here. Bivouacking at the station would leave them at deadly risk in the morning. From Doubtful, they'd march to the San Simon River, from there straight across the valley to the post in the Chiricahua Mountains. With luck, they'd make it by tonight. There was plenty of daylight left.

He formed the column. Jimmy to ride with his mother. Jamie on a halter-led horse, Donaldson's old mount. Lead the pack mules: if they slowed the march, cut the slowest ones. Miguel would take point as usual.

Hardin and Powers and Crider dusted in. Hardin said: "They're comin' down the mountain. Helluva big bunch!"

"We're headin' out now for Doubtful. Let's form the rear guard as before."

Chapter Twenty

As they filed out of the mesquites, the Apaches massed as if to charge. Instead of halting, Jesse kept the column moving and wheeled the rear guard around, now eight strong, and began firing rapidly. Brakebill's high-pitched yelling was audible above the gunfire.

The Apaches didn't charge. It was only a feint. They were wily fighters, dashing in and out on their swift horses, yelling all the while, staying just beyond carbine range. But when Hardin opened up with the Big Fifty and shot a warrior off his horse, they broke up and dashed away, even beyond the big gun's range.

"Hold your fire, Ben. Don't waste a shot. You've driven them back. Their game is to hound us, hoping we'll get strung out. About how many cartridges left for your Sharps?"

"Thirty some. Didn't figure we'd need many."

"Enough if we're careful. If they get in close, they'll sure as hell pay for it. Now, let's move out!"

They held to a steady trot. In the glittering distance rose the jagged Peloncillos where Doubtful Cañon lay. Jesse rode back and forth like an outrider, keeping the column closed. If a horse or mule went lame, it would have to be abandoned. The Apaches followed far back, always there, stalking, waiting, biding their time. It steadied in Jesse's mind that their charge wouldn't come at the stage station — too open there. Or on the open San Simon, their last brief halt. But it would come. Maybe just at dusk. These unknowns pecked at his mind. Meanwhile, they had to keep moving.

Through field glasses he spotted the big buckskin among the front riders. Juh's presence meant pursuit to the end. Having already lost two warriors, they had the additional purpose of revenge, besides recapturing the boy.

The miles fell behind without change. Susan Lattimore and Jimmy seemed comfortable riding double. A smiling Jamie rode beside them, Gabe leading his horse. Susan radiated happiness, her attention enveloping both boys. It was apparent that she had acquired another son. When Jesse told her they were marching straight through to Fort Bowie, with only the two short halts, she understood at once. No more need be said. He was glad to see that the cavalryman's daughter packed her holstered Army revolver at the ready.

Time ruled them now. Little things took on undue importance. When a horse stumbled, everyone turned to look. Was he going lame? When the boys asked for water, Susan let them drink from her canteen. Jesse assured her there was plenty of water, with extra canteens. When the cinch on Dave Wallace's saddle broke, the column had to halt. It was Enoch Tatum, brought up on an Iowa farm to fix whatever broke, who shortly made repairs, using pieces of leather from a heavy quirt. *The Reverend Tatum,* Jesse thought, *who'd brought along a bottle of whiskey and still hadn't fallen to temptation.* They marched on. And trailing ever behind them, biding their time, followed the dusty cloud of warriors.

They reached the station at Stein's Peak without further delay.

From atop the station's stone wall, watching through glasses, while the outfit watered and rested, Jesse saw the war party suddenly break into a hard gallop. *They think we'll bivouac here.* He waved for Hardin to join him.

The first slug from the buffalo rifle crippled a lead horse, the second missed, but the third took down a rider. And, immediately, they pulled up and halted.

"You're a helluva good shot, Ben," Jesse said, glasses on the war party. "That's enough now. They've eased up. It's getting costly for Juh . . . three warriors. Apaches aren't used to losing many warriors. But I guess it will just make old Juh all the madder."

He let them rest a little while longer. Over there the graves of Donaldson and Shelby, the wasted lives of two good men — men needed right now. He saw Susan glance that way, then avert her eyes. When he saw Miguel mount up and hold a hurrying look on him, he called out to saddle and hastened them down into Doubtful Cañon.

By the time they halted on the other side of the shallow San Simon, it was mid-afternoon. Horses and riders were starting to show the wear of the hard march. Jesse decided to rest them a bit longer than before, in preparation for the toughest stretch yet. As of now there was no reason they couldn't make it on in to Fort Bowie, which he estimated some thirty miles distant in the Chiricahuas, if they could hold Juh off. *If . . . if!*

He formed them in a tight column of twos, and they were trailing out, when, looking back, he saw the warriors break out of the Peloncillos at a gallop. He thought he could almost read Juh's mind. Picking up the pace now to make up for time spent at Stein's to water their horses.

And, shortly, the old cat-and-mouse game began again. The Apaches pretended to dash in, although beyond the range of Hardin's boomer, then drawing off. Sometimes a party of four or five would race off on a flanking move, still out of range, while the column persevered forward. Hardin was holding his fire on order.

After that, the Apaches began signaling with hand mirrors in the direction of the Chiricahuas. Jesse rode up to Miguel

257

and asked what the signals meant. Miguel's face brushed amusement. "They try to scare us. Make us think Apaches in mountains will come out and attack us. It is nothing. No flashes come from mountains."

"What else do you think Juh will do, Miguel?"

Miguel's eyes sent Jesse a concern that stiffened him. "Juh will attack before we reach the mountains . . . before dark. He will come. Be ready, *amigo*. He will come."

Drifting back to observe the pursuit, Jesse found himself gauging the distance to the fort against the time left. Now time was on the side of the warriors; they could attack at their choosing, overrun the outnumbered volunteers — if willing to pay the price.

Some miles on, when he figured they were about halfway across the valley, Jesse felt they could wait no longer, and he rode up to Juan. "I want you to take my horse and ride to the fort for help. Tell 'em there's a woman and children with us. Tell 'em to come quick. Big war party. We're outnumbered." Jesse pointed toward the mountains to a big cañon, which he said led to the fort. "First, you'll see where the road to the fort breaks off the main trail we're on. Just follow it."

Juan looked uncertain. "Won't your horse throw me?"

"He's snuffy, but you can ride him. Hell, you're a horseman, Juan! Now, ride! I'll stand by while you mount."

As Jesse expected, the red horse stepped away, when Juan took the reins and prepared to mount. Jesse caught the bridle, pulled the horse's head around, stopped the dance. Juan seized the saddle horn and sprang cat-like to the saddle.

"He'll settle down fast, when you get going," Jesse said. "Now and then, change your pace to rest him. Run a while, trot a while, gallop a while. You'll know when to change. He's tough. He can go the distance. Good luck!"

Afterward, the dragging afternoon turned into a grim

258

waiting game. Nothing seemed to change. Juh's warriors were no closer, no farther back than before. Jesse wondered why they waited. It was now past five o'clock. Purple shadows darkened the lower reaches of the massive Chiricahuas. The pass leading to the post wasn't far now.

Ever watching, Jesse gave a start. Little by little, the Apaches seemed nearer, suddenly growing in detail, their dust rising. He could see the buckskin quite clearly now. And all at once the certainty swept through him. They were coming at last, before dark, as Miguel had said.

He yelled at Hardin to start firing and posted several others in a tighter shield around the rear and flanks. On the run, he yelled at Miguel and told Susan Lattimore and the boys to stay low. Gabe, carbine ready, had already assumed a protective position.

There was something unforgettable about the particular way Susan looked at him, a strand of light-brown hair playing under her hat. In one flashing instant, he saw it, then resolve quickening across her tanned face and stirring in the blue-green eyes. There was something, more sensed than defined.

Now the Apaches came, yelling in chorus, charging head-on for the rear of the column, riding crouched like jockeys, difficult targets. Their horses shook the ground. There sounded the single crack of a rifle, the answering *bang-bang* of carbines, and the fading desert light was filled with the dust of running horses and blooming powder smoke and stabs of red-dish-yellow light. Above it all, Brakebill screamed hate at the screeching enemy.

The charge didn't lessen despite the steady firing from the rear guard, even as an Apache horse reared and its rider fell, and another horse broke down, rider tumbling. Jesse emptied the Spencer, reloaded.

Brakebill kept screaming: "Murderers! Brutes! Heathens!"

What happened next came without warning, without reason, and fast. Brakebill charged the Apaches, straight at them, firing his carbine. The volunteers had to cease firing to avoid hitting him. His carbine was soon empty. Still, he charged, still screaming. He smashed into a tangle of riders, swinging the carbine like a club. He knocked one warrior off his mount, then another. An Apache swept up and shot him. Brakebill threw the carbine at him, cleared that saddle, swayed, and, clinging to his mount, raced back for the column.

But Jesse saw that Brakebill had broken the charge. The Apaches were milling. Would they come on again? At the same time he saw his own men slowing down, as if thinking it was all over. He rushed among them, yelling: "Keep moving! Keep moving! Come on!"

Even as he urged them on, he could see the warriors forming again, Juh on the buckskin the central figure. They massed once more. But instead of charging as before, they slanted off at a run. On their fleet horses, they could outrun the outfit to the pass. Jesse saw that and was unprepared for this turn of the day.

They swept by, firing and hooting. Two pack mules floundered. Jesse saw Powers and Truett take hits, but hang on, Tatum helping. In a very short time, he saw his worst fear take absolute shape. Juh had won the race to the pass. They were cut off.

He called for a halt, and, as he looked toward the pass again, he saw Miguel slumped in the saddle. He rushed over. Miguel was clutching his chest. Jesse bit his lip and led Miguel's mount back through the middle of the column to Tatum. Everything here was confused. Brakebill looked out of it, barely able to ride. Jesse shouted them into a semblance of order, and saw about Susan and the boys, and posted more men in front, and told Hardin: "Pick your targets. I want them to hear the boom at Fort Bowie."

All he could do here was form a tight front and stand fast. He had a field of fire. He'd heard of groups on the plains throwing their mounts and using them as barricades, but he rejected it at once because of the utter confusion while doing it, and losing your mobility was only a last resort. Glancing around, he saw Susan bent over Miguel, and Gabe sticking close to the boys.

Hardin said: "I'm down to eight shells."

"Keep firing," Jesse said. "Space 'em out a little more."

Hardin shot again. He got a horse. The range was easy for a Sharps, about half a mile. The mass of warriors seemed to stir uneasily as Hardin scored again, this time a rider.

Jesse was counting the shots and watching the pass. It was just after Hardin's next shot that Jesse heard the scrambling *rat-a-tat-tat* bugle blast of "Charge!" Within moments he saw cavalry tearing down the pass and Juh's war party breaking up, dashing alertly away. Juh would live to fight another day. And foremost with the cavalry was a rider on a red horse, waving wildly.

When order prevailed, Jesse informed the young lieutenant in charge of the troopers about the wounded, and they strung out for the post.

It was dark when they reached Fort Bowie, which seemed primed for their arrival. The officer of the day immediately escorted them to the hospital and sent for the surgeon and assistant surgeon, who arrived shortly and dispatched orderlies to take in the wounded. A troop mess hall opened.

Jesse waited for word along with Susan and the boys and Gabe. Others went to the mess hall.

After what seemed a long time, a surgeon motioned Jesse over, spoke tersely, and left. Jesse came back, looked down. "Brakebill didn't make it. He broke the charge. We'll always remember that." Susan bowed her head. "Powers and Truett have minor wounds, thank God." He hesitated, and said: "Miguel's in a bad way. We better go in."

She left the boys with Gabe.

Miguel recognized them. Jesse took his hand, feeling no strength there. Susan caressed his brow.

"Hang on, old friend," Jesse said.

"Oh, Miguel," she said, "we dearly love you. You've done so much. Gave us both boys. Been so brave. We want you to get well. Please. We love you so, Miguel."

He attempted a weak smile, while struggling to speak. His black eyes had a far-off look. He swallowed. His words tumbled out in a rush, hurrying. "I . . . saw myself in Jimmy. In you, brave *señora,* my own little *mejicana* mother." He struggled on, to hurry. "At last I am in peace. I go now to join my little mother. Ride Ghost Pony to Happy Place."

"Oh, Miguel. Don't say that. We love you."

He smiled at them, and that was the last he said.

They wouldn't leave him, even after they knew Miguel García had left them. They still stood there weeping, looking at him, holding each other. Not until the surgeon came in did they leave, and then with reluctance.

A little later, while they stood outside in the cooling mountain air, Jesse said: "In a way, Miguel died of a broken heart."

"How do you mean?"

"You remember his story? How Chiricahuas captured him and his mother? Killed his father? How he grew up as an Apache? But he had no home, no people, really. You could say he was a man without a country. His own people in

262

Sonora turned their backs on him, when he went back, expecting to be accepted and understood. They said he was an Apache, and walked away. But he never forgot his home at Bavispe by what he called the singing river. His mother died in Cochise's *ranchería*, his Apache wife died . . . he had no children. That's when he went back. He could have stayed with the Chiricahuas, but he wasn't Apache. He was *mejicano*. One time he told me he was nothing. I tried to convince him otherwise . . . that he was a man. I believe he had found peace, as he said. We can be thankful for that. I've never known a braver man. Among all the Chiricahua bands he was known as the Horse Stealer. His signal was a series of coyote barks. That way he rode up to Juh's camp without being shot. Even so, Juh might have killed him. I was posted above Miguel, when he parleyed with Juh. I had them in range. I saw Juh grab Miguel. I had Juh in my sights . . . was going to shoot Juh, if he tried to kill Miguel. But suddenly he let Miguel go, and Miguel made the deal. He said you never knew about Juh. He was not only cruel, but unpredictable. Miguel pulled it off. I think he sensed something was wrong, when we brought Jamie in. He said Juh was sly. Next time we rode together into the camp for Jimmy, leaving the others posted above the camp. He never showed fear, but he must have felt it when he faced Juh. I know I did."

"It's a wonder you both weren't shot."

"There was one fortunate reason. Miguel had found out the night before Juh's people were making *tizwin*, Apache beer. There was a celebration. Some of the band had come in from Mexico. The men were sleeping off the *tizwin*. So he figured that. His knowledge alone made the mission possible. Knowing where to camp, where there was good water, and, above all, where Juh's meat camp was."

"Oh, yes. Dear Miguel. And now he's gone."

"A most uncommon man."

"As if, somehow, he was sent to help us. Among us only for this short time."

"I could believe that, too."

The boys were tired and hungry and noisy, so Susan sent them with Gabe to the nearby mess hall where the rest had gone, saying she would come soon.

She and Jesse lingered, held there by the sad aftermath, comforting arms around each other, each needing the other. He looked at her. In a voice not entirely calm, he said: "Father Alberto told me there was still a way to go after he shot the *hacendado* bent on killing me, and we still have a way to go from here. Sometimes I think we put off saying what's in our hearts . . . only to regret it later. That is why, now, I want you to know that I love you very much. I also respect you and admire you. You've been through a great deal. I want you to know that, Susan. So now it's said, whatever may come. I hope maybe you've sensed that a little."

She turned to him completely, her hands on his shoulders. "I have . . . it was true and sweet. Sometimes it made me weep at night, and I wanted you beside me. As you must suspect, I come from very proper people and from a very proper background. Unbending manners. Strict conduct as a family, where divorce is a stigma. For that reason, as a married woman, I've been trying hard not to care about you . . . just keeping you at a proper distance, one might say, while not wanting to. But I love you, Jesse, no matter what awaits us."

It was a long and wonderful kiss, and, when they kissed again, he discovered that his eyes were wet, and she was crying softly.

Chapter Twenty-One

On the third morning the volunteers assembled on the parade ground for the long, two-day march to Tucson. Miguel García and William Brakebill lay in plots near the military cemetery. The Reverend Tatum had officiated. Shaw and Wallace were missing. Susan and her boys looked fresh and happy after staying as guests of the surgeon's family. Powers and Truett should be able to ride to Tucson in a week or two with a mail detail. Good byes had been said last evening.

Jesse asked if anyone knew about Shaw and Wallace. The outfit had bunked at one end of the enlisted men's barracks. Tatum said he'd seen them early in the evening. No one else offered.

Then Jesse saw the officer of the day approaching at a fast walk.

"Sir," he said, "I regret to inform you that two of your party are under arrest in the guardhouse."

"Creating a disturbance, I guess? Maybe found a bottle."

"More than that. Apprehended last night for breaking and entering the post trader's store and trying to open the safe. They'll have to be detained."

Jesse groaned. "I'd better see them first. That all right?"

"Yes, sir. I'll take you."

Shaw and Wallace sat morosely in a cell. Wallace pleaded: "Can't you get us out of here, Captain?"

"Afraid not." Jesse couldn't restrain his disgust. "Whatever prompted you to do this, when all you had to do was ride to Tucson for your five hundred dollars?"

"Well, sir, we had some drinks durin' the day, an' we saw this fat safe behind the bar. Looked like a bird nest on the ground."

"Did you hurt anybody?"

"Oh, no, sir. Didn't hurt a soul. Just sorta pried ourselves in."

"Good thing you didn't." His disgust only deepened at the lame excuse. They were just shiftless wanderers, products of the times and adrift like many others on the Apache frontier. He knew very little about them because they'd offered virtually nothing when interviewed. Yet, after Shaw's desertion, they seemed to have gone willingly about their duties, never complaining, more than he could say for Crider and his little clique of Long and Webb. They'd helped fight off Juh's warriors and hadn't hung back. They'd been out front with the rest, stood up when needed. However, this damned-fool escapade also left the outfit two men short.

"I'll see what I can do," he told them. "Maybe they won't hang you." He turned to the officer: "I happen to know Colonel Chilton. Can you get me in to him?"

"Yes, sir. I think so."

After a short wait, he went in to see the commanding officer, Colonel W. S. Chilton, a hard-tailed cavalryman if ever there was one, Jesse remembered. He saluted out of respect. Chilton snapped a salute and strode to meet him, hand outstretched. "I thought you'd be in balmy California by now, Captain Wilder. Enjoying the sea breezes, sipping wine, waited on by a bevy of pretty *señoritas*." He was a tall, soldierly type, of middle age, with a short, grayish beard that framed a thoughtful face. This man had been a brigadier under Sheridan.

"Never got farther than Tucson, General."

"Only a short time ago we were both in Sonora. You as

scout for Major Gordon's little handful posing as miners, who freed Governor Reyes's daughter held by a big band of cut-throat *bandidos*. I'm still under somewhat of a cloud for busting down there without orders, when Gordon was cut off. But a senator from my home state happens to have an influential voice in War Department appropriations, and the situation looks hopeful."

"I hope so, too, sir."

"Time for a quick drink?"

"A pleasure with you, sir. You bet."

Chilton stepped to a cabinet and from it took a bottle and two small glasses. At his desk he filled the glasses and handed one to Jesse. Lifting his own, he said — "Here's to better times, Captain." — and downed his whiskey without as much as a blink. Jesse took his in two smooth swallows, thinking the colonel was a good judge of whiskey.

"I believe you and Gordon and I had a drink here before you sallied forth to Sonora," Chilton recalled.

"Yes, sir. Might say a good luck drink, as it turned out."

"You still have the red horse?"

"Yes, sir. A Mexican kid rode him in here for the help you sent us."

"Ah . . . as you rode for help from Gordon to my command on the border that night. Some forty miles, I believe it was."

"Something like that."

"Would you sell the horse?"

Jesse smiled. "I can't, sir. I've promised him to a very fine lady."

"Missus Lattimore?"

"Yes, sir."

"I remember meeting her here with her attorney. A courageous lady. Come West looking for her boy, captured by Apaches. So damned little we could do. And feeling sorry for her. I understand her boy and another captive lad have been rescued. Remarkable! Now, Captain, bring me up to date on everything. Tell me all that happened. Details! Details!"

"Glad to, Colonel."

Chilton was an attentive listener as Jesse laid out the story before him like a concise field report, detail by detail, beginning with Miguel's key rôle that made the mission possible.

Chilton nodded again and again. "And Miguel went to Cochise's stronghold and actually bargained with Juh, who knowingly gave you the other boy, though that was good in the long run. And Missus Lattimore volunteered herself." He had to shake his head in amazement and admiration. "Now what is this other matter you want to see me about?"

Jesse explained.

Chilton frowned. "Frankly, I hardly know what to do with this pair, being civilians. Have enough problems with enlisted men drunk and fighting on payday. However, since they haven't destroyed any government property, or stolen anything as valuable as an Army mule, I see no reason to hold them for a U.S. marshal."

"These men started out rough," Jesse said, "but soon settled down." (Desertion was the last thing you mentioned to a veteran officer, if you wanted him to be lenient.) "Did their duty. Never hung back in our running fight from the Burro Mountains on in. Two volunteers are still in your hospital, but expected to recover soon. Yesterday we buried Miguel García and William Brakebill. Brakebill ached to fight Apaches, any Apaches, after losing his entire family in the Catalinas. Brave man. He charged the Apaches, broke their charge. If he hadn't, they might have overrun us. It cost him his life. That just about sums everything up, sir."

Chilton nodded, understanding, seeing it all in the

mind's eye of a veteran.

Jesse waited.

"I'll have to detain them a while," Chilton said, leaving it there, with the implication that nothing drastic awaited them.

"Thank you, sir."

"Glad to see you again, Captain. Good luck."

Jesse saluted, about-faced, and left. He would always have utmost respect and liking for the intrepid colonel, who had dashed to the aid of fellow soldiers below the border, international relations and Washington be damned! His own career also at risk.

It was time to go.

He placed Susan and the boys in the center, the squirming two occupying one saddled horse led by the unflappable Gabe. Jamie looked a different boy. After the services, she had bought clothes for both at the trader's store. Tatum rode up beside her, chatting in his pleasant way. Juan and Webb would handle the remaining pack mules. He sent Crider and Long back as the rear guard with Hardin, and headed out. Although he expected no trouble, they were still in Apache country and not strong enough to discourage attack. This late they couldn't make the San Pedro as planned earlier, instead bivouacking at the Dragoon Springs station.

It hit him hard as he rode alone how much he missed Miguel. True friend. Good man to camp with on the trail. Never complained. A warrior in his own right. The Horse Stealer and his three coyote barks. Jesse smiled at the memory. Miguel must have flinched, when he rode into the stronghold after a five-year absence, no longer one of them. Would they welcome him or kill him? The same when he rode up to Juh's camp to bargain with the most fierce of all the chiefs. But he had never faltered. Was he *mejicano* or Apache? Or some of both? Having time to reflect and look back, he chose the latter. Miguel's knowledge as an Apache warrior had made the mission possible, abetted by his memory of his *mejicano* mother and himself as a boy captive. God rest his brave soul!

Furthermore, the column was down to his four "reliables," as he had begun to think of Hardin, Tatum, Juan, and Gabe. He couldn't be sure about the threesome, no more than he had been earlier. Crider had resented being ordered back to the rear guard, when they rushed out of the mountains with Jimmy. You didn't forget his surliness. As for every man doing his part during the running fight, that was a matter of survival. No other choice but to fight.

As the morning wore on, Tatum rode up to Jesse, and they talked. The reverend was thinking of starting a church in Tucson for wayward souls. Maybe doing a little preaching in the saloons. What did Jesse think?

"You'd probably get thrown out most places. However, you might start with the drunks that shoot at bottles behind the hotel."

"That's a thought."

"Do you play the piano?"

"As a matter of fact, I do. Self-taught. Not bad at it. Some raggedy tunes."

"That's a start. From there some hymns. Almost every saloon has a piano."

"Sounds good."

"Better still, if you can sing."

"About as good as I can play."

"Might practice a little before you make your debut."

"But wouldn't I have to practice in a saloon?"

"Something would work out. It's also a form of entertainment, and not costing the saloon anything." Jesse chuckled. "You'll have to pass the hat. I mean the collection plate. Don't forget that."

"I hadn't come to that yet."

"Even a preacher has to eat."

"Back in Ioway I used to get invited out to Sunday dinner. Fried chicken . . . gravy . . . mashed potatoes . . . biscuits . . . vegetables from the garden . . . sweet milk . . . coffee . . . cake and pie."

"You recite that almost like scripture."

"Didn't mean to. Remember what Jesus told the devil . . . 'That man shall not live by bread alone, but by every word of God.' Yes, I hope someday I can have a little church again."

"You will. I know you will. You've been a mighty good man on this mission, Enoch. Besides manning the ramparts, you've been our chaplain and doctor. Tended to the wounded. Been good to Susan and the boys. Always cheerful. Yesterday you conducted services a second time for two good men. I'm glad you could be there. We've needed you, and I thank you."

They chatted on, their talk swinging to what prospects a man had in Arizona and what he might find out in California. It helped to have the reverend riding point today with Miguel gone.

As Tatum swung back, he winked and said: "By the way, Captain, I still have my jug."

Later, glancing along the column, Jesse saw that Crider had ridden up beside Susan. That irked Jesse, but he wouldn't make an issue of it unless it lasted a while. Not long afterward, when he looked again, Crider was back with the rear guard where he belonged.

Susan started a bit, when Crider suddenly rode up beside her. "Nice morning, ma'am," he said, touching the brim of his hat.

"Yes, it is." And said no more. She disliked having him this close, his suggestive eyes undressing her as they had that day at the spring.

"That orphan kid sure looks a heap better. What you aim to do with 'im?" It was obvious to her that his last words hadn't reached Jamie, busy listening to Jimmy. Jamie was trying so hard to speak English again.

"I suppose . . . try to locate his kinfolks, which will be difficult with his parents killed on the Mimbres, and we don't yet know his family name."

"You can always put 'im in an orphans' home."

His words raised an anger in her. "That's the very last thing I'd want to do, I assure you."

"Be just another mouth to feed."

"I would welcome that. He's a fine little boy and needs a home."

"Depends on how you look at it, I reckon."

"That is all I have to say about the matter, Mister Crider. Your remarks are not appreciated. Good day, sir!"

Crider's pitted face seemed to swell. His pale eyes narrowed, raked her over again, then he jerked his mount around and rode back to the rear guard.

For a split second she was tempted to say something to Jesse, but why worry him? He'd done so much. There'd been so much tension and heartache. She could handle this herself, and would. The next time Crider approached her, she would remain silent and ignore him until he went away. And she sensed there would be another time before they reached Tucson.

They reached the stage station in the Dragoon Mountains at dusk, watered and fed. Jesse put Susan and the boys behind the rock walls, and Gabe made the fire and prepared supper for them.

After his own supper with his reliables, Jesse dropped by and asked her: "How are you all doing here?"

"Fine. Jamie's doing much better with his English words," she said. "Before long I hope he'll recall his surname. He and Jimmy laughed and tugged on each other all the way in. And the minute we unsaddled, they started romping. At night they sleep together."

"Like brothers," Jesse said. "Well, tomorrow we'll get an early start for Tucson. Sleep well." When he bent down and kissed her lightly on the cheek, she feigned hurt and said: "Can't you do better than that, Captain Wilder?"

"Yes, ma'am."

He laughed and kissed her fully on the lips, held her, then left to set the pickets. Hardin had the first watch, next Crider, then Tatum, Jesse the last. Again, he missed Miguel.

He lay down, and, before he fell into a light sleep, the pleasant thought occurred to him that, when they reached Tucson, he would make certain there was a place for the likable and indispensable Gabe Jackson. Susan would like that, too.

In what seemed a short while, he woke up, disturbed by a wrongness. It wasn't the picketed stock, cropping the short grass. It was voices, low voices, from where Crider and the other two were bedded down. It was the raised tone, still audible, that had awakened him. All at once the voices ceased.

On some vague sense, he moved his pack to the station's entrance and decided to sit a while by the wall, fully awake now, the Spencer across his lap. A half moon rode the sky.

Not many minutes later he heard light steps approaching. The sound seemed to hang, as if the walker was looking around, before turning to enter the station.

"That's far enough," Jesse said. Against the light he recognized Crider's bulk.

Crider jerked back, startled. "Was just gettin' ready to go on watch."

"Hardin's not off yet. Besides, you know you don't stand watch inside the station."

Crider flung away without another word. Damn the man! He knew that Susan and the boys were inside the station. Every man did.

An hour or more later Jesse heard Hardin cross the bivouac to bring Crider on.

The rest of the night passed without incident.

A beautiful morning greeted them, cool and bright under a vast bowl of turquoise. They marched off in a column of twos. Jesse in the lead, following the trail over which Miguel had led them. Hardin and Crider and Webb formed the rear guard. They halted briefly on the San Pedro and moved on. In a few hours they'd be in Tucson. Jesse could see anticipation glowing in Susan's face as she gazed about, so happy with her boys.

The sun slipped into early afternoon. Jesse was thinking ahead, envisioning the obstacles facing him and Susan, when a blast of gunfire behind him shook the day's perfect peace. A sharp cry mixed with the sound.

He spun around to find himself looking into Crider's smoking carbine, and Webb and Long covering everyone else. Hardin was shot — on the ground by his mount.

"Don't be so surprised," Crider gloated. "I aimed to take over last night, but my boys said it was too early."

"What about your five hundred dollars in town?" Jesse placated, blaming himself for this, thinking he should have shot the bastard last night. Susan was very still, her eyes never leaving Crider.

Crider sneered. "Five hundred, you say. Hell, we're gonna take everything that fat Mexican Murillo's got. He's a walkin' bank. Then it's on to Californy. You see, we're in kind of a hurry. Busted outta the Fort Bliss guardhouse . . . killed two guards." He was enjoying his recital.

"You're takin' too much time," Long called out. His eyes kept darting here and there as he played his carbine about. "Let's get this over with."

"Yeah," Webb joined in nervously, "hurry it up." He sat humped in the saddle, his paunch overflowing the saddle horn, his hooded eyes like icy slits over his carbine.

"You git it first, *Captain* Wilder!" Crider shouted, slurring the rank. "You, the fancy Southern gent, orderin' us around like niggers. No man orders Nick Crider around an' gits away with it for long. Reason I didn't take to soldierin'." His pent-up rage growing, he glared at Susan. "You're goin' with us . . . Missus Highfalutin. You an' yer high-an'-mighty ways . . . too good for Nick Crider! Well, you'll see what a common man can do . . . once I rip off all them clothes. You'll find out before we git to Tucson, you will!"

"My boys," Susan pleaded. "Don't harm my boys." Somehow her voice sounded remarkably cool.

"Oh, I might jest turn 'em loose on the desert. Maybe they can crawl into town . . . if the coyotes an' wolves don't git 'em."

"Get it done!" Long yelled.

It was coming now, Jesse knew, figuring fast. He'd jump the red horse into Crider and go for the Spencer at the same time, hoping he had that split second before Crider fired. But as Crider looked from Susan to Jesse, an ear-splitting blast rocked the quiet, and a second quick blast. A vast astonishment flew into Crider's face as he dropped the carbine and fell headlong to the ground.

Smoke bloomed from Susan's Army Colt. Time seemed to stand still as Webb and Long stared, slack-jawed, at Crider. In that hanging instant, Jesse drew the Spencer and, earring back the hammer, shot Long in the chest, and felt the carbine buck in his hands as Tatum and Juan shot Webb off his horse. When Long struggled to bring his carbine around, Jesse shot him again, and this time he dropped from his horse and didn't get up.

It was over.

Jesse looked at Susan. The cavalryman's daughter was trembling, but she still held the Colt. And Gabe still shielded the wide-eyed boys.

They all hurried to Ben Hardin — his eyes nearly closed, his mouth sagging, his hawk-like face gray. His mount stood by, reins dragging. Tatum took one look and rushed to his pack and began tearing up a shirt for bandages.

"Juan," Jesse said, "take my horse and ride to *Señor* Murillo's. Tell him to bring a doctor and a light wagon or buggy, so we can get Ben into town."

"Ah, *Señor* Ben," Juan said. He was away in moments, the red horse stretching out into a run.

They all crowded around Hardin, wishing they could do something. He had taken Crider's slug on the right side of his chest. Susan bathed his face. After Jesse got him to take a few sips of tequila, Hardin stirred a little. "Just ridin' along. Suddenly that snake Crider turned an' shot me. Been a lot of low talk between the three of 'em all day. Should've warned me."

"Looks like the bullet went through," Tatum said shortly. "That's good. Bleeding seems to be just about stopped. Maybe we dare move him. Sooner the better."

After much trying, they knotted the ends of blankets together and rigged up a crude litter between two gentle mules and started out at a slow walk, Jesse and Gabe leading the mules. They would go a short way, then stop. Hardin didn't complain.

In less than two hours, they saw fast-approaching dust. Juan and Murillo dashed up with some twenty armed riders and a light wagon with a canvas top, much like an Army ambulance. A Mexican doctor took over at once. After examining the patient and giving him laudanum, he ordered a bed made on the floor of the wagon. When the bed was ready, he got in beside Hardin. Also with Hardin went Jesse's tequila.

While that was going on, Jesse gave Murillo an account of what had happened. Murillo said he would send out a burying party tomorrow. Meantime, his friends would gather up the loose horses and help any way they could. And then Murillo, looking to Susan, said: "*Señora,* I am happy to tell you that your husband arrived two days ago. I told him the good news. He is anxious to see you and the boy."

She thanked him graciously, but Jesse saw dread fall like a shadow across her face before she turned to her boys.

Jesse looked away, thinking again: *Whatever may come.* Well, it was coming, and he sure as hell would stand by her in every way.

Chapter Twenty-Two

The sky was hues of sunset pink shading into lavender when they reached town. Murillo insisted that Hardin be brought to the hotel.

The others rode to the corral, where Jesse told Susan to wait for him before going to the hotel, while he unsaddled and watered and fed their mounts. No more was said. He soon joined her and the boys. They started walking toward the rear entrance of the hotel, which led through the courtyard.

A man was waiting there. A tall, dark-haired man with a patrician bearing and heavy beard. His sternness was evident, Jesse thought, even from this distance.

Susan paused. There was no embrace, neither moving toward the other. Jimmy, who was holding Jamie's hand, stuck close to his mother. He looked afraid.

In a forced effort at civility, Susan said: "Rutherford, I'm sure *Señor* Murillo has told you briefly what happened. How we got Jimmy back, and, too, this fine little boy, Jamie."

"He did. I heard enough."

The voice, Jesse thought, fit the man: inflexible.

"But don't you understand? Jimmy is safe. To me, it's a miracle. And brave men died to rescue Jimmy."

"The agreement was, Susan, you were to hire a respectable person, say a former U.S. Army officer, to look for Jimmy. You were not supposed to go yourself, a white woman with these uncouth frontier characters. I saw you and this man here, when you rode up to the hotel. I caught the look on

278

your faces. Even Jimmy's. I refuse to accept this. By God, I won't!"

"I went because I felt I could help, and because I felt I should share their dangers."

"Mister Lattimore," Jesse said evenly, "you don't understand what it took to bring Jimmy back. There was a running fight with Apaches from the Burro Mountains in New Mexico almost to Fort Bowie. As for hiring a former U.S. Army officer, I am a former captain in the Confederate Army. I was in charge of the mission. But the one who made it possible was Miguel García, who died of wounds at Fort Bowie."

"You stay out of this, sir!" Lattimore's face was livid.

"I can't because I'm part of it, as I just explained. And if Susan hadn't been along, none of us would have survived. Three of our outfit . . . Army deserters, they admitted . . . tried to take over this morning. She shot the ringleader. I can assure you that she is a very brave and fine woman, and in no way did she shame herself by going on the mission."

Making a visible effort to compose herself, Susan took an uncertain step toward her husband, another, and another, until she stood before him and looked up at him appealingly. "Rutherford, please try to understand what it took. The many sacrifices. I feel so grateful to everyone, and I'm also very saddened."

"You and these uncouth men!" He was shouting. He fisted his right hand. "You and Jimmy are going home with me on the next east-bound!"

Seeing Lattimore's readiness to strike her, Jesse felt his own anger burst. And following on that, swiftly, like a shaft of light, he sensed something else, just now bared here, that went back in time before this.

"No more," he said, stepping between them. "No more of

this. Susan and Jimmy aren't going back East with you, Mister Lattimore. They're staying in Arizona with me. I love them and will protect them. They'll be happy here. They're not going."

Lattimore's furious eyes left Jesse, and he fixed an incredulous stare on Susan. "You . . . Jimmy? You'll stay here . . . with him? I can't believe this!"

Her lips firmed. She nodded emphatically. "Yes."

Lattimore lowered his fist and took a deep breath and stepped back, in shock. His dark gaze wavered as he appeared to realize fully what was happening. His mouth trembled. And then he turned and walked slowly and heavily away.

When he had gone, Susan said: "I never told you that Rutherford struck me at times. I thought I should endure it for Jimmy's sake. I was wrong, of course. I was prepared to break away from him, when Jimmy was captured. If you hadn't spoken up, I still wouldn't have gone with him to have it start over again. If you hadn't, I would have been hurt. But I knew you would."

Jesse took her hand. "It won't be easy out here, Susan. You won't have the comforts you had back East. It'll probably be ranching and raising good horses. I don't figure I'd make much of a miner or storekeeper."

"I already treasure what we have and what Jimmy will have growing up . . . a good father. Jamie, too. Both our boys." Her eyes fastened on him, glowing. "You often hear people talking about tomorrow. They forget that today was yesterday's tomorrow. This is our today."

"There'll be a nasty legal fight getting you free."

"Why, I'm already free, Jesse. Can't you see?" Her face was radiant.

He had to marvel at her spirit, this cavalryman's daughter

who could put two .44 slugs into a vicious killer, dead center, and yet be so thankful and understanding of others, and so gentle and loving. In the days to come he would likely marvel at her again and again.

About the Author

Fred Grove has written extensively in the broad field of western fiction, from the Civil War and its postwar effect on the expanding West, to modern Quarter horse racing in the Southwest. He has received the Western Writers of America Spur Award five times — for his novels COMANCHE CAPTIVES (1961), which also won the Oklahoma Writing Award at the University of Oklahoma and the Levi Strauss Golden Saddleman Award, THE GREAT HORSE RACE (1977), and MATCH RACE (1982), and for his short stories, "Comanche Woman" (1963) and "When the *Caballos* Came" (1968). His novel, THE BUFFALO RUNNERS (1968), was chosen for a Western Heritage Award by the National Cowboy Hall of Fame, as was the short story, "Comanche Son" (1961).

He also received a Distinguished Service Award from Western New Mexico University for his regional fiction on the Apache frontier, including the novels, PHANTOM WARRIOR (1981) and A FAR TRUMPET (1985). His recent historical novel, BITTER TRUMPET (1989), follows the bittersweet adventures of ex-Confederate Jesse Wilder training Juáristas in Mexico to fight the mercenaries of the Emperor Maximilian. TRAIL OF ROGUES (1993) and MAN ON A RED HORSE (1998) are sequels in this frontier saga.

For a number of years Mr. Grove worked on newspapers in Oklahoma and Texas as a sportswriter, straight newsman, and editor. Two of his earlier novels, WARRIOR ROAD

(1974) and DRUMS WITHOUT WARRIORS (1976), focus on the brutal Osage murders during the Roaring 'Twenties, a national scandal that brought in the F.B.I. Of Osage descent, the author grew up in Osage County, Oklahoma during the murders. It was while interviewing Oklahoma pioneers that he became interested in Western fiction. He now resides in Tucson, Arizona, with his wife, Lucile. His next **Five Star Western** will be A DISTANCE OF GROUND.